Tales from Grace Chapel Inn

Life Is a Three-Ring Circus

Rebecca Kelly

Guideposts

CARMEL, NEW YORK

Acknowledgments

All Scripture quotations are taken from
The Holy Bible, New International Version. Copyright © 1973,
1978, 1984 International Bible Society. Used by permission
of Zondervan Bible Publishers.

www.guideposts.org
1-800-431-2344
Guideposts Books & Inspirational Media Division
Series Editors: Regina Hersey and Leo Grant
Cover art by Edgar Jerins
Cover design by Wendy Bass
Interior design by Cindy LaBreacht
Typeset by Nancy Tardi
Printed in the United States of America

Life Is a Three-Ring Circus

Chapter One

"Autumn is near," Louise Howard Smith said to Jane Howard, as they walked through the gardens of Grace Chapel Inn. "You can smell it in the air."

Like the many artfully planted flowers in the garden, the sisters complemented each other. Both were slender and graceful, and from the similarities in their pleasant features, it was easy to guess that they were siblings. Yet it was the contrasts between the two women that people noticed first.

Louise, the eldest of the three Howard sisters, possessed the timeless beauty of a pale and perfect rose. Her crisp, practical manner was reflected in the precise, short cut of her silver hair and the directness of her blue eyes. Her love of subtle colors showed in her beige tweed skirt, pearl white blouse and mauve cotton cardigan. Reading glasses hung from a silver chain around her neck and added a note of order and competence.

Jane, the youngest sibling, was as exotic as a hothouse tiger lily. This morning, instead of her usual ponytail, she had braided her long dark hair and had woven a bright orange ribbon through it. The ribbon matched the vividly striped orange and white work shirt she had paired with her black denim overalls. Polished beads of tiger-eye gleamed in her ears, and similar beads interspersed with chunky gold nuggets formed a triple-tiered bracelet around her right wrist. On one strap of her overalls she had pinned a whimsical enameled marmalade cat.

Though their personalities were as different as their appearances, the two still radiated a strong sense of mutual affection, for they were friends and business partners as well as loving sisters.

Today Louise and Jane were attending to one of the many chores involved in running Grace Chapel Inn, their childhood home that they had transformed into a bed-and-breakfast. The inn boasted two gardens, one devoted to flowers and decorative plants, the other reserved for growing many of the vegetables they used. Keeping the gardens tidy and attractive required constant attention, but it was a task that the outdoors-loving Jane relished. Louise and their sister Alice regularly volunteered to be garden helpers since Jane, a former chef, also handled most of the cooking.

Jane turned her face up toward the sun and breathed in deeply. "That's not autumn in the air. That's just smoke from Bellwood Farm."

"The Bellwoods must be clearing out brush," Louise said. Their friends were sheep farmers who produced some of the finest wool in the county, and their extensive property also included several heavily forested areas. Samuel Bellwood grew Christmas trees in one section and would annually clear out brush and dead leaves to make it more accessible to his customers.

Jane shook her head, making the cable of her dark, braided hair twitch. "Rose told me that Samuel brought home so many fish from his trip down South that he'd have to cure them. He must have started up his smoke house." She bent to tug at the head of a dandelion poking up from an otherwise perfect bed of violet-blue blooms.

"It's not only the scent of wood smoke," Louise said as she extended the clippings basket, in which Jane deposited the offending weed. "The quality of the air is changing too. It's becoming drier and softer."

"That's only because we haven't had any rain in weeks," Jane reminded her as she patted down a clump of soil. "Besides, we have a couple of weeks before autumn officially begins. Then there's days of Indian summer, and there hasn't even been a frost yet."

Louise frowned. "What does frost have to do with it?"

"You can't have an Indian summer until *after* the first frost hits," Jane said, "which Fred Humbert said will arrive on October twenty-eighth this year."

Fred Humbert, owner of Fred's Hardware and the general handyman around the town of Acorn Hill, was an avid weather prognosticator. Over the years Louise and her sisters had grown to respect his surprisingly accurate forecasts, which were based on careful observation of signs in nature, but this seemed rather exact, even for Fred.

"How can he possibly predict the precise day the frost will arrive?" Louise asked.

Jane thought for a minute. "I can't remember, but it had something to do with hearing a cicada during the summer. He counts the days from the first time he hears it. Or maybe it was the last time. Anyway, it's definitely cicadas." She rubbed her chin. "Unless it was crickets."

"I can't see how insects—whether they are cicadas or crickets—have anything to do with Indian summer."

"Ask Fred the next time you see him," Jane advised. "Also, don't you think calling it 'Indian summer' is politically incorrect?"

Louise always tried to keep up with which expressions were currently considered inappropriate because they could inadvertently cause offense. In this case, however, she had knowledge of the phrase that her sister did not. "The word

Indian in Indian summer does not refer to Native Americans, my dear."

Jane looked up. "It doesn't?"

"Cargo ships crossing the Indian Ocean in the fall months always waited for good weather before sailing, so they could carry the heaviest loads of cargo without danger of the ship foundering in a storm and losing the cargo. They referred to the time of year as 'Indian summer' and would mark ships' hulls with 'I.S.' to indicate the load limit thought safe for the crossing."

"How do you know all that?" Jane asked, astonished now.

"I read it in a book about maritime history. Viola had it in a special display of her favorite new works at the bookshop. It was really quite fascinating." Louise glanced up at the sky, which was streaked with high, feathery white clouds. It was a much lighter blue than it had been last month, another sign that the seasons were changing. "Whatever we call this weather, it is lovely."

"A true gift from Mother Nature," Jane agreed.

"'Every good and perfect gift is from above,'" Louise quoted from the Bible, as a gentle reminder to her sister to Whom they should be grateful, "'coming down from the Father of the heavenly lights'" (James 1:17).

"Father of the abundant pumpkins too," Jane said as she dusted off her hands and stood. "I have so many good ones this year I might sell the extras over at the Farmer's Market."

"Are they ripe already? It's only the first week of September."

"They're getting there. The smallest ones are about this big now." Jane held out her hands to demonstrate the size. "Let me get a bag of mulch. I left some stacked behind the house."

Louise followed her sister around to the back of the inn. "I can't believe the pumpkins are nearly ready. All our trees are still green." To Louise, the arrival of harvest time was heralded by the changing colors of the leaves, which gradually turned gorgeous shades of scarlet, tangerine and gold. The change of leaves would also bring a wave of visitors, for many people enjoyed coming to this rural area of southeastern Pennsylvania to see the display of nature's glories.

A low, noisy rumble from the road beyond the inn prevented Jane from replying immediately. The sound swelled into a grumbling roar that vibrated through the air and the ground and caused several of the inn's windows to rattle.

"What was that?" Jane asked when at last the din faded.

"It sounded like a caravan of trucks," Louise said.

Such traffic sounds were highly unusual in Acorn Hill. Aside from recreational vehicles and the occasional tour bus, the roads usually remained blessedly free of traffic. Even the trucks and vans from businesses in the larger towns of Riverton and Potterston only came to town once or twice each week to make deliveries.

It was also odd to hear such traffic this close to the inn. One reason Louise enjoyed living on the outskirts of town was the peace and quiet of the country, something she hoped was not changing. She had lived for many years in Philadelphia, and the one thing that she didn't miss about her home in the city was the ceaseless traffic noise.

It wouldn't do much for our business, either, Louise thought. *No one wants to stay in a bed-and-breakfast where the windows rattle and exhaust fumes greet you when you walk out the door.*

"Fred said that they're building a new off-ramp over on the interstate," Jane said as she tucked a bit of stray sweet pea vine back into the white, cross-hatched slats of a latticed arch over the path. "Maybe they shut down part of it for the new construction and the truckers got lost taking a detour."

"They would have to become seriously misdirected for that to happen." Louise could not recall any major conventions or tours scheduled to take place in the near future in any of the surrounding towns. "Was there anything in the newspaper about activities going on nearby?"

"Nope," Jane said. "The Catholic church in Riverton had its back-to-school carnival, but that wrapped up last weekend. I'll check today's paper, though, to see if there's something I missed."

Trade shows, bus tours and conventions sometimes brought unexpected guests to Grace Chapel Inn. The four guest rooms were empty at the moment, and no reservations had been made for the next several weeks. Still, Louise believed in being prepared. "I'll make the rounds upstairs and make sure that we're ready for any walk-ins."

"Good idea. I'll see what we have in the fridge." Jane took the clippings basket from her. "Alice should be home from work any minute, so she can help if we get any unexpected guests."

"Putting me to work already?" a cheerful voice called out.

Louise and Jane looked over and smiled as their middle sister Alice Howard appeared in the doorway leading from the inn's kitchen to the garden. Alice, who was wearing her white nurse's uniform, carried a large cardboard box piled high with ripe apples. The dark red apples were unusual in that they had a very round shape, rather like tomatoes.

"Are those Winesap apples?" Jane asked, sounding quite incredulous.

"That's what Dr. Meecham told me," Alice said. "He brought these in for us."

Louise frowned. "I haven't heard you mention a Dr. Meecham before this."

"Drew—Dr. Meecham—actually works in the ER, but sometimes we have lunch together in the cafeteria," Alice said. "A few days ago he mentioned that he has relatives who own an orchard up North, and they sent him a crate of apples from their first harvest for his birthday. Drew is single and doesn't cook, so he was afraid they'd go to waste. When I told him what a great chef you are, he brought in this box for us."

"Bless Dr. Meecham's generous heart," Jane said. "I'll have to send something over to the hospital for him. Unless you think that would be, *um*, trespassing . . ." Ever the romantic, she gave Alice a hopeful look, which only earned her a laugh.

"Sorry, little sister, but Dr. Meecham is barely in his thirties, young enough to be my son," Alice said. "We're just friends who share a meal together now and then."

"Too young for me too." Jane sounded glum. "Drat."

"Cheer up. He also gave me his aunt's recipes for apple butter, spiced cider and brown-bag apple pie." Alice peered into the box. "I think I stuck them down in the side here somewhere."

"What is his aunt thinking? You don't need to spice cider made from Winesap apples. They have a great spicy flavor on their own." Jane said as she went over to inspect the fruit. "And please do not tell me there is an apple pie recipe in existence that calls for a brown bag."

Jane's training as a chef often made her somewhat militant about proper food preparation.

"It's not an ingredient, my dear," Louise said. "You put the pie in a brown bag to bake it, to prevent it from over-browning. Something from the days before cooking parchment and aluminum foil became widely available."

"That's interesting—barbaric, but interesting." To Alice, Jane said, "All right, sweetheart, hand over the apples, and no one will get hurt."

Alice handed Jane the box. "With pleasure. By the way, if you'd rather make something other than pie, I'd love some old-fashioned apple dumplings."

"Oh, yes, with cinnamon and nutmeg and golden raisins and *tons* of brown sugar," Jane said as she carried the box into the kitchen. "But no bags. Tell me more about this doctor. Is he dating anyone? The new dental hygienist is single, you know, and . . ."

Louise began to follow her sisters in, and then hesitated as she heard a faint and very curious sound. It was not the rumble of large trucks. It was unlike anything she had ever heard before around her home or in town. It was a strident, trumpeting sound like one would hear at the zoo or while watching an old Tarzan movie. It was followed by a similar but much higher-pitched sound. Both faded away and were not repeated.

Louise tugged together the lapels of her sweater. *I'd better make an appointment to see the doctor and have my ears checked*, she thought as she walked into the kitchen. *I'm starting to hear* elephants *in Acorn Hill.*

Chapter Two

Dinner at Grace Chapel Inn was never a hurried affair. Jane's superb cooking made it impossible for anyone to rush through the meal, and the three Howard sisters had fallen into the habit of using the occasion to update each other with news of friends and the community, as well as to discuss the many details involved in keeping an inn.

Alice usually refrained from discussing her work at the hospital as, according to her, some of the events of her day would kill everyone's appetite. Tonight, however, she was happy to report that three of her patients had recovered enough to be discharged.

"So what do nurses do when they have no patients to look after?" Jane asked as she brought to the table a fluffy golden angel cake topped with thin, red-brown streaks.

"There are *always* patients to look after, I assure you." Alice held out her plate for a slice. "Why were you so skimpy with the icing, Jane?"

"That is glaze, not icing," Louise corrected. She sampled the piece Jane had given her. The cake was as light as air and the glaze a delectable blend of flavors. "Raspberry-chocolate, isn't it?"

"It is, and I made it with a natural, low-calorie sweetener." Jane looked over at Alice. "Last week you were grousing about those five pounds you gained over the summer, remember? You said you wanted to start a six-week diet so you could cut down on your calorie intake. You marked on the calendar when you wanted to start the diet, and it starts tomorrow."

"Yes, yes, but my going on a diet doesn't mean you have to stop making your amazing desserts." Alice stabbed the cake with her fork. "The diet is a terrible idea anyway. If all I have to live on are turkey sandwiches without mayo and skimpy diet cake, I'll be miserable." She took a bite and closed her eyes for a moment. "On the other hand, maybe not. This is . . ." she took another bite.

"The word you're looking for is *sinful*," Louise said.

Jane grinned. "I don't know if you can call it sinful. Wouldn't that make it fallen angel food cake?"

"Now *that's* sinful," Alice said.

"If there is something sinful going on," said a familiar voice from just outside the kitchen, "then I want to hear all about it."

The three sisters looked over as the plump, petite figure of Ethel Buckley came through the doorway. The Howard sisters' aunt wore one of her best church dresses made of striking red and black linen. Atop her short red hair she had perched a dramatic beret hat made of plaid felt. Two white feathers sprouted from the red braid hatband, which was decorated with a large, ornate Celtic medallion. To complete the unusual outfit, Ethel had draped a length of plaid over one shoulder and tucked the ends under the belt of her dress.

Louise wasn't surprised by her aunt's demand, as Ethel was the unofficial town hub for news and gossip, which she collected the way other women did knickknacks. Louise was a little startled by the older woman's appearance, however, for even though Ethel liked vivid colors and to coordinate her accessories with her garments, this ensemble was rather extreme even for her.

"You can have a wee bit of me sinful cake," Jane teased, imitating a broad Scottish brogue, "but only if you'll first play us a tune on your bagpipes, lassie."

"I knew I should have changed out of this getup before coming over here." Ethel looked down as Wendell, the family's tabby cat, came over to sniff the hem of her dress. He scooted away from her before she could pat his head. "See? Even the cat hates it."

"There is a story behind this costume, I presume," Louise said.

"It was for the monthly Seniors Social Circle meeting. I told them that I didn't think I should have to be Scotland just because I'm the only member with red hair, but it was that or Ireland, and my green dress is at the cleaners. That and I hate to disappoint Florence Simpson when she gets one of her notions."

Jane went over and gave her aunt an affectionate hug. "Come and sit down and I'll get you some cake."

"What notion did Florence have that required you to dress like that?" Louise asked.

"Florence insists on having themes whenever she hosts the meeting," Ethel said as she removed the hat and the plaid drape and placed them on the counter before taking a seat at the table. "Tonight it was 'Countries of Europe.'"

"How like Florence. What does she plan for her next theme?" Louise asked. "'The Purses and Shoes of Italy'?"

"I hope not," Ethel said, missing the joke. "Mine are all from the discount shops in Potterston."

"I'm sure Florence can lend you something from her vast collection," Louise said.

Jane coughed, while Alice pressed her lips together and gave all her attention to her slice of cake.

Florence Simpson was a wealthy woman, and the Acorn

Hill resident most devoted to promoting culture. Her abrasive personality, snobbish attitudes and perpetual vanity had created or contributed to some problems for Louise and her sisters, but they tolerated her, for Florence and Ethel had always been very good friends. Louise sometimes wondered if Florence knew how fortunate she was to have such an obliging soul as her aunt for a friend.

Jane brought a dessert plate and fork for Ethel. "I bet you were the best country at the circle."

"I tried, and so did the other members, but as usual, Florence outshone us all." Ethel didn't sound resentful. "She had the best country, of course."

"England," Louise said promptly.

"When I saw that crown she was wearing, I said—" Ethel stopped and gave her a sharp look. "How did you know Florence was England?"

Louise knew Florence would never pass up the chance to dress like a queen, but all she said to her aunt was, "Lucky guess."

"Well, it was a very nice get-together, I suppose, until Rose Bellwood's cousin Nan told us the awful news. Nan was Spain, but I didn't think the flounced dress she had on was much like what real flamenco dancers wear. She shouldn't wear bright red lipstick, either. It makes her lips look so thin."

"What news?" Alice asked.

"About the detour." Ethel glanced at the window. "It's all because of those terrible hail storms west of here. Their equipment was damaged, and they needed to stop to make repairs or something like that, and next thing you know, there they were, driving right through town."

"They who, Aunt?" Jane asked.

Ethel seemed surprised. "Didn't you hear them? Nan said they came this way, and the noise must have shaken windows from here to Pittsburgh."

"We did hear some trucks earlier," Louise said.

"That was them." Ethel shook her head sadly. "It's all these tourists we've had coming through town, according to Florence. You let some of them stay, you have to let the rest of the riffraff come too. When Nan told us the news, Florence was fit to be tied."

"What sort of riffraff? What news?" Jane asked.

"The worst kind," Ethel said. "A circus has come to town."

"A circus! That should liven up things around here," Jane said.

Acorn Hill was too far off the beaten track for carnivals, parades or circuses. Louise couldn't remember a circus ever before even passing through their little town.

"We already have plenty of life in this town," Ethel said. "A circus is something we don't need."

"I bet I know why Florence got her scepter into a knot over it," Jane continued. "A circus is fun. She considers it her mission in life to keep everyone from having any fun."

"Florence may not devote her time to saving whales, dear, but as a resident she has the right to be concerned about the impact something like this will have on our community," Ethel said, and sighed. "I'm worried, too, but hardly anyone else is. Why, to hear Nan talk about it, you'd have thought we were being visited by that fancy French to-do they have on cruise ships now."

"Somehow I doubt that the *Cirque de Soleil* has come to Acorn Hill," Louise said, her voice dry.

"It wasn't anything French. Nan told me the name, but I can't recall it. Something with an *M*."

"That eliminates Ringling Brothers," Jane said.

"Will they be giving a performance here?" Alice asked. Before Ethel could answer, Alice went on, "That would be wonderful, you know. Hardly any of the local children are able to go when the big circuses come into the city. They'd be so thrilled to have one right here in Acorn Hill. I know I was overjoyed the first time I went with Father and Louise to see the circus."

"Didn't you and Louise once take me to see the circus in Philadelphia?" Jane asked. When Alice nodded, she rubbed her chin. "I vaguely remember that. I think I wanted to run off and join one of the acts."

"You were seven at the time." Louise patted her hand. "Somehow I doubt you would have gotten far."

"Which act, Jane?" Alice asked.

"Definitely the trapeze. That made a very big impression on me. I couldn't take my eyes off them the whole time they were performing. The trapeze artists were a family from Italy, weren't they? The men were so dark and handsome, and their sister was breathtaking." Jane looked up at the ceiling. "That was the first time I ever saw anyone wearing that many sequins."

"Now there is something I've waited forty-three years to understand." Louise glanced at Alice. "Remember what Jane did with Mother's jewelry?"

Understanding dawned on Alice's face. "That's why she glued all of it to her little bathing suit?"

Jane's chin dropped. "I did *what*?"

"That was the same summer we took her to the circus," Louise reminded Alice. "It had to be the trapeze artist."

"It was only library paste, dear," Alice reassured Jane, who was still gaping at them. "It washed out of the suit, and we took in the jewelry to be cleaned."

"That might also explain why you kept trying to climb up the Bellwoods' oak trees." Louise rubbed her temple. "We never understood why you insisted on taking that jump rope up with you."

Jane nodded. "That I *do* remember. Lucky for me, it was too short for me to tie a decent knot, or I'd have been swinging from those branches."

"Jane!" Horrified, Alice covered her mouth with her hand, while Ethel chuckled and shook her head.

"I take that back," Louise said. "It was better when we didn't know."

"Just don't ever ask me why I showed up dripping wet at Delilah Jones's ninth birthday party," Jane suggested. "And a circus isn't bad news, Auntie. Circuses are fun."

"The popcorn and the cotton candy always tasted better at the circus. So did the peanuts." Alice's gaze became dreamy. "I fed half of mine to the elephant the first time we went, remember?"

"Indeed. I was surprised at how gentle that giant creature was." Louise turned to Ethel. "Jane is right, Aunt. A visiting circus isn't such a tragedy. If they put on a show, it will provide some welcome entertainment for the residents. It may not be to Florence's taste, but she can hardly object to what others enjoy."

"That's how their type distracts everyone from what they really do when they come into a town," Ethel warned. "Whatever they call themselves, those circus folks will be up to no good around here."

"Why do you say that, Aunt?" Alice asked.

"I remember the carnivals that used to come to town when Bob and I had the farm. We'd have to chain one of the dogs to the chicken coop at night or risk losing half our flock. Light-fingered thieves, the whole bunch were. Wouldn't do an honest day's work but glad enough to steal from those of us who did."

"But a circus and a carnival are very different things," Alice protested. "I agree, there are some seedy carnivals out there, but they put on rides and games. Circuses hold performances in tents with acrobats and clowns and animal acts. Like the elephant I hand-fed when I went as a girl."

Animal acts—elephants. That might explain the noises

Louise had heard earlier. She touched Ethel's arm. "Did Nan say if there were any elephants with this circus?"

"No, but I wouldn't be surprised if they brought a whole menagerie with them," Ethel said. "Traveling people have no sense of propriety. Jane, dear, would you cut me a tiny slice of that cake?"

"You can have more than tiny, it's low in calories and high in deliciousness," Jane told her.

"I would, if Florence hadn't served a big tea. I think she's been spending too much time in Viola Reed's bookshop. You know what an Anglophile Viola is." Ethel rolled her eyes. "Anyway, I thought the tea was very nice, although Florence insisted everyone have a scone because she made them herself."

Louise winced. Florence regularly hired caterers whenever she had parties, not only to impress her friends, but because she was not a particularly talented cook. "How were they?"

"Tasty, but a bit heavy," Ethel said. "She told me afterward that she might have forgotten to put in the baking powder."

Alice, who was not a gifted cook either, nodded. "I've done that with biscuits, and they generally turned into doorstops."

"Let's just say that if a high wind comes along in the next day or so, I don't think I'll tip over." Ethel pressed her hand against her stomach. "Anyway, Florence and I agreed that we would go straight into town tomorrow morning to talk to Lloyd about these circus folks. She wanted me to call him tonight, but he had a meeting with another mayor and won't be getting home until late."

"There goes our fun," Jane muttered.

"Aunt Ethel, I don't think it's a very good idea to use your position as Mayor Tynan's special friend to persuade him to do as Florence wishes," Louise said carefully. "These people haven't done anything to anyone. We don't even know if they're going to have a show. All they've really done is drive through the town."

"Give them time and opportunity and they will, Louise." Ethel scowled as she collected her things. "I promise you, we'll be very lucky if they don't steal us blind." She kissed Jane's cheek. "Thank you for the cake, dear. Goodnight, girls."

After Ethel left, Louise gave Jane a direct look. "Now, my dear sister, you will tell me *exactly* why you showed up soaking wet to Delilah Jones's ninth birthday party."

"Because jumping into a pond was better than being stung by the two thousand wasps chasing me," Jane promptly said.

Alice gave Louise a beseeching look. "That sounds sensible, doesn't it?"

"Why were wasps chasing ... no." Louise held up one hand. "I don't wish to know. I won't sleep a wink. Good night."

But as she left the kitchen, Louise distinctly heard Jane say to Alice, "Good thing I didn't have to explain the part about the stray cow on the trampoline."

Chapter Three

The next morning the phone rang just as Louise was finishing updating the inn's books. It was Laurie, the clerk from Time for Tea, Wilhelm Wood's specialty tea shop in town.

"Your china order has come in, Mrs. Smith," Laurie told her. "Mr. Wood said that he'll deliver it to the inn this afternoon, if you like."

It was another beautiful, warm day, the perfect weather for a drive. "Thank you, but I think I'll drop by and pick it up myself," Louise told her.

"We'll keep it at the counter for you," Laurie promised.

"I'm going into town," Louise said as she stopped in the kitchen to find Jane coring an apple. "Do you need anything while I'm there?"

"I'm running a little low on vanilla extract and brown sugar." Jane placed the peeled, cored apple in the center of a large square of flat dough, and spooned a fragrant mixture of dark sugar, spices and pale raisins into the empty center of the fruit. "Would you see if they have any decent avocados? I have a recipe for fruit salsa I want to try."

Jane's tone was absent, because she was completely absorbed in her cooking. Louise glanced at the deep dish baking pan, in which her sister had placed eleven apples wrapped in dough. "May I ask you a question, my dear?"

Jane didn't look up. "Sure."

"Are we having the Seventh Fleet for dinner?"

"Not unless their ships ran aground outside the inn." Jane finished wrapping the apple in the dough square and crimped the edges together. "Why?"

Louise tapped the edge of the baking pan. "You're making enough apple dumplings to feed them."

Jane looked at the pan and laughed. "Good grief, how did that happen? I was only trying a couple of different types of dough. I guess I lost count."

It was not the first time Louise had heard this. Jane loved to experiment with food and often got carried away with a new idea. "Can they be frozen after they're cooked?"

"Yes. I'll share some with Aunt Ethel too." She tossed an empty flour sack in the trash bin and picked up the ceramic flour container. "You'd better add flour to the pick-up list," she said after peering inside.

"I will, as long as you promise me something," Louise said. She thought of the extensive collection of cookbooks Jane had brought with her when she moved back to Acorn Hill. "Do not start making quail in aspic after I leave."

Jane pursed her lips. "But I've never made that for you and Alice."

"Precisely." Louise kissed her cheek, picked up her purse and walked out to the front desk, where Alice was doing some filing. "I'm off to town, dear. Do you need anything? Other than apple dumplings?"

Alice straightened. "Thanks, but I ran all my errands the other day on the way home from work. Please don't mention apple dumplings, I'm on a diet."

"Is this diet really necessary?"

"Yes. I'm having trouble buttoning some of my

waistbands." Alice sighed. "If you hear anything about the circus putting on a show, call me. I want to be the first in line to buy my ticket."

That puzzled Louise. "Don't you think we're a little old to be going to a circus?"

"How often do we have real, live elephants anywhere within the vicinity of Acorn Hill?" Alice countered.

Louise could argue with Alice, but not with her love of animals. "I'll see what I can find out."

Louise always enjoyed driving her beloved Cadillac, which still ran like a charm after twenty years. On the way to town, Louise noticed that the meadows around Grace Chapel Inn were still speckled with wildflowers. With the warmer weather, she and her sisters could continue to enjoy them on their walk to church on Sunday.

Wilhelm Wood's tea shop was one of Louise's favorite spots in town, and she often went there simply to browse. She had always thought the ritual of serving tea was as soothing as it was civilized, and Time for Tea reflected both aspects.

In the front window the proprietor had draped soft white linen and lace curtains. Beneath them gleamed fine bone china pots and the polished wood of different-sized tea chests. A crystal snifter contained a jumble of silver ball tea infusers, which could be filled with one of the varieties of boxed loose tea Wilhelm had stacked in neat pyramids. Fanned linen napkins and decorative, Victorian-styled posters with instructions on how to prepare the perfect cup of tea provided a pretty backdrop for the displays.

A number of small, round silver tins with Asian lettering on the labels caught Louise's eye. The labels sported different animals, such as tigers and pandas, which were painted with a Chinese brush technique.

I wonder what those are. Wilhelm was an avid traveler who always brought back from his excursions something new for the shop. *I'll have to ask*, she thought as she went inside. *Jane does so love exotic coffees and teas.*

The bell tinkled as the door opened and alerted the clerk at the counter, who glanced up from the textbook she was reading and smiled. Wilhelm's sound system, which provided soft, classical music for his shoppers, was currently playing the Goldberg Variations. The delightful fragrance of tea, starched linen and potpourri scented the air inside the shop.

As she always did, Louise paused for a moment to admire Wilhelm's wares. One section of Time for Tea was completely devoted to the necessities of tea-making: shelves of canisters, kettles, strainers, infusers, caddies, drip catchers, honey pots, dippers and tongs. In the center of the store was an island of elegance, with draped tables upon which sat several pots paired with matching cups and saucers, as well as sugar bowl and cream pitcher sets, in stoneware, bone china and porcelain. The linen bins that lined one wall offered towels, aprons, napkins and tablecloths in a variety of fabrics and styles. There was also a food section, with scone mixes, boxed English biscuits and miniature mince pies, and a rack of recipe books.

"Hello, Mrs. Smith." Laurie, a friendly girl in her early twenties, came from behind the counter. Wilhelm had hired her over the summer to give some time off to his mother, who often worked the counter and always ran the shop when Wilhelm traveled. Laurie stopped at the carved walnut side table that held an electric tea kettle, tea samples and novelty mugs. "Would you like to try one of our new chai blends today? We're featuring chocolate and mango-strawberry."

"No, thank you. I just had breakfast a short time ago." Louise disguised a shudder at the thought of chocolate-flavored tea and went over to admire a plate of tiny tea cookies. Such treats were something Wilhelm usually did not set out for browsing customers. "These look tempting. Are they from the Good Apple?" she asked, referring to the town bakery.

"No, ma'am. A customer brought them in for Mr. Wood this morning." Laurie looked around before she lowered her voice. "She lives in Potterston but she comes to the shop at least three or four times a week. I think she's sweet on him."

Despite stirring similar sentiments among a number of his other lady customers, Wilhelm was a confirmed bachelor. When he wasn't traveling, he remained very content with sharing his mother's beautiful old colonial home. "How unfortunate. I presume that she doesn't realize how comfortable he is with his single life."

Laurie nodded sadly. "She's totally clueless that he's happy being single. I tried to drop some hints, you know, to spare her feelings, but she's really determined."

In that moment Louise could understand how her aunt had become so addicted to gossip. The urge to speculate was almost irresistible. "Well, I hope she doesn't take it too hard." Louise looked around the empty shop. "Where is Wilhelm this morning?"

"He decided to go for a walk so he could . . ." Laurie stumbled over her words. "Get some fresh air."

Or not, Louise thought. Wilhelm was fond of smoking a pipe, but did so secretly and almost never inside his shop, where the scent of tobacco might linger.

The bell sounded as another customer came through the door, and Louise returned to her reason for visiting the shop. "You called earlier about my special order. May I see it, please?"

"Yes, ma'am." Laurie went back around the counter and brought out an open gift sack with Louise's name written on a lavender tag tied to the handle with a bit of purple silk ribbon. "Here it is." Carefully she lifted out a small box and removed the lid to show Louise the contents.

Louise took the small porcelain creamer, which was embellished with a distinctive pattern of hydrangeas, from the clerk's hand. "It's lovely."

Louise had ordered the creamer as a gift for Viola Reed, who had a set of china in that pattern. Viola used her good china the same way other women did their everyday dishes. Unfortunately, Gatsby, one of Viola's many cats, had jumped up on the dining room table while Viola was answering a phone call and knocked the original creamer onto the floor while trying to get at the last bit of cream inside.

Louise knew how much her friend loved her elegant dishes, which had been brought over from England when Viola's family immigrated to the United States. She also felt partially responsible, as she had been the person on the phone with Viola when the accident happened.

Wilhelm Wood was regarded as the local expert on fine china, and Louise immediately enlisted his aid. He discovered that Viola's china pattern was no longer produced by the manufacturer, but he found a china replacement service in the United Kingdom and obtained the new creamer from them.

The customer who had come in earlier suddenly called to the clerk, "Excuse me, young lady, but do you have any large cozies in a dark red or purple? With lace, preferably?"

"Yes, ma'am, I think we do." The clerk gave Louise a rueful look before going to assist the other woman.

Louise didn't mind waiting for her order to be rung up. One of the pleasures of being one's own boss, she had discovered, was not being subject to an inflexible work schedule. Running the inn required a significant amount of daily effort, and Louise liked following a very structured routine, but now and then self-employment proved quite convenient.

The bell tinkled again, and the proprietor himself appeared. A tall, slim man, Wilhelm Wood had graying blond hair and the lean, aesthetic features of a thespian or philosopher. He always dressed tidily but comfortably, preferring cardigans to jackets and corduroy slacks to dress trousers.

Louise detected the very faintest scent of cherry tobacco

coming from his cardigan and suppressed a smile. "Good morning, Wilhelm."

"Louise, a pleasure to see you." Wilhelm set a paper sack and a rolled-up copy of Acorn Hill's community newspaper, *The Acorn Nutshell*, on the counter before shaking her hand warmly. "Did Laurie give you your special order?" His gaze moved to the creamer. "I see that she did. May I offer you a cup of tea?"

"No, thank you, Wilhelm. I'm having a problem with the concept of chocolate-flavored tea." She nodded toward the front of the store. "I was wondering, though, what are those pretty round tins in the window? The ones with the Asian labels?"

He glanced toward the display. "Those are filled with white tea. It's all the rage now."

"White tea?" Louise had never heard of such a thing. "It's not white chocolate, is it?"

Wilhelm happily explained how the new brands of white tea differed from green and black varieties and had nothing to do with chocolate at all.

"The leaves come from a particular variety of tea plant called the *chaicha* or narcissus. Growers pick its fuzzy leaves, which are so light green they appear white—hence the name—just as the leaves sprout around a new bud." Wilhelm showed her one of the commercial brands of white tea he stocked, which showed the plant on the outside of the box. "Finally, rather than steaming, as would be done if making green tea, white tea leaves are put to dry in the sun."

"It must be very fresh," Louise said.

"The process is vital in order to preserve white tea's unique properties," Wilhelm said. "It has three hundred times the antioxidants found in black or green tea, not to mention how wonderful it is for the skin. Mother has started using it as a mask and she looks twenty years younger."

Louise knew Wilhelm's mother, and thought that the tea would be wonderful, indeed, if it could have that effect on Mrs. Wood.

"Well, what do you say, Louise?"

"I think we'll have to try some." Louise couldn't see giving up her favorite cold cream for tea, but knew Jane was always looking for natural beauty treatments.

Wilhelm brought her a tin with a panda painted on the label and rang up her order. "Have you heard the latest news? The Majeska Circus has come to town."

"Yes, my aunt told us last night." Louise paid for her purchase with her credit card. "Didn't bad weather bring them here? She mentioned something about hail storms."

"From what I heard at the Coffee Shop this morning," Wilhelm said, referring to the little restaurant frequented by most of the townspeople, "they're staying on Bellwood Farm for a few weeks. Because of the hail damage, they have to make repairs on some of their vehicles and their tents. It'll also give their animals a chance to rest."

"Goodness, that must have been some storm. I hope everything will turn out all right for them."

"Someone said the Majeskas have been putting on a minimum of three shows per week for the entire summer." Wilhelm wrapped the creamer in protective paper and put it back into its box. "I must say, it was very kind of Samuel and Rose Bellwood to let the circus stay on some of their vacant pastureland. Some people claim to be good Christians, but the Bellwoods are the real thing."

"Has there been any word if they'll have a show here in Acorn Hill?" Under the circumstances, Louise rather doubted that they would, but felt that she had to ask for Alice's sake.

Wilhelm handed her the credit card receipt and a pen. "No word yet, but we can hope."

"*You* would go to see the circus?" Louise asked, startled. Wilhelm was such a refined man and so seasoned a traveler that she would never have imagined him to be the type to enjoy such entertainment.

"Pass up a chance to see a show that bills itself as having the most magnificent menagerie and multitudes of magical marvels? One that is practically on my own doorstep?" He winked. "Not on your life, Louise."

Chapter Four

Her purchases neatly stowed in a shopping bag, Louise bid Wilhelm good-bye and went out of the shop. She walked over to Town Hall, thinking she would pop in and say hello to Mayor Lloyd Tynan—and promptly found herself in the middle of an argument.

"I will not!"

"You will too!"

"Will *not!*"

At first glance Louise thought that the two people who were standing toe-to-toe and having this dispute on the sidewalk were two nicely dressed children. Both had dark curly hair and possessed angelic, if somewhat reddened, faces. She glanced around but saw no mother or father.

"You *will*," the boy said. He had on a tailored shirt, tie and dress pants, and carried a jacket over his arm. "I'm the oldest, so it's my decision. We're going to change the act and that's final."

"Not if you want me to be in the act, it's not," the girl facing him said. Her dress was a denim jumper over a frilly blouse, and she had a bandana tied around her small head to hold back her longer curls. "You are not my boss, Billy. Mr. M. is, and he lets me do whatever I want. Unlike some people I know who are too pea-brained to know what's good for the act."

"I'm your brother!" the young man fumed. "Not to mention your partner!"

Louise thought about stepping in to calm down the two children, except that she noticed something very odd about them. Despite standing barely three feet tall, their dress, features and voices were not at all childlike. It took her a moment to realize that they were, indeed, adults.

The young woman glanced up at Louise. "Oh, look what you've done now. Sorry, we didn't mean to block the sidewalk. We're just a little lost." She grabbed her brother and yanked on his arm. "Move out of the way."

"I am not lost, you are," the young man retorted before giving Louise a sheepish look. "Excuse us, ma'am."

"No harm done." Louise looped her shopping bag over her arm. She had never before encountered such an extraordinary pair, but suspected now was not the time to marvel at their uniqueness. "May I direct you somewhere?"

"I'm looking for a shop that sells fabric, the kind you can use to make clothing," the young woman told her. "Someone mentioned there was one here in town."

"That would be Sylvia's Buttons." Louise told them how to get there. "Sylvia Songer, the owner, stocks a selection of dress fabrics, patterns and trims."

"Thank you, ma'am. I'm Roberta Bratwick, by the way, and this is my brother William." The young woman elbowed William, who glared at her. "We go by Billy and Bobbi."

Louise introduced herself and nodded toward the outskirts of town. "My sisters and I run Grace Chapel Inn, the local bed-and-breakfast."

"Now that's a great name," Billy said to Bobbi. "Dignified and easy to remember."

"We perform as clown tumblers for the Majeska Circus,"

Bobbi told Louise. "Our act is called 'The Tiny Tumbling Terrors.'"

"Which I hate," Billy tagged on, "and which my sister refuses to let me change to something better. Like our act. And our costumes, which are *stupid*."

"If the shoe fits," Bobbi said sweetly. "It's also a good warning for nice, normal people like Mrs. Smith here."

Louise found herself a little offended by that remark. Still, she realized that Bobbi might feel a need to characterize the people who likely stared at her every day. "My favorite writer, C. S. Lewis, said, 'Nothing is yet in its true form.' I try to keep that in mind when I look at other people."

Bobbi gave her an admiring look. "That's a nice way to think." She turned to her brother. "See? It doesn't matter what we look like, so we don't have to change our act."

Louise almost groaned. She had not intended to give the young woman more ammunition to use against her brother.

"You want to keep doing the same old tired thing forever? People never stop laughing at us as it is," her brother stated flatly. "What's wrong with putting some dignity into our performance?"

"*Dignity*?" Bobbi made a hooting sound. "We're clowns who run around and do minor gymnastics and a little tumbling, Billy. What's so dignified about your idea, anyway?"

"Everyone is crazy about fantasy these days," Billy said in a tone that indicated he had repeated this often and patiently. "We'll just be playing characters from the movies, like I told you before, okay? I'll be the warrior king and you'll be the beautiful fairy. We can still tumble."

"I *hate* those movies," Bobbi said flatly. "They're ridiculous and misogynistic, not to mention boring and—"

"They are not!"

Louise saw shopkeepers starting to look out through their

doors and windows. Certainly the Bratwicks were entitled to their disagreement, but it would be more diplomatic if they had it somewhere other than directly in front of Town Hall. The noise alone would surely draw Mayor Tynan out of his office any minute now to seek the source. *Has Ethel already called to talk to him about the circus?*

"Excuse me, madam," a deep voice said, and the largest man Louise had ever seen in her life eased past her. He appeared to be at least seven feet tall, and he had the physique of a dedicated body-builder. His head was shaved, but a thick brown mustache that curled at the ends graced the space between his mouth and his high-bridged nose. His eyes were very gentle and twinkled as he reached down to catch Bobbi's hand.

"Heya, now, no more arguing," the big man said. "I told you, you gotta stop doing this."

The big man's accent, Louise guessed, was Italian, as were his beautiful, handmade leather shoes, which looked to be bigger than those an NBA basketball star might wear.

"You walk too much around, I think, no? Come on." The man crouched down and held out his arms, and each of the Bratwicks reluctantly went and sat on one of his forearms. He stood and held both as he spoke to Louise. "Scusa the little ones, madam. They forget to behave sometime when they tired."

"As do we all," Louise said. She couldn't help feeling a bit like the Bratwicks as she stared up at the towering man.

"I am Gianni Talero," the man told her as he put Bobbi on one of his wide shoulders and took a colorful rectangle of stiff paper from his shirt pocket. "My card." He presented it to Louise with a proud flourish.

On the card was the rainbow-colored logo of a big top tent, an elephant standing on its hind legs and a clown's face, along with the words *Majeska's Most Magnificent Magical Marvels* and *Goliath* in lettering that resembled balloons.

"Goliath is our strong man and primary roustabout," Bobbi said as she put an arm around the big man's thick neck.

"Roustabout?" Louise repeated, not familiar with the word.

"That's what we call the people who do all the physical labor for the circus. Performers are the people who put on acts for the show." Bobbi gave the big man a fond pat. "Goliath does both and keeps me and Billy out of trouble too."

"Mostly," Billy said.

"With these two is full-time job," Goliath joked.

Louise smiled but she was beginning to feel the weight of many stares. "I do hope you all enjoy your stay in Acorn Hill." On impulse, she took one of her own business cards from her purse and handed it to Goliath. "If you need anything while you're in the area, this has my number."

"That is very kind of you, madam. Have a nice day." Goliath carefully tucked the card into his pocket. "We go to this store together now, eh, Bobbi? And we buy the fabric." With one more nod to Louise, Goliath strode off, still carrying the siblings.

Louise watched the trio head toward Sylvia's Buttons. She was so engrossed that she didn't at first hear her name being hissed.

"Louise. *Louise.*"

As she turned toward the new voice, she saw her aunt's friend Florence Simpson coming out of Time for Tea, in the same manner that a SWAT officer might creep up on a gun-wielding criminal. Florence's stealthy movement was only made more ridiculous by her attire, a chartreuse designer pants suit that did nothing for her sallow skin tone and even less for her stout figure.

"What in heaven's name did you think you were doing?" Florence asked, holding her expensive purse tight against her chest. She looked from side to side as if afraid of being seen speaking to her.

"I've been shopping, Florence," Louise said mildly. "Would you like to see what I've bought?"

"You know what I mean. You were *talking* to those *people*." Florence gestured in the direction Goliath had carried Billy and Bobbi. "You know where they're from, I hope?"

Louise sighed. "I didn't inquire as to their hometowns, but I would guess that the large fellow is from Italy. He has the loveliest accent."

"They're from that *circus*," Florence said in a whisper, as if the word was too horrible to speak out loud. "They're *performers*."

"Yes, that much I gathered." Louise was beginning to feel impatient. "I do have other errands to run, Florence, so perhaps you'll excuse me now."

"I can't believe you're so calm about this." Florence clutched her purse tighter. "What did they say to you? Did they want money? Are they going to panhandle, right here in town?"

"They wanted directions to Sylvia's Buttons. That's all." Louise noticed a number of townspeople who were trying casually to move closer to them to hear what was being said. "They're actually very nice people," she said in a slightly louder voice. "Just like any other visitors to our town. It would be nice if we could treat them as such."

"But that man was a giant." Florence looked over Louise's shoulder. "And those other two were m—"

Louise raised her index finger. "Do not use that word, Florence Simpson. It's insensitive."

"Oh, very well. You know what I mean." As she saw that the circus performers were not returning, she relaxed a little. "I just don't think you should be encouraging those people, Louise."

Louise had always prided herself on being slow to anger, however, around certain people, like Florence, her temper always seemed to shift into high gear. "Encourage them to do what? To shop? To feel welcome? To see Acorn Hill as a place that accepts everyone, regardless of his or her appearance, occupation or height? What, may I ask, is wrong with any of that?"

Florence scowled. "You always try to make me feel wrongheaded."

Louise took a deep breath. *I will remain civil.* "I was merely trying to help some visitors, Florence. Whatever it looked like to you, that's all it was."

"I'm not trying to pick a fight with you, Louise." She lowered her voice before she added, "I've been attending counseling sessions with Rev. Kenneth Thompson. I've been working on how I express myself to others. Caring what people think of me is not a crime."

Louise was taken aback by this. She knew Florence and her husband Ronald had gone to Kenneth Thompson, the head pastor of Grace Chapel, for some limited counseling in the past, but Louise assumed she had finished or abandoned the practice.

"I think that's wonderful, Florence." What else could she say that would sound appropriate? It wasn't as if she and Florence confided in each other on a regular basis. "Um, good for you."

"Yes, well . . . thank you." Florence looked a little uncomfortable for a moment. "The reason I'm worried about these people is your aunt. She lives alone in that carriage house. You should think of her before you go chatting up strangers."

"Ethel is very self-reliant, as you well know," Louise said. "She doesn't take chances with her personal safety, and she is only a few hundred feet from any help she might need."

Florence lifted her penciled eyebrows. "You can't be too careful these days, and as an older woman you should know that. Why, if I were a thief, I'd be staking out Ethel's place, or your inn."

"I believe thieves *case* houses, while the police conduct

stakeouts. I can't agree with your opinion, either. We can be alert without living in fear of being victimized." Louise managed a smile. "I do appreciate your concern for our aunt."

"You only . . . wait." Florence threw up her hands and took three deep breaths. "This is when Rev. Thompson says I should politely end the conversation, take some time for myself and recite my prayer for inner peace. Excuse me." Florence turned on her heel and paused to look back. "Have a nice afternoon." She walked quickly away.

Louise glanced through the window of Town Hall but saw no sign of Mayor Lloyd Tynan. The mayor was not only Ethel Buckley's special friend but someone the Howard sisters considered practically family. Lloyd had a talent for defusing tense situations, and she wondered if it might not be wiser to bring the circus matter to his attention now. Florence would probably not be the only person who had a negative reaction to the circus folk visiting town.

That was another strange thing. After any argument with Florence Simpson, Louise generally felt as if she'd been pummeled. This time she didn't feel that way at all. She acknowledged that her aunt's friend could still be incredibly annoying, but something was different. Perhaps it was learning that Florence was still in counseling and making an effort to change. She had never known the other woman to walk away from a dispute the way she just had.

Heavenly Father, Louise prayed, *please bless Florence with whatever inner peace she needs.*

The excitement of the day was not yet over, as Louise soon discovered on her way back to the inn.

Usually the drive home was uneventful, as few people had a reason to take Chapel Road past Fred's Hardware. The only time Louise ever encountered any amount of traffic was on Sunday mornings, when members of Grace Chapel drove to attend church services.

Her father, Rev. Daniel Howard, would have loved to meet Goliath and the Bratwick siblings, Louise thought as she drove past Fred's Hardware and waved to the owner, who was helping a customer carry out some rain gutter sections. Her father had spent most of his life in Acorn Hill as the head pastor of Grace Chapel, but he never missed an opportunity to learn something about the world outside their cozy little town. She felt certain he would have regarded the circus folk with intense interest and excitement. *Knowing Father, he probably would have taken them to have coffee and pie with him at the Coffee Shop.*

A low but growing rumble startled Louise. She peered ahead and saw a motorcycle coming directly at her from the opposite direction.

She only had time to form a short impression of the rider approaching her Cadillac. He appeared to be an adult, dressed in a black windbreaker and jeans and wearing a black helmet.

What is *that?* Louise thought as she peered at the rider in black. It looked almost as if his helmet was *burning*. He wasn't moving into his lane, either. *Why is he riding in the center of the road? Doesn't he see me?*

Louise felt a flutter of panic and put her hand on the Cadillac's horn. Before she could use it, the motorcycle moved into the right lane and went around her car.

It was then that she realized that what had appeared to be flickering flames were actually realistic, glittering orange, yellow and red decals on the helmet. The flaming helmet matched the blazing art painted on his motorcycle's fenders, tank and saddlebags.

Although she felt an immediate surge of relief, Louise gripped the steering wheel tightly as the motorcycle's engine seemed to roar in her ears as the machine went past her.

"I believe that I liked the elephants and the trucks better, Lord," she said as she glanced into her rear view mirror. The motorcyclist continued driving along Chapel Road toward town.

Louise reached the inn a few minutes later, where she parked and collected her shopping bags from the trunk before hurrying inside. Her heart was still pounding from the unexpected encounter with the motorcycle, and she didn't think she would feel safe until she was indoors and away from the road.

As soon as Louise closed the kitchen door behind her, she felt utterly ridiculous. *It was a motorcycle, Louise, not Abbadon leading swarms of locusts up out of the Bottomless Pit.* She looked up at the ceiling. *Lord, thank You for loving me, even when I behave like a doddering ninny.*

"Hey there." Alice came into the kitchen to help Louise with the bags she carried. Once she saw Louise's face, she frowned. "Are you feeling all right, Louise?" Always the nurse, Alice gently touched Louise's cheek. "You look so flushed."

"I'm fine." She leaned back against the door. "I scared myself on the drive home. Silly, really. It was only a motor-cyclist. When I saw that black jacket and flaming helmet, and the fact that he was driving down the middle of the road—"

"His helmet was *on fire?*" Alice's voice squeaked on the last two words.

"No, it was only covered with decals that looked like flames. Although for a moment I could have sworn he was . . ." She shook her head and laughed at herself. "Then there is everything that happened while I was in town." She handed a bag to Alice. "Let's put these away and I'll tell you all about it over lunch."

"Why do things like that never happen to me?" Jane wanted to know after hearing the description of Louise's brief but panic-inspiring experience with the motorcyclist. "I could drive up and down every road in this county and never see a biker with a flaming helmet. Or even a biker with a boring old ordinary safety helmet. Why is that?"

"You're lucky, I guess." Alice brought the glasses to the table while Louise set out three place settings and a pitcher of mandarin-orange-flavored iced tea.

"I can't imagine what a motorcycle rider is doing in Acorn Hill," Louise said as she filled the glasses. "Unless he works for that circus."

"A biker, Louise. They call themselves bikers," Jane corrected.

"Biker," Louise said. She intensely disliked the word already. "I'll try to remember that."

"He might work for the circus. I saw a program on TV where bikers drove around inside a huge steel cage ball," Jane said. She stood at the counter stuffing dark chopped greens, flaked smoked salmon and a spicy mayonnaise mixture into saucer-sized rounds of rye pita bread. "They had to use precise timing or they risked colliding with each other. Not a good thing when you're riding upside down."

The image that produced in Louise's head made her shudder. "I imagine not."

"Maybe he's stopped here on his way to attend some sort of meet," Alice suggested. "Bikers do like to congregate and socialize, just like any other special interest group."

Louise had heard of motorcycle enthusiasts flocking to various bike rallies and custom shows, but those events were usually held in metropolitan areas. "I can't recall ever seeing anything about a motorcycle rally or show in the area. Surely this motorcyclist—biker, I mean—didn't come here for one."

"Or she," Jane said. When Louise glanced at her, she shrugged. "Women do ride motorcycles too. All the time."

"This was a man." Louise felt sure of that. Although the helmet's tinted face shield had concealed the rider's face, his jeans and windbreaker had looked like men's wear. "A young man, I'd say, considering his taste in vehicle adornment."

"Customizations." Jane laughed. "Adornment is something you do to yourself, or to your Christmas tree."

"Whatever you want to call it." Louise felt irritable. Why should she know motorcycle lingo? "I simply wish he hadn't driven in the center of the road like that. It genuinely frightened me."

"I don't think he meant to scare you," Jane said as she handed Alice a dish of apple slices. "And you, madam, can stop making that face. You must eat more fresh fruit. The dumplings are for dessert after dinner, and if you're a good girl and don't snack, you may have one."

"I have to wait that long? Sadist," Alice grumbled as she brought the fruit to the table and took her place. "I have to agree with Jane, Louise. Not about the dumplings, but the biker's intention. I don't think he was trying to frighten you."

Louise placed folded napkins by each plate, and then sat down. "Why was he driving in the middle of the road like that? For his own amusement? It obviously wasn't for mine. Doesn't he know how much damage a classic Cadillac can do?"

"Most bikers do drive down the center of roads when they can, to avoid getting flat tires," Alice said. "There are all sorts of debris on the sides of roads that can puncture their tires." When Louise and Jane stared at her, she blushed. "I've never ridden one, of course, but I knew some boys in high school who rode them."

"Alice Christine Howard, you sneak," Jane said. "You never told me you dated bikers when you were a girl."

"I never dated them. I knew them, as in I had classes with them and friends who dated them. Father would have never permitted me to go out with a boy with a motorcycle. He would have thought it far too dangerous."

"Because of the bike or the boy?" Jane wanted to know.

A wry smile curved Alice's lips. "The bike, I think. Although in my younger days, all bikers really were regarded as 'Wild Ones.'"

"Things have changed. Lots of people own motorcycles, and take rides in the country on them," Jane said. "The man you saw could be just a weekend rider or a tourist, Louise."

Louise thought that highly unlikely and said so.

"I wonder why he would come to Acorn Hill. This town is not exactly what I'd call a biker mecca." Jane brought the stuffed pita sandwiches she had prepared for lunch and set beside them a split dish of bread-and-butter pickles and stuffed green olives before taking her seat.

"Alice, would you say the blessing?" Louise asked.

The sisters joined hands and bowed their heads as Alice thanked the Lord for their meal.

"Dear Lord," Alice prayed aloud, "You watch over us every day and are always there to help us wherever we go. You are our safety and our refuge, and we trust You with all our worries. Thank You for this food and for the loving hearts around this table and for the spiritual nourishment that You give us. It is through You and Your love that we can face any challenge and welcome new experiences, and for that we praise Your name, through Jesus Christ our Savior. Amen."

"Amen." Louise glanced at Alice. "Putting in a good word for me or the circus folk?"

"Or the motorcycle rider?" Jane asked, a twinkle in her eye.

"It was for everyone." Alice passed around the sandwich platter. "I'm also practicing the lesson for my next ANGELs meeting. I'm trying to help the girls learn how to pray more spontaneously while keeping in mind a specific purpose."

"As in, 'Hi there, God, can we talk about my problems?'" Jane teased.

Alice smiled. "Something like that."

"But aren't you worried that the girls may connect prayer

with momentary crisis, rather than with constant faith?" Jane asked. "Couldn't teaching them spontaneous prayer defeat the fundamental purpose of teaching them prayer, which is to make it a daily part of their lives?"

"Their lives are not any more planned or predictable than ours, Jane," Alice told her. "Spiritual crises can happen to them at any moment. My girls can't say 'Next Tuesday I'll see my best friend shoplift or I'll hear my parents have an argument, so I'll plan how I'm going to pray about it now.' No, when the next crisis happens, they need to have the means to reach out to God at that moment. Spontaneous prayer allows them to do that for any situation."

Louise cut her pita in half. "I often use spontaneous, informal prayer when something suddenly troubles me."

"Well, I do too," Jane admitted. "I just wonder if youngsters shouldn't first learn that prayer should be a process of careful reflection, meditation and entreaty. Otherwise they might forget that they're speaking to God."

"One of the things I stress to the ANGELs is that spontaneous prayer is informal, but never is it disrespectful," Alice assured her. "The girls learn to go through the same steps of honoring the Father, acknowledging sin, making requests of Him and expressing gratitude for His Love. What I teach them is to do it in their own words rather than repeated Bible verses or traditional prayers they've learned at church. They learn that it's okay to speak plainly and from the heart, which helps them relate better to traditional worship. Through spontaneous prayer, they stop automatically repeating words and start sensing the true meaning and power of prayer."

"Yes, I can see that. I should have known that our wise Alice would have all the bases covered," Jane said. "Thank you for explaining it."

After the Howards finished their lunch, Alice cleared the dishes to load the dishwasher for Jane. On a rack on the counter was the pan of apple dumplings where Jane had put them to cool. Louise suppressed a smile as she watched Alice lift a corner of the aluminum foil lightly covering the pan. Jane was busy wiping the table.

"Lord in heaven," Jane said just as Alice was about to dip her finger into the corner of the pan, "Your knowledge spans the universe, and so I'm sure You know what's going on here at Grace Chapel Inn. Please help my sister Alice resist the temptation of my apple dumplings until dinnertime, or I'm afraid she's going to *gain* five pounds. If You would do that, I'll try to remember not to leave them out on the counter again. Amen."

"Foiled by spontaneous prayer." Alice sighed as she replaced the covering on the pan without sampling the contents. "Thanks a lot, Jane."

Jane walked over to the sink and paused on the way to peck a kiss on Alice's cheek. "You're welcome."

Chapter Five

Louise had related the details of meeting Goliath and the Bratwick siblings, but decided not to mention her subsequent run-in with Florence Simpson or what she had said about the circus performers. Neither Alice nor Jane was particularly fond of Florence, and Louise didn't want to start off anyone on a rant about her. Florence once per day was enough Florence for just about anyone.

The sisters were just finishing with tidying up after their meal when the front door of the inn opened and slammed shut. The sudden, forceful bang made the window panes above the sink rattle.

A cry followed the noise. "Girls! Help!"

Jane shut off the sink faucet. "That's Aunt Ethel." She ran out of the kitchen, with Louise and Alice close behind her.

Ethel and Florence Simpson stood just inside the door. Both were breathing heavily, and Ethel's hat was askew. Florence, who was quite a bit heavier and in visible distress, groped the wall for support.

"What on earth?" Alice gasped.

"Here, now, it's okay." Jane went to Ethel, while Louise and Alice flanked Florence, and they guided the two frightened women to chairs in the living room. "Is anyone hurt?"

"No—yes—no," Ethel began babbling rapidly as soon as she sat down. "Bolt the door. Shove furniture against it. Call Lloyd. Call the police."

Jane knelt down in front of their aunt. "What is it? Did you have an accident?" She looked over at Florence, who was still too distressed to answer.

Alice was already giving both women a professional visual exam. "I don't see any blood or bruises."

"We're all right, but only just." Ethel dragged in a deep breath and gripped the chair's arms. "There is a maniac out there, and he chased us all the way from the carriage house." Her eyes filled with tears. "I swear to you, Jane, I thought we were done for."

Jane put her arms around Ethel and hugged her. "It's okay. You're safe with us now."

"He tried to run us down, right where we stood!" Florence chimed in breathlessly.

Alice went to the window and pulled the curtain aside. "I don't see any cars out there but ours, Aunt."

"He's on a motorcycle. It's black with flames on the sides," Ethel said as she pulled back from Jane's comforting embrace. "Land's sake, Louise, why are you standing around like you're waiting for a bus? Go and bolt the door before he comes into the house."

Louise joined Alice at the window and saw the biker whom she had encountered on the road earlier walking up to the front of the inn from the driveway. She shifted her gaze and saw that he had parked his motorcycle at the very front of the small parking lot, where it would not block any of the cars. She felt her heart rate speed up as he unbuckled the strap under his chin and removed his helmet to reveal his face. Who was this mysterious man?

"I don't know him," Alice said as she studied the middle-aged man's pleasant features and silver-streaked red hair, which he wore in a tidy crew cut. "Do you?"

"No, I don't. What should we do?" She nodded toward Ethel and Florence. "They're scared out of their wits."

"We'll get some answers," Jane said as she walked past them and opened the front door. To the man standing outside, she said, "Hi, I'm Jane Howard. Welcome to Grace Chapel Inn."

Alice covered her mouth with one hand. Without thinking, Louise stepped forward to put herself between the man and Ethel and Florence.

"Hello. I'm looking for a room. Did you happen to see . . ." the man hesitated as he came in and saw Ethel and Florence in the living room. "There you ladies are. I thought you might have run in here."

A room? Louise was confused now. Why would he chase Ethel and Florence over a room?

Florence appeared ready to keel over in a faint. Instead, she slumped back in her chair and, after covering her face with her hands, began softly reciting the Lord's Prayer.

"About what happened out there," the man continued. "I didn't realize how much I must have startled you when I drove up. I'm sorry."

"Sorry? *Sorry?*" Ethel rose to her feet and jabbed a finger in the direction of the biker. "Don't think you can come in here and pretend you did nothing wrong."

"What did I do?" the man asked, bewildered now.

Florence was so outraged that she stopped praying and dropped her hands. "What did you do? You nearly killed us!"

"What?" The biker's dark eyes widened, and he nearly dropped his helmet. "How could I possibly—"

"You tried to mow us down with that diabolical machine of yours," Ethel added. "Deliberately. In broad daylight. Not two steps from my own front door."

"Mrs. Buckley's nieces are going to call the police and have you arrested," Florence said as she came to stand beside her friend. She folded her arms and gave the man a triumphant look. "Aren't you, Louise?"

Louise bit back a groan. "Florence . . . Aunt Ethel . . ."

"I do sincerely beg your pardon, ma'am, but I should explain what happened out there." The man looked very upset as he turned to address Ethel. "I saw you ladies come out of that little house and I assumed that you both worked here." His expression changed. "Is this Grace Chapel Inn?" he asked Louise.

"Yes, it is."

The man gave Ethel an unhappy smile. "I couldn't quite read that sign out there. My eyes aren't as good as they once were, I'm afraid. That's why I stopped, so I could ask you two ladies if this was the inn and if there were any rooms available. I was told by the hardware store owner in town that there might be. But before I could park and get my helmet off to speak to you, well . . ." he glanced at Florence. "That lady began screaming and you both ran away from me."

A complete silence fell over the room as everyone digested this.

At last Alice cleared her throat. "Well, that seems to explain things."

The ridiculousness of the situation made Louise's stomach clench. She also suspected that soon there would be one of her tension headaches settling in behind her eyes. "Indeed, it does."

"So." Jane looked at Ethel. "I guess we won't have to call the police."

"For which I am very grateful," the biker said, sounding relieved.

"Aunt Ethel?" Louise said, trying to keep her tone even. "Under the circumstances, I think another apology is in order."

"Oh, very well." Ethel faced the biker. "I apologize

for assuming that you were chasing us on that loud, evil-looking—"

"It's just a motorcycle, Auntie," Jane said.

"Motorcycle." She held out her hand to the man. "I'm Ethel Buckley, by the way, and I'm very sorry that we jumped to the wrong conclusions, Mr. . . ."

"MacElroy Wilde," the biker said and shook her hand. "I answer to almost anything, but I prefer Mac."

"How do you do, Mac," Jane said and quickly made introductions all around. Only Florence seemed reluctant to shake his hand, but, after a glance at Ethel, she did so and murmured something terse but polite under her breath.

"I'd better get back on the road and see if I can find another place to stay," Mac said, preparing to put on his helmet.

"How long will you need accommodations?" Jane asked, ignoring the startled looks that Ethel, Florence and her sisters directed toward her.

"I wouldn't want to ask for a room from you ladies after the commotion I've caused," Mac said, and chuckled.

"Nonsense. We'd love to have you stay here at Grace Chapel Inn," Jane assured him. "Come over to the desk and we'll talk about rates and dates."

"But—" Ethel began to protest.

"Let's go back into the living room for a moment," Louise said, and put an arm around her aunt. "So you can catch your breath."

The moment Louise closed the door, Ethel began to talk. "How could she invite that man to stay at the inn? Doesn't she realize that he's a maniac?"

"An extremely well-mannered maniac, I'd add," Louise said. "We do run a business here, Aunt, and we have no reservations booked for several weeks. We can always use the income." She didn't admit that she wasn't entirely happy that Jane had offered a room to the man.

"He seems like a very nice man, doesn't he?" Alice asked.

"I suppose so." Florence went to the window and looked out. "What are people going to think when they see that evil-looking motorcycle parked in your drive?"

"They'll assume it belongs to a guest," Louise said, keeping her tone even but firm.

"I don't trust these biker types," Florence said. "A man his age has no business riding around on one of those things. What sort of name is Wilde, anyway? Sounds like he made it up. You should think about his finances too. If he can't afford to drive a proper car, then he might try to avoid paying his bill."

"That motorcycle is not cheap, Florence," Alice pointed out. "It looks new. Some motorcycles can cost as much as a car."

"Money matters aside, Florence is right. I don't like the idea of that man staying here. Not with you girls always alone in the house." Ethel shook her head. "There's something wrong with someone who chases two women with a vehicle."

"He did explain why he did that." Louise sat down next to her aunt and took her hand in hers. "I know it was a frightening experience for you." Indeed, Louise was feeling guilty about her own earlier assumptions, particularly since her encounter with Mac had been completely harmless and far less dramatic. "I think it would behoove us to remember that first impressions are very often wrong."

Florence gave her an incredulous look. "You can't tell me that you *approve* of that man."

"I've never met anyone like him before," Louise replied. This seemed to be her day for such things. "I will not make any snap judgments about him. Remember what Christ said in Matthew 7:1? 'Do not judge, or you too will be judged.'"

"So, Louise, you're going to treat him the same way you did those circus people." Florence started to say something else, stopped herself and made a face. "I'll need to pray a bit more for guidance this afternoon."

Alice tried but couldn't hide her surprise at Florence's words.

Louise decided a change of subject might be prudent, and so she told them about Jane's enthusiasm in making apple dumplings earlier that morning. She had everyone relaxed and smiling when Jane came in a few minutes later.

"Mac is all checked in and settled in his room." She eyed her aunt and Florence. "For those of us who have watched too many reruns of a certain movie starring Marlon Brando, you should know that he's a retired bank executive from Washington, D.C."

"I don't know what you're talking about, Jane Howard," Ethel said, obviously offended. "I never liked Marlon Brando."

"How long will Mr. Wilde be here, Jane?" Alice asked.

"A few weeks. He's leaving his stay open-ended." Jane sat down beside Louise and smothered a yawn. "Excuse me. Some odd noise woke me up before dawn, and I couldn't go back to sleep. I'll have to have a little snooze later."

"How can you talk about sleeping with that man living right here under your roof?" Ethel demanded.

"I don't think he'll pay to stay in the garden shed, Auntie," Jane said with a laugh. "What do you imagine he'll do? Throw wild parties in the parlor? Chase Alice around the garden? Ride his bike up and down the stairs?"

Florence muttered something about inner peace.

"You can do as you like, Jane." Ethel sat back and rubbed one temple. "You always do, don't you? Regardless of the consequences."

Jane's expression changed from amused to militant. "Now, wait a minute—"

"Ladies, please," Louise said quickly, "Mr. Wilde is a guest here now. We shall treat him as such and refrain from antagonizing each other over his presence. Civility under duress," she added when she saw that Jane was about to speak again, "requires no small effort, but is appreciated by all who are treated with it. Quite unlike anger, or sarcasm, for that matter."

Jane ducked her head. "Got me on that one." She looked over at Ethel. "Sorry, Auntie."

"I can be civil, Louise, even when your sister teases me to distraction. I just hate feeling so helpless," Ethel said bitterly. "I didn't realize until just now that I'm too old to run away from someone chasing me. If that Wilde man had meant to rob us or hurt us—and yes, Louise, I *do* understand that he never intended to—I couldn't have stopped him."

"Of course you could," Florence said promptly. "The fact that you're an older woman has nothing to do with it. You could take a self-defense course."

"That's for young women in good shape, the kind who can bend over and touch their toes." Ethel glanced over her knees. "I feel lucky that I can still *see* mine."

"You know, the Mature Years Center in Riverton offers self-defense courses for seniors," Florence declared. "Some of the women in my prayer circle have talked about attending them."

"I don't think that's necessary," Louise put in.

Florence shook her head. "I disagree. Women our age have to be more cautious. We're walking targets for any sort of mugger or purse snatcher."

"Now that you mention it, one of my high school friends who now lives in Ohio took a self-defense course offered by her company," Ethel said. "She wrote to me about it. I thought at the time that she was crazy for taking it. Then she called me and told me how a man tried to mug her not two weeks after she completed the class. She knocked him out with a single punch." She made a choppy motion with her hand.

Louise tried to imagine Ethel defeating a mugger. "It would have been smarter for her to run away. What if he had been armed?"

"I don't know. I didn't know what to do when that Wilde person started chasing us." Ethel looked at Florence. "Do you have to be a member of Mature Years to take the class?"

"No, from what Sue told me, the class is open to anyone over age fifty-five. I can't remember the teacher's name, but she's a police officer who works for the Riverton PD." Florence was beginning to sound excited now. "Why don't we sign up for the class together? I think I'd feel much safer if I knew how to properly defend myself."

Alice gave Louise a panicked look. "Aunt, really . . ."

"What would be the harm in taking a class like that?" Jane asked. "I'm just sorry I'm too young to sign up with you both."

Louise shook her head at Jane's comment. *Always ready to leap to the defense of the underdogs, even when she doesn't agree with them. That's our Jane.*

"Come, Florence," Ethel said as she rose to her feet. "We'll go back to my house and call Mature Years to see what the class schedule is and how we can sign up for the next one."

Louise smothered a sigh. Her aunt was determined, and when Ethel Buckley set her mind on doing something, there was little anyone could do to change it. *If nothing else, it should keep her from worrying about our new guest.*

"One more thing, girls." Ethel leveled a stern look at all three of her nieces. "If that man doesn't behave himself—and I wager he won't—I expect you to evict him from this house at once."

"If they actually do take this self-defense course," Alice said after their aunt and Florence had left for the carriage house, "one of us should probably tag along to the first class, just to make sure it isn't too much for either of them. I'd go, but with the inn being empty, I told my supervisor that I'd work some extra shifts at the hospital this month."

"I'd love to go, but I'm using what spare time I have to experiment with some new chocolate recipes," Jane said. "Exquisite Chocolatiers in Philadelphia asked if I'd come up with something new for our Madeleine and Daughters truffles collection." Jane had developed the collection in partnership with the Philadelphia firm as one of her many interests that added to the inn's coffers.

"New truffles?" Alice perked up.

"They have plenty of raspberry and hazelnut flavors, so I'm going to try whipping up some different centers from assorted nuts and fruits." Jane glanced at Alice. "Don't even think about it. There is no such thing as a diet truffle."

"There *should* be," Alice grumbled.

"The point is, neither of you can go," Louise said, giving in to the inevitable. *I should talk to Rev. Thompson about that prayer for inner peace he gave to Florence.* "Very well. If they sign up, I'll take them to the first class."

Chapter Six

Contrary to Ethel's dire predictions, MacElroy Wilde proved to be one of the most considerate guests who had ever stayed at Grace Chapel Inn. Each morning he came down to the dining room at precisely 7:00 A.M. for breakfast, and always asked for items that required little preparation. After breakfast he left the inn. He returned each evening just before dark and spent the night in his room.

"All he ever wants is two pieces of toast, grapefruit and a pot of coffee," Jane complained one morning after Mac had been at the inn for a week. "I went out to the dining room yesterday to talk him into trying one of my special omelets—I even offered to make it with egg whites or egg substitute, in case he's watching his cholesterol level—but he turned it down and ordered the same thing he does every day."

"He always leaves his place at the table so neat," Alice said. She was glumly cutting an orange into slices.

Jane snorted. "He doesn't eat enough to make a mess."

"I mean, he leaves the cloth so clean I don't really have to change it," Alice explained. "Same thing with the guest bathroom. I go in to clean and find it spotless."

"He keeps his room very neat, as well," Louise confirmed

as she popped bread into the toaster. "Alice, do you want whole wheat or white this morning?"

"Whole wheat. I wonder if he sleeps the whole time he's up there," Alice said. None of the Howards had seen Mac in the parlor or anywhere in the inn other than the dining room and going to and from his room.

"You could set your watch by when he comes and goes," Jane said, "but I hardly know he's here. I never hear a peep out of him."

Louise put the toast on a plate and regarded both of her sisters. "Are we actually complaining that a guest is *too* quiet, polite and courteous?"

"Well . . ." A dimple appeared in Jane's cheek. "I confess I was hoping that he'd live up to his surname, even just a little bit, that he'd add a little spice to our lives."

Alice's mouth rounded. "Jane!"

"Come on, admit it, you expected him to be completely different too," Jane challenged. "He's not anything like those boys you never dated in high school, right?"

Alice mulled that over for a minute. "He certainly is the *nicest* biker I've ever met."

"Same here." Jane went to the refrigerator to retrieve the plum preserves that Louise liked for her toast, and her own strawberry jam. "So what do you think he does all day when he's not here?"

"I know that he's been to the used bookstore over in Potterston," Louise said. "When I went to dust his room yesterday, I saw a couple of books on the night table with the store's stamp on the edge of the pages."

"We should tell him about Nine Lives," Alice said, referring to the bookshop in town. "If you don't think it would upset Viola to have a biker as a customer."

Viola Reed, the owner of the Nine Lives Book Shop, was one of Louise's friends. "Knowing Viola, she would probably try to sell him books by Hemingway and Kerouac," Louise said.

"So what does he read?" Jane leaned forward, eager to know. "Mysteries? Thrillers? Adventure novels?"

"From the titles, I would say Mr. Wilde has a keen interest in economics and politics," Louise told her. "All of them are very analytical works by well-respected experts." In fact, some of the titles she had seen on Mac's night table could have been at home on the bookshelves of a university professor or stockbroker.

"I guess that's understandable. After all, he was a bank executive, and he is from Washington, D.C.," Alice said.

"But he's a biker." Jane shook her head. "Shouldn't he be out doing a little carousing or something?"

"Where would he do this carousing, dear?" Louise asked her. "At the Coffee Shop? Or perhaps at the Good Apple Bakery?"

Alice chuckled. "I know, at Fred's Hardware. Think of all the fun those men have, trying out the hammers and screwdrivers in Fred's demonstration section."

"Not just the men," Jane told her airily. "I really like that cordless electric drill Fred has on display this month."

Louise eyed her. "Playing with power tools? Don't you have enough gadgets in the kitchen?"

"Gadgets are like bracelets," Jane said, and shook her wrist so that the Celtic charm bracelet she was wearing jingled. "A girl can never have too many."

"Good morning, girls." Ethel came through the kitchen door. "Can you spare a cup of coffee? Mine didn't turn out too well this morning. It tasted like I'd filtered it through old socks. I think I need to clean that machine. Do you have any of that solution, Jane?"

"Sure, Auntie, a whole bottle." Jane exchanged a look with Louise that spoke volumes before she went to get another mug.

Louise brought another place setting to the table, but

Ethel refused any breakfast. "I already had some cereal at home, and I'm trying to watch my weight these days," she told her nieces, and gave her stomach a pat.

Alice glanced down at the plain cereal, skim milk and sliced oranges that Jane said were all she could have for her breakfast. "Would you watch mine too?"

"That's my job," Jane said.

As Ethel chatted with Alice and Jane, Louise got up to load the dishwasher. It seemed lately that their aunt was using any excuse to pay daily visits to the inn. The visits themselves were not unusual, for Ethel tended to come and go as she pleased, often interrupting the sisters during meals or in the midst of work. But the frequency of her appearances was increasing, which was suspicious. Louise couldn't remember her aunt's ever spending as much time at the inn before Mac Wilde's arrival.

"Florence and I finally were able to enroll in the Mature Years Center's self-defense class," Ethel announced.

"Finally?" Jane asked. "Was there a problem?"

"They insisted Florence and I have our doctors provide them with fitness certificates before we were allowed to enroll. It has been over a year since Florence's last physical, so her doctor insisted on seeing her first." Ethel flapped her hand. "Doctors. Always fretting about your blood pressure."

"You should never do anything like this class without your doctor's approval," Alice said. "These classes will probably be very tiring, especially in the beginning. Be prepared for some sore muscles."

"I hope the instructor teaches me how to do one of those over-the-shoulder throws." There was a certain amount of grim enthusiasm in Ethel's voice. "That always looks so impressive on television, doesn't it?"

"I'd like to know how to toss someone through the air like that," Jane said. "When you get that technique down, Auntie, will you teach it to me?"

"Is this a class to learn self-defense," Louise asked mildly, "or how to commit assault and battery?"

"There, I knew it." Her aunt put down her coffee mug with a thump. "I knew you'd say something like that, Louise. You always do, in just that tone, like you're being reasonable and I'm not."

Louise raised her eyebrows. "Then I'm pleased that I haven't disappointed you."

"You know what I mean." Ethel shook her finger. "You think the solution to every problem is prayer, and every solution that isn't prayer is worthless. Well, prayer isn't going to protect me from criminals or hooligans. The Lord helps those who help themselves."

Alice gave Louise an uneasy look. "Aunt Ethel, that's not exactly true, and not exactly what that means."

"It's all right, Alice." To her aunt, Louise said, "I am not *entirely* against this notion of yours. Every woman should be sensible about her personal safety, but I think there are other ways you might protect yourself that don't involve physical violence. As for prayer, I do believe it can help bring about solutions to any problem. I can't speak for the Lord, of course, but Father taught us that He helps everyone. All you have to do is ask Him."

"I'm going to do one better," Ethel said. "I'm going to show Him that I can take care of myself."

There was no arguing with such determination, Louise thought. "I think He already knows that, Aunt."

"Mrs. Smith, do I have to?" Charlie Matthews stared at the sheet music in front of him and wrinkled his nose.

Louise looked over his shoulder to make sure she had not inadvertently given him the wrong lesson. Charlie's sister was her most advanced piano student, and on one memorable occasion she had mixed up their lesson folders. Trying to play

Sissy Matthews's lesson, a complicated piece by Bach, had thrown Charlie into a complete panic.

She saw that this time the music sheet was correct. "Yes, Charlie, you do."

"Okay." With a hangdog look, the boy put his hands over the keyboard and began slowly picking out the notes for "Twinkle, Twinkle, Little Star."

Louise went over to where Charlie's mother Carol sat listening. "I thought he was much further along than this," she told Louise quietly, so Charlie couldn't hear.

"He was, in terms of what he could play," Louise whispered. "The return to basics is just so he can improve some of his skills."

"But don't you think that will discourage him? He did so well playing 'Hey Jude' at his father's birthday party. I had hoped . . ." Carol glanced at her son and lowered her voice again. "I know Charlie will never be as proficient a pianist as Sissy, but I still think it's important he get some grounding in music."

"I agree," Louise said, "but at this point in his education, he must learn how to recognize and correct his mistakes. That is why we've returned to the beginner lessons."

"Was he making so many?"

"Not really. All of his problems, in fact, are directly related to his note reading," Louise told the concerned mother. "I noticed that despite his proficiency at reading sheet music, he was continually hitting the same wrong notes when he played. I did some testing and discovered that he is doing something we call 'mirror reading.' He sees one note but he mistakes it for another when he plays. The only way to resolve it is to return to the basics and use very simple pieces while we focus on reinforcing correct note recognition."

Carol looked over at her son. "Could he be, you know . . . musically dyslexic or something?"

"No, not at all," Louise said. "There are some children

who have this problem because they have reading problems, or poor symbol recognition skills, but that isn't Charlie's problem. He is a very active boy who I suspect would prefer playing soccer to playing Tchaikovsky."

"In a heartbeat," Carol said, and chuckled.

Louise smiled. "How has he been doing with his piano practice at home?"

"I have him play his practice sheets every day after school, just as you recommended." Carol described the scales and music her son had been playing at home, and added, "He never wants to practice, of course, but we use the 'sports rule' method."

Louise frowned. "I've never heard of that one."

"Tim's idea," Carol said, referring to her husband. "We told Charlie that if he doesn't do his piano work, he can't go to soccer practice."

That could be the root of Charlie's mirror reading problem, Louise thought. "How long does it take him to get through a typical practice session, Carol?"

"I don't know, really." She considered that for a moment. "Ten or fifteen minutes at the most."

"The practice sheets I give him generally should take twice that long to play. Rushing through them is probably where he picked up his note recognition problem."

Over at the piano, Charlie hit a wrong note and immediately stopped playing. Louise excused herself to return to his side. "Good, you heard it this time." She had instructed him to stop whenever he realized the note he had played was wrong. Working on simple songs also made it easier for him to "hear" a mistake. "Now, where is the note you misread on the sheet?" She waited until he pointed it out. "Please tell me, what is that note?"

He looked at the sheet. "It's a B, Mrs. Smith."

"Excellent. Now, please look at the keyboard. Which note did you play?"

Charlie peered at the keys. "Gee. I played a D instead." He played the correct note, glanced up at her and said, "Start over from the beginning, right? Focus on the sheet music and play B not D this time."

She rested an affectionate hand on his shoulder and smiled at him. "That's the spirit."

When the lesson was over and Charlie and his mother had departed, Louise tidied up the parlor and went out to see if she was needed at the front desk. There she found Jane filling out a form for some supplies from a paper goods distributor.

"How many rolls of paper towels do you think we typically go through in a month?" Jane asked.

"I'm not sure." Louise tried to recall how many times they usually changed the roll in the kitchen. "Twenty?"

"Sounds about right." Her youngest sister wrote a number on the form. "All done with Charlie?"

"Yes, and I've solved the mystery of his missing notes." Louise looked at the desk, but it was clear of any paperwork waiting to be done. "Anything need my attention?"

"Nope. Dinner is ready to go into the oven, the gardening is done and Alice changed Mac's linens while you were teaching." Jane waved a hand toward the stairs. "You can relax for a couple of hours if you like."

Louise felt too energized by her success with Charlie to rest or read. "Is Alice at work?"

"No, she's in Father's study with Pauline Sherman." Jane gestured toward Daniel Howard's favorite room. "They're working together on something for the next ANGELs meeting."

Louise frowned. "I didn't hear Pauline's car."

"One of her friends dropped her off here." Jane flipped over the order form. "I think it was Joyce Wilson."

"Maybe I can help them." Louise walked back to the study, the door to which Alice had left open, and looked inside. Her sister was at Daniel's desk, while the younger woman was seated on a chair, making out a list.

The mother of two of Alice's ANGELs, Pauline Sherman was one of those women who sometimes inspired envy in others. Although she was in her mid-thirties, she looked quite a bit younger, thanks to good skin and a model's figure. She wore her smooth, light brown hair in an angled fall to her shoulders, and she had the same soft blue eyes and pretty features that she had passed along to both of her daughters. Pauline always dressed beautifully, too, in classic styles. Today she had on a foam-green linen dress and hunter green jacket, and wore a narrow gold chain around her throat. On the chain was a modest cross pendant that sparkled with three gemstones.

Louise liked Pauline Sherman, who had attended a Bible study class with her and had some interesting opinions on the Scriptures. She always seemed in such a hurry, however, and had often missed the class because of some conflict with a family commitment.

Pauline looked up as if sensing her presence and smiled. "Hello, Louise."

"It's nice to see you, Pauline." Louise glanced at Alice. "I'm done with piano lessons. May I help you two with anything?"

"Pauline and I are just going over the ANGELs call list, to see who can carpool for a day trip," Alice said. "We're going to Bellwood Farm so the girls can see the Majeska circus animals."

"Have they decided to put on a show?" Louise asked. Although the circus had been in town for over a week, there had been no announcement of a local performance.

Alice shook her head. "Not yet. I called Rose Bellwood to ask her about it. Apparently they're still trying to repair some damaged vehicles and torn tents. It was Rose's idea to bring the girls over to see the menagerie."

"I hope they do put on a show," Pauline said. "I adore the circus."

"You do?" Louise wouldn't have guessed that.

"I used to play circus when I was a girl," Pauline said. "My mother gave me a couple of her old cocktail dresses and allowed me to wear them as my costumes. I would set out all my stuffed animals and pretend to put on a show." She laughed softly at herself. "Not in front of anyone, of course. I was too shy for that."

"Pauline?" Jane appeared in the doorway. "Your husband and your daughters are here looking for you."

"Stanley and the girls? But I told them to be here at—" Pauline glanced at the thin gold watch on her wrist and a look of panic came over her face. "Five o'clock? Already?" Without another word she grabbed her purse and hurried out of the study.

Louise and her sisters followed Pauline out to the front hall, where Stanley Sherman and Pauline's daughters were waiting. Stanley looked as if he had just left work, while the girls were dressed in light sweaters and shorts over black leotards and dance shoes.

"I lost track of the time," Pauline was saying to her husband.

"That's okay, honey," Stanley said, and chuckled as he put an arm around her shoulders. "You're always running behind schedule these days."

Stanley Sherman was a tall, broad-shouldered, good-looking man who had gone to college on a football scholarship. A hip injury had dashed his hopes for a pro career in the sport, so he had fallen back on his accounting major and gone into the tax consultant business. Louise knew that he now had four different offices and had more than thirty people working for him.

The Shermans were members of Grace Chapel, and although Louise didn't know him very well, Stanley seemed like a kind man.

"So, we'd better hit the road and make up for lost time," Stanley said, his voice deliberately hearty. He looked around the room. "Where are the grocery bags?"

"I . . . I don't have any," Pauline said. "I meant to ask Joyce if she could stop by the store and the cleaners on our way here, so I could do my errands, but we were talking about the fund-raiser and . . . I forgot to ask. I forgot all about it."

Stanley dropped his arm. "You didn't pick up the groceries or the dry cleaning?" Clearly astonished by this, he consulted his own watch. "But, sweetheart, the cleaners is closed by now."

"I know." Pauline ducked her head. "I'm sorry, Stanley."

"This is going to create some problems," her husband continued, as if he hadn't heard her apology. "I need my gray suit for a morning meeting. Iberon Electronics is a family-owned business, and old man Iberon isn't going to give his accounts over to someone in a golf shirt and chinos."

"Mom," Briana, her older daughter, said, and tugged on Pauline's wrist. "We're going to be late. Let's go."

"All right, dear, just a minute. Stanley, you could wear your green suit," Pauline suggested, a note of bright desperation in her tone. "I picked up that one with the last dry cleaning order over the weekend."

"That's looking out-of-date," Stanley said, shaking his head sadly. "I wanted to wear the gray one. Never mind about it," he added when she began to apologize again. "What's done is done. I'll figure out something else. Now, we have to get the girls to their dance lessons." He patted her shoulder. "You can drop me off at the club on the way there and go shopping while they're in class."

Louise couldn't help noticing how tired Pauline's face looked as she muttered a meek, "Yes, dear, of course I can."

"Speaking of shopping, while you're at the store, would you pick up a copy of the *Nutshell*? It wasn't delivered this week for some reason."

Pauline looked confused, opened her mouth and then closed it.

She forgot to pay the paper boy, Louise thought with sudden clarity, *and she has just realized it.*

"Our dance teacher hates it when we walk in late, Mom," Tiffany, Pauline's younger daughter, complained, pulling on her mother's sleeve. "Can we go now?"

"Yes, darling." Visibly embarrassed, Pauline turned to Alice. "Would you mind terribly finishing the car pool calls without me?"

"Not at all, I'll take care of it," Alice assured her.

"Thank you." The younger woman smiled before hurrying out of the inn with her family.

Louise could hear Stanley's voice, still mildly reproving Pauline, as the Shermans walked out to their car. She knew that in addition to being a homemaker and helping Alice with her ANGELs group activities, Pauline served on at least two other church committees, volunteered at her daughters' school and held regular dinner parties for friends and Stanley's business associates. In fact, she had often wondered how Pauline managed to do so much for her family and friends from church. *She is obviously overloaded.*

"I don't know how Pauline does it," Jane said, unconsciously echoing Louise's thoughts. "If I tried to keep up with her, even for a day, I'd have a nervous breakdown."

"She tries so hard to be supportive of Briana and Tiffany and all the ANGELs." Alice sighed. "I wish some of the other mothers would help out half as often as she does."

Over the years Louise had known many women like Pauline, who thought nothing of taking on too many responsibilities. Some thought that the more they did without complaint, the better wife and mother that made them. Others felt guilty for not working outside the home, as if being a homemaker had become something to be ashamed of. They tried to "justify" their lack of paid employment by keeping busy every moment of the day. Naturally their families took it for granted, and often added more burdens. She hoped that this wasn't happening in Pauline's case and that the carelessness Stanley had shown toward her was simply an isolated incident.

That night at dinner it was Jane's turn to say grace, but Louise asked if she could offer the prayer instead.

"Dear Lord," Louise prayed, "I thank You for this meal and my two wonderful sisters, with whom I share it. Your bounty is everywhere, in the food we have and the care with which it is always prepared. Your presence is known to me in the life I live with my sisters and the love they show me without reservation. Sometimes I take that affection and devotion for granted, Heavenly Father, and I ask Your forgiveness for that. My sisters are, like all Your gifts, the greatest blessings of my life. Help me be the same for them, in all that I do, through Christ our Lord. Amen."

"Same goes for me, Lord," Jane said, tears glistening in her eyes.

Alice squeezed their hands. "Amen to that."

Chapter Seven

The following Wednesday morning Louise received a phone call from Rose Bellwood, who invited her out to the farm to meet the owners of the visiting circus.

"Samuel and I have been going to the Majeska circus every year since our kids were small," Rose told her. "Over time we've gotten to know the owners, Aldo and Ilsa Majeska. We usually have to drive across the state every year to see their show, so you can imagine how happy we were when they called and asked to stay on the farm."

"Thank you for the invitation, but I wouldn't want to intrude," Louise said. She was curious about the circus folk, of course, but wondered why Rose would invite her. She didn't think that she gave the appearance of someone who would be interested in the circus.

I think I've just called myself a snob, Louise thought with mild surprise.

"They're very friendly people," Rose assured her. "Now that they're settled in . . . well, as settled as a circus can be in any one place . . . I was hoping to introduce them to some of our friends and neighbors. I know they'll be happy to show you around their camp. Bring your sisters along, if you like."

Louise found that she would rather visit a circus and

please Rose than stay at home and feel like a snob, and so she agreed to drive out to Bellwood Farm at noon. Alice was working a shift at the hospital, and when she asked Jane if she wanted to accompany her, her youngest sister groaned.

"I wish I could." She looked down at the tray of hand-dipped truffles she was working on. "But I've got to work out this vanilla-almond cream combination. I can't get the ground almonds to blend very well with the vanilla whip. I've almost reduced them to the consistency of powder, and they still make the center taste gritty."

Louise eyed the little nut grinder Jane had been using. "Why don't you try that paste you use to make marzipan? That's smooth, and it's made from almonds, isn't it?"

Jane grinned. "You're a genius. I take back every bad thing I ever said about your cooking."

"You could repay me by coming out to Bellwood Farm," Louise suggested.

"I've still got to dream up some more combinations for Exquisite Chocolatiers," Jane said, making an apologetic face. "Also, I don't want to leave these where Alice can find them. Don't worry, you'll have fun." She gave Louise a hug. "I'll want to hear all the details, the minute you get back."

"I'll take notes if I have to," Louise promised her.

Walking out to her Cadillac, Louise heard a faint sound of an approaching engine and shaded her eyes to see Mac Wilde riding past Grace Chapel. He was headed away, not toward the inn. *What* does *he do all day?* She wondered.

Bellwood Farm was located in an area where Amish families had once farmed most of the land. Most of the original Pennsylvania settlers had moved farther west, forming tight-knit communities within Lancaster County, but there were several families that had stayed behind and continued to farm while maintaining their faith and the pastoral simplicity of their way of life.

Rose and Samuel were not "plain people," and had started out on Bellwood Farm with little experience as sheep farmers. Rose, the daughter of an auctioneer, and Samuel, the son of a potato farmer, had learned a great deal about raising sheep from their Amish neighbors, and they put those lessons to good use. As a result, their stock of Merino sheep produced some of the finest wool in the state and provided steady jobs for a number of local farm hands, shearers and wool-makers.

Louise had always thought of Bellwood Farm as a lovely retreat from the modern world. Wide, green pastures surrounded the long white two-story farmhouse, which Rose and Samuel had enlarged and modified over the years to suit the needs of their growing family. Along the edges of the property were the wooded acres that Samuel kept preserved for future generations, thinning out dead or diseased trees only when necessary to prevent brush fires.

As Louise parked in the drive and walked up the stone path to the house, her eyes were drawn as always to the round, red and green hex sign that the Bellwoods kept above their front door. In the center of the sign, surrounded by folk art-styled tulips, hearts, birds and a star, was the German word *Wilkum*, greeting anyone who came to visit.

"I thought I heard a car." Rose Bellwood said as she appeared in the doorway before Louise had a chance to knock. A petite brunette who wore her long dark braids pinned around her head like a crown, she had the quiet smile and patient eyes of someone used to living by the change of seasons rather than the flipping pages of a calendar. "How are you, Louise? Come inside."

Louise followed her into the house and back to the kitchen, the room the Bellwoods considered the heart of the house and in which they regularly congregated with family and friends.

Samuel had done most of the carpentry in the kitchen himself, installing glass-fronted blonde burl oak cabinets along with the wide, dark green marble-topped counters. Rose enjoyed cooking big meals for her extended family and had every appliance a cook could desire, all in cream colors to complement her cabinets. Sunlight shone through the room's large windows and bathed with warmth the little brass herb pots Rose kept on her windowsill.

Rose offered Louise a glass of her homemade cider. "Excuse me while I finish this stew. I want to put it on before we ride out to the pasture."

As Rose finished chopping vegetables and chunks of lamb to add to her crock pot, she told Louise the latest news about her five children, four of whom lived in the area and remained close to their parents. Her youngest daughter, who was in her first year at college, had yet to decide on a major.

"I keep telling Samantha that there is no such thing as a career in liberal arts," Rose said, and sighed as she added a handful of diced potatoes to the pot. "She's always been the butterfly, fluttering here and there, never content to settle down."

"Jane was like that," Louise said, thinking of how eager her youngest sister had been to escape Acorn Hill and travel the world. "Give Samantha time, and I'm sure she'll find a place for herself."

A black-and-white Sheltie dog trotted into the kitchen and came over to greet Louise with a wagging tail. She was followed by Rose's husband.

"Hello, Missy." Louise scratched behind the delighted dog's ears before she smiled up at Samuel. "How are you, Samuel?"

"I'm staying out of trouble, as usual, Louise." Rose's husband was a big man and towered over his petite wife. His deep tan from years of working every day in the sun made his hair and eyes appear very light. "Aldo and Ilsa offered to come up to the house, but I told them you might like to drive over to see their setup. Is that agreeable to you?"

"Yes, that will be fine. I'd like to pay them a visit."

Samuel preferred to get around the farm on horseback, but today he brought the family car, a sturdy Range Rover, around to the front of the house.

The Bellwoods had provided ample space for the circus, which Louise would have had no trouble finding even without Samuel, since someone had posted small yellow signs with black arrows at regularly spaced intervals along the back road to the pasture that the circus presently occupied.

"I thought circus life was nothing but fun, until I watched the Majeskas set up their operation after they arrived here," Samuel said as he drove down to the pasture. "These folks practically build a town for themselves in a single day. A day to a week later, they have to tear it all down, pack it up, and move on to the next town, and then do it all over again. They work nearly every day of the year. The only vacation these folks get are a couple of weeks at Christmas."

"I'm a little confused," Louise said to Samuel. "I thought the circus was stopping here simply to make repairs and allow their animals to rest. Why would they be setting up?"

"The performers still need to practice, and for that they need the tents, rigging and equipment set up just as it would be for a show," Rose said. "I think that if all goes well, Aldo and Ilsa might consider giving a special performance for the local residents while they're in town."

As the camp came into view, Louise saw that, indeed, the circus nearly took up the same amount of space as a small town. Dominating the center of the pasture was an enormous tent made of canvas striped in red, blue, yellow and white, which she assumed was the "big top." From the open entrance of the tent, which was large enough to comfortably admit a tractor-trailer, ran a corridor of grass flanked on both sides by small, boxy tents and open-sided booths. Sawdust had been liberally applied over the ground wherever the grass was thin or where animal cages were standing.

"Aldo hasn't raised the big top yet," Samuel said, unknowingly correcting her presumptions. "Some of the canvas panels were damaged in the storm. That one in the center there is a temporary practice tent. The smaller tents along the midway are for the menagerie, arcade games and some of their traveling displays." He pointed to the different tents as he spoke. "See that red wagon with the gold wheels in the front there? That used to be a World-War-I-era fire truck. Aldo's grandfather bought it from a junkyard and fixed it up. It's been used to sell tickets since the Depression."

"Has this circus been in operation that long?" Louise asked as a man in jeans and a plaid flannel shirt waved Samuel over toward a parking area.

"Ilsa told me that the Majeska family started their first circus in eastern Europe during the eighteenth century," Rose said. "Aldo's family came over to the United States just after the Civil War."

The parking area was to one side of the temporary practice tent, behind which Louise could see a section that had been roped off. Equipment, cages and packing crates were stacked neatly behind the ropes. "What do they do back there?" she asked Samuel, pointing to the area.

"That's where they keep everything they need on hand for their performances," Samuel told her. "Aldo calls it their 'backyard.'"

Although the big top had not yet been raised, and there were ongoing vehicle repairs being made, the circus seemed ready to open for a performance at any moment. In the wooden booths, games were set up and ready to be played, while stuffed animals, plastic toys and trinkets hanging in clustered garlands from the booth frames waited to be won as prizes. From the concession stands came the smells of popcorn, caramel apples and cotton candy, and Louise could see concessionaires bagging and wrapping those goodies. Air hissed from a large tank as one woman stood filling balloons shaped like elephants, clowns and tigers and tying them to long, thin wooden dowels.

"The circus looks ready to open," Louise commented to Rose.

"There may not be a performance under the big top, but the midway will be open every day, and there will be access to the animal cages and the tent exhibits," Rose explained. "Aldo doesn't charge an admission unless there is a show. We've passed the word around to the local schools and churches, in the event someone wants to bring kids over on a field trip."

As Rose and Samuel walked with Louise to the midway, some children playing kickball ran across the wide strip of grass. "I didn't realize that the circus people brought their families with them," she said to Rose.

"In the circus, the whole family travels along with the show." Rose smiled and waved at the kids, who took off running toward a purple and gold RV parked to one side of the big practice tent. "The Majeskas have their own school tent, where the children go to classes, which are much the same as those that home-schooled kids have."

Louise knew a small number of mothers in the community who chose to home-school their children. They sometimes met at the Acorn Hill Library to exchange ideas and lesson plans.

But there was more to life than work, travel and education. "Do the Majeskas have church services for the circus's employees and their families?"

"Every Sunday morning." Samuel pointed to a large, light blue tent that had been erected some distance away from the practice tent and the midway. "The performers are of different faiths, so Aldo and Ilsa simply gather the entire troupe together for readings from the Bible, singing hymns and silent prayer. No one is required to attend, but most everyone does. They also give time off on Sundays to those who wish to hold special worship services for their particular faith."

Hearing that made Louise admire the Majeskas. Her father had always considered worship one of the most important elements in any family's life, and she was glad to see the circus owners also thought that it was important.

The sound of music came from a little clearing next to the entrance to the practice tent, and there Louise saw an unhitched, horse-drawn wagon. Sitting in the wagon's bed was what at first appeared to be a miniature church organ with abbreviated brass pipes. At the keyboard was a man in his mid-twenties, who had carrot-orange hair. He was wearing worn denim overalls with colorful patches over a blousy white shirt covered with red polka dots.

"Dilly's playing the calliope," Rose said to Samuel. She turned to Louise. "I know what a music lover you are. Want to stop and listen for a moment?"

Louise nodded, fascinated by the instrument, the sound that it produced through its golden pipes and the confidence of the musician playing it. "I've only read about calliopes in books," she confided to Rose. "I've never seen one up close."

"*Calliope* is such an odd word. I wonder what it means?" Rose asked.

"It was the name of the Greek muse of epic poetry," Louise said. "The word means 'beautiful-voice.'"

"Outlandish name for a pipe organ," was Samuel's comment.

"It is a little different from a pipe organ, which is usually built into the structure that houses it," Louise said. "Pipe organs have hundreds of pipes and often multiple sets of keyboards, too, while the calliope is smaller and generally has one, shorter keyboard. The internal mechanisms for producing the calliope's music are not as sophisticated as a pipe organ's, either, which explains its simple but powerful sound."

Louise told him how the first calliopes were powered by steam and had to be carried on sturdy wagons during circus parades because of their weight.

"It appears they've adapted this one to run off an air compressor," she said, nodding toward the small block of equipment on the ground beneath the wagon.

Rose peered at the compressor. "Why would you need air for a piano?"

"The calliope isn't a piano, but a very sophisticated version of the steam whistle. Instead of vibrating strings struck by a key's hammer, as you have with a true piano, the instrument produces sound through pressurized air sent over and through the slits in the pipes." Louise pointed to the juncture of the keyboard and the wind chest. "The higher the pressure, the louder the sound it produces."

"Aldo got that instrument from one of those old steam-powered paddlewheel boats on the Mississippi," Samuel said, as the young man at the keys finished the cheerful tune he was playing. "They used the calliope whenever they docked someplace along the river. Like a train whistle, I reckon."

"The sound would have carried for miles," Louise agreed. She saw the calliope player looking down at them and smiled as he leaped nimbly over the side of the wagon and walked over to greet them.

"I didn't know I had an audience or I would have dressed up this morning," the young man said. He pulled from his pocket a round red foam ball and placed it on the end of his nose. "There, that's better."

Louise had guessed from his hair that the calliope player was also a clown, but the red nose clinched it.

"Louise, this is Dilly, also known as Piccadilly the Clown," Rose said. "Dilly, this is our friend Mrs. Smith."

The young man bowed deeply. "A pleasure to meet you, Mrs. Smith," he said.

"Thank you," Louise replied. "I enjoyed your music."

"Rose, Samuel," a man's voice called out.

Louise turned to see an older man and woman walking toward them. The man was dressed in a red and white striped jacket, white shirt and pants, and had a dramatic mane of fluffy white hair. He limped slightly and walked with the aid of a beautifully polished dark wood cane topped with a brass knob shaped like a lion's head. The woman at his side was the same height, but plumper, and wore an exotic black caftan richly embroidered with scarlet, gold and blue thread. Her silver curls were mostly concealed by an elegant black turban, the front of which was decorated by a large ruby brooch set in gold.

"Aldo and Ilsa Majeska," Rose said to the man and woman, "may I present our friend, Louise Howard Smith?"

"The lovely Mrs. Smith! We have heard nothing but praise about you. Delighted, madam." Aldo Majeska took Louise's hand, but instead of shaking it, he bowed over it. His voice was the sort that one could hear clearly from the back of a room, colored by the faintest of European accents. "I am Aldo, and this is my wife Ilsa."

"You are very welcome here, Mrs. Smith," Ilsa said warmly, reaching out to pat her arm. Her accent was quite a bit heavier than her husband's, and she spoke much slower, as if not sure of the words.

"Thank you." Louise smiled at both.

"Come, come." Aldo threaded his arm through Louise's. "We will give you the grand tour."

Louise glanced back at Rose and Samuel, who were grinning at her, and then allowed the circus owners to escort her down the midway.

Chapter Eight

The Majeskas first stopped at the games booths and concessions along the midway to introduce Louise to the people who ran them, whom they called the "butchers." Some of the midway workers were retired performers and others were fairly young married couples. Many had family members working as roustabouts or performers for the show.

"Do you know why we call them 'butchers'?" Aldo asked, and pointed to the colorful rows of prizes and snacks displayed in rows on the posts and rafters of each stand. "They hang out their goods the same way old-time butchers did their hams and sausages."

Louise was offered samples of everything, from the salty, buttery circus popcorn to the puffy, lacy funnel cakes that were still made as they had been for over a century. She watched the art of spinning melted, flavored granulated sugar into fine strands of candy "floss" and chuckled over candy bars and snack cakes that were coated with a tasty batter, deep-fried and served piping hot, their centers melted to a gooey consistency.

"No, thank you," Louise said as she was offered another exotic treat. Ilsa did the same, which prompted Louise to say, "It must be difficult to resist such goodies when they are available every day."

"I know if I eat too many, Aldo will put me in the ring so I can perform with Hannah, our elephant," Ilsa joked.

Along the midway Louise peeked into the tent exhibits, which had both natural marvels, such as a three-foot-tall amethyst geode that Aldo had found during their travels out West, and charming artifacts, like the collection of antique circus costumes on display, some of which had been kept in such excellent condition that they looked ready to be donned for the next performance.

The Majeskas were obviously very proud of their circus heritage, and over time had preserved many other interesting mementos from the show's long history. There were framed photographs of Aldo and Ilsa with dozens of performers, along with rare playbills, some hand-lettered and dating back to the mid-nineteenth century, when Aldo's grandfather had been ringmaster.

Ilsa's personal collection was a small library of books devoted to the history of circuses and other traveling shows. Unable to resist, Louise glanced inside one heavy volume, which described circuses that dated back thousands of years, when ancient Egyptians celebrated the annual recession of the Nile's floodwaters with performances and games of skill, during the feast of Osiris.

As they entered the practice tent, Aldo explained how the larger tents, such as the one they were in and the big top, were erected.

"All of this canvas is too heavy to be pushed up by the poles, as we do with the smaller ones out on the midway," he said as they walked around a horse trainer grooming a large, white stallion. "That is why we must use special ways and ask our dear Hannah to help us."

Louise was amazed by the ingenuity of the circus people when it came to constructing their place of business. Aldo showed her how the practice tent was fashioned from canvas panels, which were first laid out on the ground and stitched together with rope passed through large, metal grommets at the seams. Once assembled in sections, the edges of the tent were fastened to tent stakes already hammered into the ground, while the center poles were raised by Hannah, the Majeska's prize Asian elephant and star performer of their show.

"Hannah doesn't mind helping?" Louise asked Ilsa.

The older woman chuckled. "Oh no. Our Hannah always likes seeing the tent go up, because she knows this means she can perform. I think sometimes she is more ham than elephant."

"Hannah is expert at tent-raising," Aldo put in. "She is very strong, but careful, and never makes a mistake with the ropes."

While they had walked through the practice tent, which Aldo had explained was only half the size of their big top tent, Louise was introduced to the bale rings, which were metal rings around the bottom of each center pole. Aldo demonstrated how the rings were attached by pulley to the top of the pole, and then attached to the assembled canvas tent sections. The pulleys and a little more of Hannah's elephant power were used to raise the roof of the tent as well as the support, sidewalls and marquee for the entrance.

As Louise listened, she spotted Bobbi and Billy Bratwick in one of the rings, where they were practicing their tumbling act, and waved to them when they saw her. Goliath stopped to say hello and then went out of the practice tent. Today he carried two large bales of hay on his shoulders as if they weighed no more than the Bratwicks had.

"Now you must meet our star," Aldo said.

Louise followed the Majeskas out to the area where the animal cages were parked. There she saw that two temporary corral-like structures had been erected with aluminum fencing that could be broken down into small sections. One pen contained five magnificent white horses like the ones she had seen in the practice tent. The other pen held Hannah and her new baby.

"This is the star of the Majeska circus," Aldo said as he walked with Louise up to the elephant pen. "Hannah, come and meet our new friend."

Louise felt a twinge of alarm as the enormous gray Asian elephant turned her massive head to look at them and then lumbered over toward the fence, while the baby stayed behind, a little shy of the visitors. With each step Hannah took, the ground trembled faintly under Louise's feet.

"She is as sweet as a lamb," Ilsa said, reading Louise's expression accurately.

Hannah stopped a foot from the fence and lifted her trunk. This revealed her mouth, which was roughly diamond-shaped. Inside Louise caught a glimpse of the enormous flat teeth Hannah used to chew her food. She jumped when Hannah's trunk brushed her arm as it curled lightly around Aldo's neck.

"I am glad to see you, too, Hannah." Completely unperturbed, Aldo rubbed the elephant's trunk.

The prehensile end of the trunk resembled fingers and the lips of a mouth at the same time, and air rasped in and out as Hannah breathed. The breathing turned into a snuffling sound as Hannah nudged Aldo's pocket.

"She knows I always have something for her." The ringmaster grinned at Louise as he removed a ripe purple plum from his pocket. Hannah delicately plucked the plum from his hand and used her trunk to deposit it in her mouth.

Hannah was certainly the most interesting member of the Majeska troupe, Louise decided as she studied the gigantic creature. The elephant had very dark eyes, which were surrounded by long eyelashes. Her hide was not as bald as it seemed from a distance, but sported very fine hairs, particularly on her head and twitching tail.

Louise smiled at Aldo. "She's beautiful, and so gentle."

"So tame she follows her trainer around like a faithful dog," Aldo said, and chuckled. "Sometimes we wonder if she thinks she is one."

As the elephant shambled off to rejoin her baby, Ilsa told Louise that Hannah currently spent most of her time in the pen. "Hannah would not run away, she is too well-trained. The pen is to keep the baby from wandering away."

After Louise was introduced to the tigers, lions, monkeys and a wonderful collection of performing poodles, along with their trainers and the many performers who worked with them, the Majeskas invited her to have lunch with them at the "pie car."

The long trailer, which served as the circus's traveling kitchen, was painted in the red, white and gold signature colors of the Majeska circus. Inside, two men and three women were cooking, as they would all day, according to Ilsa.

"It is hard work to feed the entire troupe," Ilsa told Louise. "We have two cooks, but everyone takes a turn helping them one day each month."

The trailer's wide, extendable awning provided shade for rows of folding tables and chairs that served as the troupe's open-air dining hall. About a dozen people were dining there. Aldo explained that the troupe also ate in shifts.

Louise marveled at the interaction between the Majeskas and their performers. It was as if they all were members of the family. While the performers had all been uniformly polite to Louise, they treated their employers' with obvious affection.

Louise and the Majeskas helped themselves to the buffet-style baked chicken, fresh corn on the cob and spicy barbecued beans, and took their plates to an open table. Louise found the food unusually seasoned but delicious.

"Strovi must be cooking today," Ilsa said after she tasted

the chicken. "He is Hungarian and cannot resist putting paprika in everything."

After the meal the Majeskas took Louise to meet the members of their trapeze act and three of the athletic-looking rope dancers, and then walked with Louise to the purple and gold RV, which served as their management office as well as their home.

"It is not a house," Ilsa admitted, "but it *is* home."

"It's very charming," Louise said as she admired the interior walls, which the Majeskas had decorated with a kaleidoscopic series of framed playbills and posters. A partially drawn curtain revealed a rack of costumes, mostly striped ringmaster's jackets. Space was limited, naturally, but everything was as neat as a pin.

"Would you like water, wine or juice?" Aldo asked as he went to the RV's tiny kitchen area.

"Water, please, thank you," Louise said. The tour had been fascinating, but she was tired, a little hot and quite thirsty now.

As Louise sat with Ilsa at the small table inside the RV, she noticed that the other woman was rubbing her hands as if they were aching. "Is something wrong?"

Ilsa shook her head. "Just some age pains. I am fine."

"You are expert on the circus now," Aldo said to Louise as he brought her a glass of water. "So, when can you come and work for us?"

Louise almost laughed. "Thank you, but I already have two jobs. I teach piano and operate a bed-and-breakfast with my two sisters."

"Ah, well." Aldo shrugged. "Do you wish something to nibble on, perhaps?" He made as if to search the little pantry. "Ilsa, what did you do with those pretzels?"

"I'm really not hungry, not after that lovely lunch we just had," Louise assured the elderly couple.

"Stop making the fuss, Aldo," Ilsa said. To Louise, she

said, "This is why I am so fat. Him. I think he *does* wish to put me in the ring with Hannah."

"What is this fat?" Aldo demanded. "You are only *zaftig*, my love."

"That means pretty," Ilsa translated for Louise, "but still fat."

"I do not like skinny women," her husband said. He gave Louise an apologetic look. "*Most* skinny women."

She chuckled. "I will take that as a compliment." She glanced at the older man. "What nationality are you, Aldo, if you don't mind my asking?"

"I consider myself like all Americans—I am the melting pot," he joked. "My mother was an Austrian Jew, and my father was Swiss Catholic. I have German and Czech blood as well. And there's a bit of Protestant blood to keep things interesting. All circus performers, of course." He made an expansive gesture. "The circus has been in my family's blood for generations. We would not know what to do with ourselves if we could not perform."

"I will be glad when we can open," Ilsa said, rubbing her hands again. "It never feels right to put up the tents and not have the big top go up or a show scheduled."

"How many performances do you usually schedule?" Louise asked.

"If there is no problem with the setup, we open with one show the first night," Aldo said. "During weekdays people work, so we will have an afternoon and evening show. On weekends we do morning, afternoon, twilight and evening shows. We perform in rain, sleet, snow, hail—well, maybe not hail." He gave his wife a wry look. "Even when there are only five or six people in the stands, we perform." He gave her a saucy look. "Better than the post office, we are."

"Not always," Ilsa scolded. To Louise she said, "We cannot put on our regular show schedule while we are here. We have yet to repair the canvas for our big top tent. Also,

Hannah is still recovering from having her baby, and we do not wish to risk her health by having her work a full schedule of shows too soon."

"Couldn't you have shows without Hannah's performance?" Louise asked.

Both of the Majeskas appeared shocked.

"Oh no," Aldo said. "Hannah is the *star* of our show. If she cannot go on, no one else will."

Louise could see that the Majeskas regarded the huge creature as parents would a much-loved child, and so decided not to comment on this. "Have you any names in mind for Hannah's baby?"

"Aldo and I cannot agree on anything," Ilsa admitted. "We want a joyful name, because Hannah loves her so much, and she is such a happy little thing."

Little? Louise thought of the baby elephant, which was roughly the size of a compact car.

"I say we call her Joy," Aldo put in, "but Ilsa tells me no, she does not like it."

"*Joy* is what I use to wash the dishes," his wife retorted. "Our baby deserves better." Her eyebrows drew together. "You have many children in your town, Louise?"

"Yes, many children of all ages." *And how they would love to see this circus*, Louise thought. The ANGELs had certainly enjoyed their trip to see the animals, according to Alice. From what the Majeskas had said about Hannah, however, a performance in Acorn Hill seemed unlikely.

"Children are the best at naming things," Ilsa said. "Aldo, why don't we have a contest to let the children in town name Hannah's baby?"

Aldo's eyebrows rose. "And who, Madam Majeska, picks the winner of this contest? You or me?"

Ilsa laughed. "We will put them in a hat and let Hannah pick."

There was a knock at the RV's door, and Aldo went to answer it. Goliath stood outside and said something in very rapid Italian to the circus owner. Aldo nodded and issued instructions in the same language.

"Aldo speaks six languages," Ilsa confided to Louise. "I only speak Polish and English, but I did not come to America until I was a teenager, so my English is not so good."

"I think you speak English very well," Louise reassured her.

Aldo closed the door and returned to the table, this time leaning on his cane rather heavily. He brought a packet of mail to the table. On the top was a brochure with the photo of a tropical beach setting with a palm tree.

"You called them again?" Ilsa asked him and tapped the brochure with one finger.

Aldo looked a little ashamed. "It does no harm to think about it." He glanced at Louise. "There is a retirement community in Florida. It is for old circus people like us. It would be nice, after all these years on the road, for Ilsa and me to go there."

"We cannot retire, Aldo." Ilsa sounded a little sad now. "Everyone depends on us. The show must go on."

"Yes, yes. We will not argue in front of our guest, please." He waved his hand at her. "Louise, do you know the mayor from town?"

"Lloyd Tynan? Yes, I do." She watched Aldo's frown deepen. "Is something wrong?"

"He is here talking to our friends Rose and Samuel," Aldo told her. "He will want us to pack up and leave town."

Louise walked with the Majeskas back to the midway, where she saw Lloyd Tynan in deep conversation with Rose and Samuel Bellwood. The trio stood just at the entrance to the circus's encampment, so it was impossible to hear what was being said. As soon as Rose spotted them, she patted her husband's arm and then hurried over to Louise, Aldo and Ilsa.

"Did you enjoy the tour?" Rose asked.

"I did. It was lovely." Louise looked over at Lloyd. "Why is the mayor here?"

"Oh, he just needs to talk to me and Samuel about some minor things. Safety issues, things like that." Rose gave the Majeskas an encouraging smile. "The mayor is very good friends with Louise's aunt," she told them.

Aldo smiled broadly. "That is wonderful. She can talk to him and tell him how safe we are. Why, we have the safest show on earth!"

"We have shown her everything, just like you said, Rose," Ilsa added.

"Come, Ilsa." Aldo took his wife's arm. "We should check on the lighting and see if Jimbo has repaired that generator. To show that we are safe, yes? And we cannot have a dazzling show in the dark, of course. It has been a pleasure meeting you, Mrs. Smith." The old couple walked off together toward the backyard of the practice tent.

Louise suddenly understood why Rose had been so insistent about her coming to see the circus and meet the Majeskas. "They did show me *everything*."

Rose had the grace to look a little ashamed. "I admit, when Aldo and Ilsa started talking about putting on a special performance for the town, Samuel and I thought that we might encounter some resistance to the idea from Mayor Tynan."

"Who just happens to be very good friends with my aunt and me." Louise looked sideways at her friend. "Quite convenient."

"You always seem to get along so well with Lloyd. I would have asked Alice, but she hates confrontations and Jane, well . . . she usually starts them."

"Which makes me the wishy-washy one?" Louise asked.

"Not at all. You're just the most reasonable woman I know. Who happens to be friends with the mayor, the man who might try to make the Majeskas move out of here." Rose grimaced. "I'm sorry, Louise. I should have told you. The thing is, we love the Majeskas. And when will we ever have a circus stop over in Acorn Hill again?" Rose gave her a beseeching look. "Anything you could do to intervene with the mayor would be so appreciated, not only by me and Samuel, but the performers and the Majeskas too. And then there are all the children in town who have never even *seen* a circus—"

"Stop." Louise held up her hands in a gesture of surrender. "I'm convinced, Rose. I can't promise anything, but let me see what I can do."

As the two women walked over to where Lloyd and Samuel stood talking, Louise noticed a significant number of the circus performers working around them—many more than had been on the midway earlier. While everyone was busy with some task and avoided looking in the same direction as Lloyd and Samuel, it was obvious that they were also trying to listen in on the two men's conversation.

They do look out for each other, Louise thought as she smiled and said hello to the mayor. *I suppose with this sort of life, always moving from one place to the next each week, they have to.*

"If your land were a mile to the north, you'd have to bring the Riverton Fire Marshal out to perform the inspection," Lloyd was saying to Samuel as Louise and Rose drew near the men.

"Lucky for us, we're a mile short," Rose said under her breath.

"According to the deed my father gave us at our wedding," Samuel said, sweeping his hand from right to left, "all of this was open, unincorporated land."

"At that time, it was," the mayor agreed, "but the county

incorporated all your land as part of Acorn Hill fifteen years ago. That brings this circus under my jurisdiction." Lloyd didn't sound very happy about that fact.

Louise decided this might be a good time to join in. "Hello, Lloyd."

The mayor seemed astonished to see her. "Louise, what are you doing here?"

"I was invited to meet the owners." She gave Samuel a faintly ironic look before she smiled at Lloyd. "The Majeskas have a very impressive setup, don't they?"

"It's certainly big enough," the mayor said, eyeing the midway. "That's my main concern."

"There's no such thing as a *small* circus," Rose protested. "I'd also like to remind you that the Majeskas are our friends, Mayor, and while it may be subject to Acorn Hill ordinances, this is still our land."

Louise rested a hand on Rose's arm. "Lloyd, what is the problem with the size of the show, if you don't mind my asking?"

"I'm worried about the safety issues it might create," the mayor replied. "We've never had a circus set up anywhere near town, so I'd expect most folks will want to attend, particularly those who have young kids. The road in here is two-lane, with no outlet, so traffic will be a problem."

"We already have a plan," Samuel said. "Traffic won't be a problem. The people who work the parking lot areas know how to keep the traffic moving smoothly, and we're going to rope off a turnaround in the field across the road so cars can head out as easily as they come in. My hands will be here to help out."

"Traffic is not the only issue here, Sam," Lloyd told him. "You can attract a rowdy element who may try to cause a ruckus. And while I may not be a fire marshal, I'm still responsible to see that there are no fire hazards involved here. Potterston Fire Department could respond to a blaze, but there are no reservoirs or lakes nearby to serve as a water supply—they'd have to bring out their tank truck."

"Troublemakers have never been a problem at any of the performances we've taken our family to," Rose said. "The Majeskas always hire local off-duty policemen to provide security, and our men are very conscientious."

"What about fire hazards?"

One of the men working nearby came over. "Excuse me, sir, but I couldn't help overhearing what you said and I'm one of the fire safety crew. There's an extinguisher in every camper, trailer, truck, stand and tent, and extras are stored near where any electrical, lighting or flammable items are kept. We do a safety inspection of the grounds every day and of the stands before and after every performance. The fire crew also keeps in touch with each other on its own channel." He showed the mayor his hand-held radio. "We transport our own water tanks and fire-fighting equipment, and have six men on our crew who are fully qualified volunteer firemen."

"That puts my mind at ease," Lloyd admitted.

"You know, Lloyd, you should really take a tour of the circus grounds, if you have time," Louise recommended. "I think you'll be very pleased with what you see."

"Sir, I've got some time now and can escort you, if you like," the man offered.

Rose and Samuel seemed to be holding their breath as the mayor scanned the encampment.

At last Lloyd nodded. "Good enough. Let's have a look around this place."

Chapter Nine

The first class of the Mature Years Center's self-defense course was held the day after Louise visited Bellwood Farm. Louise might have forgotten her promise to accompany Ethel and Florence, had Jane not reminded her that morning at breakfast.

"Eat something more than an English muffin, please," Jane scolded. "You'll need lots of energy today. You're driving the ladies to Riverton this afternoon, remember?"

Louise's thoughts went blank until Jane made a karate-chop in the air. "The self-defense class is *today*?"

"Aunt Ethel wrote it on the calendar." Alice reached for one of the Danish pastries on the breakfast platter, saw Jane scowl and chose a small bran muffin instead. "In red ink. She underlined it three times, and there are exclamation points after each of the words."

Louise felt her appetite disappear. "Wonderful."

"It shouldn't be too bad," Alice said. "I mean, it's not as if they're taking instruction in martial arts or fencing."

"You will not mention those activities in front of our aunt," Louise warned her sister, "and *especially* not within Florence Simpson's hearing."

That afternoon Ethel and Florence met Louise at the inn and climbed into Louise's Cadillac for the ride to the class. Louise kept the conversation light as they drove toward Riverton, but the closer they came to the downtown location of the Mature Years Center, the more her misgivings seemed to grow.

"There it is!" Ethel said, pointing to a modest one-level building at the corner of a medical office complex.

Louise made the turn into the parking lot and found a space near the building's entrance. In the past she had heard her aunt and some of the other older women in town mention Mature Years, which provided continuing education for seniors, but this was her first visit. "It looks smaller than I imagined."

"Most of the classes for college credit are held over at Riverton High School at night," Florence said from the backseat of the car. "The administrative offices are here, as is the gym for the physical therapy classes."

"Is self-defense considered physical therapy?" Louise asked Ethel as they walked up to the building's front entrance.

"It's physical, so I imagine it is." Ethel looked down at the comfortable cotton knit slacks suit the instructor had recommended as appropriate for the class. "Maybe I should have worn something dressier and brought a gym bag."

Florence, who wore designer sportswear, made a dismissive sound. "You look fine, Ethel."

At the lobby desk inside, a smiling young man asked them to sign in. When he compared their names to a typed sheet, his forehead creased. "I'm afraid I don't show a Louise Smith on my class roster."

"I'm serving as the driver for my aunt and her friend," Louise told him. "If it's permissible, I'd like to sit in on the first class."

"Relatives are always welcome," he told her. After handing Ethel and Florence two paper adhesive badges on which their names had been neatly printed, he directed them to the gymnasium at the back of the facility.

The gym turned out to be a large, well-lit room with padded walls. The floor was covered with short-pile carpets, and stacks of exercise mats sat in one corner. At the back of the room stood different-sized upright padded objects, which Louise could not identify. About a dozen senior-age women were waiting inside, seated on folding chairs.

"It doesn't seem like a very large class," Louise said softly to Ethel.

"Good," her aunt replied. "We'll get more individual attention from the instructor."

Florence recognized someone at once. "There's Delia's cousin Karen. She said she was planning to take this class too. I'll be right back." She called to her friend and went to speak with her.

Ethel studied Karen and the other women with a certain amount of curiosity. "At least we're not the oldest ones here," she whispered to Louise.

Indeed, they were not. Louise saw at least three women who appeared to be in their late seventies to early eighties. One extremely frail-looking woman had a walker placed next to her chair. Louise's misgivings increased. How could such a fragile-looking woman possibly fend off an attacker, assuming she would ever be in such a situation? What if Ethel and Florence hurt themselves trying to learn and practice these potentially dangerous techniques?

Physical fitness was one thing, but personal strength was the real issue. Strength was something that Louise had always found in the Scriptures. Why couldn't God's Word provide her aunt with the sense of security she seemed to need so greatly?

"What are you thinking?" Ethel asked. "You have the strangest look on your face."

"I was thinking of a Bible verse," Louise said, quoting, "'Fear of man will prove to be a snare, but whoever trusts in the Lord is kept safe'" (Proverbs 29:25).

"Proverbs won't help me if someone is trying to snatch my purse," Ethel complained.

Perhaps it would be best not to argue that point for the moment, Louise decided. She concluded that she would talk to her aunt more on the subject when they returned to the inn, assuming that Ethel wished to continue the course.

"If you don't like this class or it proves to be too much for you," Louise asked, "will you be permitted to leave?" Maybe she should say something to Florence about the possibility.

Ethel gave her an impatient look. "I'm not going to quit. I just got here."

Louise reined in a sigh. "What I meant was—"

"I know *exactly* what you meant." Ethel looked upset now. "You don't think I can do something like this. You think I'm too old for it."

Was her aunt worried about her personal safety or her self-image? Ethel had been making a lot of remarks about her age lately.

"Aunt, I think you can do anything you set your mind to," Louise said honestly. "If I have learned anything from you, it is that you are as young as you feel."

That seemed to mollify her. "Today I feel twenty-five."

Tonight you'll probably be going to bed feeling two hundred and five, Louise thought as she glanced at the thick floor mats and imagined her aunt falling on them. *If you're not over at Potterston Hospital getting a cast put on some part of your body.*

A young woman and two large men walked into the gym. "Good afternoon, ladies, I'm your instructor, Dana Starkey. If you're ready to begin class, please fold your chairs and set them back against the wall," the woman said in a voice that carried easily to the back of the room. "When you have done so, please form two lines in front of me." She glanced at Louise. "Any visitors may take a chair and sit next to the left wall. I ask that you please not interrupt the class while it is in session."

Louise nodded and retrieved one of the chairs to take her place, while the other women put theirs away. She took a moment to inspect Dana Starkey, whom Ethel had said was an active-duty Riverton police officer. Dana was tall and seemed more slender than muscular. Her straight black hair was angle-cut level with her slightly pointed chin, and she had very direct blue eyes. She wore no makeup or jewelry, and her clothes, a white polo shirt and plain black trousers, enhanced her no-nonsense presence. She had not a hair out of place or a single wrinkle in her garments, and even the low-heeled black shoes she wore glowed with polish.

"Thank you," the young woman said when the women were standing in two lines as she had instructed. She stood before them, her back very straight and her arms at her sides, while the men took positions on either side of her. "As I said before, I am Dana Starkey, and I will be your instructor for this class. You may call me Dana or Ms. Starkey. I am a detective assigned to the Burglary Division of the Riverton Police Department. These are my colleagues, Patrol Officer Lewis and Sergeant Morse." She indicated each man in turn. "They will be assisting me with various demonstrations throughout this course."

Dana's two colleagues were not only taller but also far more heavily muscled than the instructor.

She sounds like one of those boot camp drill instructors, Louise thought, not sure if she cared for Dana Starkey's blunt way of speaking. *These are elderly women, not recruits for the police academy.*

"You ladies have enrolled in a four-week, personal self-defense course," Dana said. "I will be teaching you how to preserve your own safety at all times, as well as how to protect others around you who are in danger. The techniques you learn here could very well save your life or the life of a loved one, so I would appreciate your undivided attention."

Dana's very presence commanded attention, Louise decided. Not a woman in the room could take her gaze away from the stern young woman.

"We will start right now by identifying one of the most valuable assets used during self-defense. It's something that each of you already has." Dana looked around the room. "Does anyone know what that is?"

Someone made a worried sound. "I'm not carrying any weapons."

"Anyone?" Dana asked. When the class participants simply looked at each other, she pointed to her temple. "It's your brain, ladies. Your brain is the most valuable thing you will use in self-defense. Because the best defense is an intelligent one, based on knowledge, experience and confidence, and that all comes from one place."

Louise found this very sensible advice. *If only there were no violence attached to it.*

Dana went to stand in front of one of her older students. "I am going to take your purse away from you." She stepped to the side. "I am going to drag you out of your car." She looked at another woman. "I am going to break into your house. What do you do first? You use your head."

"I didn't pay for this class just to learn how to think," someone, perhaps Florence, grumbled.

"That is not all you are going to learn, ma'am," Dana said. "But I want you to keep it in mind. There is not one defenseless woman in this class. You all have exactly what you need, right now, to protect yourselves. I'm simply going to show you how to use it when you're in danger."

"Ms. Starkey, I've never been attacked in my life," one of the older attendees said. "My daughter-in-law insisted I take this class because I'm a widow and live by myself, but I don't feel as if I'm in any danger."

As if on cue, Sergeant Morse stepped up behind Dana Starkey and locked one of his arms around her throat. Dana rammed her elbow backward, stomped down on his foot and whirled out of the man's loosened grip. She jabbed her fingers at his eyes, stopping just short of gouging them. It all happened so quickly that Louise barely had time to see what the instructor did.

"Most people never feel as if they are in danger," Dana said as she backed away from Sergeant Morse. "Most of you might think that an off-duty police officer would be safe from attack, because we carry our weapons twenty-four hours a day. This is not the case. Nor are you safe simply because you live in a small town or a very nice neighborhood with very little crime." She went to the stack of exercise mats and spread one of them out on the floor. "In most cases of assault and robbery, the victims never thought such a thing could happen to them. Crime is perceived as something that happens to someone else."

Patrol Officer Lewis lunged at Dana from behind, looking as if he intended to fling his arms around her waist and drag her to the ground. This time she simply made a rolling movement that avoided Lewis's clutching hands and propelled him onto the exercise mat she had spread on the floor. The throw and the impact of the big man's landing made everyone gasp.

Dana offered Lewis a hand up before continuing. "No matter who you are or where you live, there is a possibility that one day you might have to face a personally dangerous situation."

Louise resisted pressing a hand to her throat.

"Your first responsibility is to escape such a situation," Dana continued. "If you cannot escape it, your survival will absolutely depend on your self-defense skills. Crimes of violence are ugly and frightening, but they are also part of this world in which we live. This class will teach you how to live with a new awareness of that reality, and how best to respond to it."

∽

"I hate to admit it, but the class was quite riveting," Louise said later that afternoon as she helped Alice in the study sorting the paperwork to be recorded in the inn's ledgers. "Ms. Starkey was very matter-of-fact about what she expects from her students, but she appears to be a naturally forthright, no-nonsense sort of woman. Her demonstrations showing how to defend against an attack were nothing short of dazzling."

"The thinking part I could do, maybe," Alice said as she separated the yellow and pink copies of the paid purchase orders. "But kicking and jabbing and throwing someone to the ground?" She winced and shook her head.

"I couldn't do it either, my dear." The sunlight coming through the windows caused a glare on Louise's reading glasses, which she adjusted before checking the date on an invoice. "But those are all techniques she will be teaching the class."

"To seniors? Really?"

"Ms. Starkey also told the students that they have to complete daily workouts, and not just at the Center," Louise said. "Apparently most people who take self-defense courses tend to freeze up when they are faced by a real threat because they don't continue practicing at home the techniques they're taught in class."

"Why not? Are the techniques that complicated? How are they going to learn them if they are?"

"According to Ms. Starkey, 'The body must be trained to react even when the mind doesn't.'" Louise sighed. "Her theory is that with enough practice, self-defense becomes more like a natural instinct, such as putting out your hands when you fall forward. You can then gouge someone's eyes because you won't need to make yourself think about it. Your brain goes on automatic."

Alice cringed. "Dear Lord in heaven. This instructor is teaching that to our aunt?"

"That was my reaction as well. I can't approve of this, Alice. Violence is contagious." Louise put down the filled guest register sheets and rubbed her forehead. "I know that Aunt Ethel and Florence wish to feel safer, and certainly they have the right to defend themselves. But to me, learning methods with which to harm someone else isn't the way to find a sense of security. We should depend on God, prayer, family, the authorities, our friends and community for that."

"I would agree, except that I've seen victims of violence come into the hospital." Alice's expression turned sad. "Some are violent themselves, but most are good people, Louise, people who, I imagine, have never hurt anyone in their lives. People like Aunt Ethel and Florence and us."

"I understand what you're saying, dear," Louise said, "but two wrongs still don't make a right."

"I know that in my head. My heart . . ." Alice hesitated before adding, "It's very hard to know what to feel, especially when you've watched someone suffer from an unprovoked attack."

Louise felt her heart constrict. "I suppose the reality of violence is uglier—and more real—when one has to see it every day, as you do."

Alice tried to smile. "Not every day, not even every week, but yes, it is very hard to take sometimes."

"The only comfort I have is knowing that our town has one of the lowest crime rates in the county and probably the state," Louise said. "Whatever this police officer teaches Ethel and Florence, I doubt they will ever have an opportunity to use it."

The phone rang, and Alice excused herself to answer it. As her sister talked to one of their vendors, Louise made an effort to compose herself. She was far more disturbed by the self-defense class than she had admitted to Alice, but Acorn Hill was a peaceful, law-abiding community. Surely no harm would ever come to her aunt or Florence.

I think this calls for prayer, Louise thought and closed her eyes. *Lord, thank You for our home place, and the people who share it with us. In all the years I have lived here, I have never been afraid of violence or crime and have known only the love of family, friends and heaven watching over us. Please, take the fear from the heart of my aunt and her friend. Give them peace of knowing that You provide the strength and the protection that we truly need. In all things, You are our best defense against evil, Heavenly Father. Through Christ our Lord, Amen.*

Chapter Ten

When Louise came out of the study, Alice was off the phone and talking with their guest, Mac Wilde.

"Mr. Wilde, I didn't know you were back from your excursion," Louise said.

"I came in about an hour ago, when you ladies were out working in the garden, I believe. Please, do call me Mac." His gaze moved to the neat stack of bills, receipts and file folders in Louise's hands. "Now there is something I will never miss about my old job: piles of paperwork."

"There is no end to it when you have a business," Louise said. "You worked in banking, my sister tells me."

"I was an investment banker for thirty years before I retired," Mac said. "Stocks, bonds, that sort of thing. Mostly corporate investors. The exciting world of high finance." He made it sound anything but that.

Louise knew a little about investment banking, as one of her late husband's friends had worked in that field. It was not a career in which a person could advance without a great deal of intelligence, ambition and dedication. Those were qualities she couldn't quite reconcile with someone who chose a motorcycle as his mode of transportation.

An investment banker turned biker?

"I know I don't look the type," Mac said, as if he could

hear her thoughts, "but I've been making some changes since my retirement. Good changes, for the most part, although I do miss work. I think that's what most people don't like about being retired."

"I was just telling Mac about Aunt Ethel's self-defense class," Alice said. "Mac takes Tai Chi classes, but for fitness, not for self-defense."

"Do no harm, but stay in shape," Mac said. "That's my motto."

"What a world this would be," Alice said, "if everyone lived by that. Or by Matthew 5:9—that one is probably closest to my own philosophy."

"'Blessed are the peacemakers,'" Louise quoted from memory, "'for they will be called sons of God.'"

"The daughters of God too," Jane put in as she passed the desk with a vase of flowers. "Alice, if you eat those M&M's you have hidden in your pocket, you'll wreck your calorie quota for the day." Jane disappeared into the kitchen.

"How did she know—" Alice stopped and her face turned red. "Fiddlesticks." Slowly she reached into her sweater pocket. "Mac, do you like M&M's?"

"Yes, I do."

"Here you go." Alice handed him a small, snack-size bag of candy. "Compliments of my diet and Grace Chapel Inn."

Louise pressed her lips together and looked at the floor until the laugh that she didn't want to release died away.

"Thank you." Mac tucked the bag into the pocket of his windbreaker. "How is the dieting going?"

"I'm starving," Alice said deadpan, "wasting away. My sister is the one who calls it dieting."

"You're doing very well," Louise said, feeling a pang of sympathy. She did not have to watch her weight as closely as Alice did. Neither did Jane, and Louise should remind Jane of that. "I'm sure you've lost at least three or four pounds by now."

"No, I've only lost two and a half pounds," Alice said gloomily. "Jane makes me weigh in once a week on her scale. And we plan my menu every day. We have a food scale now too. I'm beginning to hate the word *portions*."

"An extra hour of vigorous exercise per day might help," Mac suggested.

"I do try to walk as often as I can with my friend Vera Humbert," Alice said. She brightened. "The weather's been so nice I could probably take a bike ride after dinner every day." She saw Louise's expression and chuckled. "I'm talking about a *bicycle* ride, Louise."

"I never said you weren't," Louise replied. She glanced at Mac. "Your motorcycle has caused quite a stir around town."

"That's what I've gathered." He nodded toward town. "I've talked to a few people when I go for coffee and tried to reassure them that I'm a regular guy. Most of the younger folks are friendly enough, but a few of the older ones are still giving me the eye whenever I drive down the street. Which reminds me, will either of you ladies be driving to town today?"

"I have some errands to run," Louise said.

"Would you mind if I tag along with you?" Mac asked. "I need to pick up a few things. Maybe you can direct me to the best places in town to get them."

"I'd be happy to," Louise said, "as long as we take my car."

"Since my Ducati's trunk space is pretty limited," Mac's green eyes crinkled with mirth, "I was hoping you'd say that."

On the way into town Mac asked Louise to tell him more about her aunt's self-defense class.

"Not that I'm trying to be nosy," he said, "but I didn't think there was much crime in this area or a need for ladies to worry about that sort of thing."

"We have very little crime in Acorn Hill," Louise said, "thank the Lord."

Louise wasn't sure if she wanted to have such a discussion with Mac Wilde. For one thing, though he seemed like a genuinely nice man, she wasn't entirely comfortable with discussing Ethel with him. At the same time, she felt he should know the part he had played in making her aunt and Florence resort to taking the self-defense course. Everyone should know what effect he has on people, Louise decided, particularly if that effect was a negative one.

"You remember what happened with my aunt and her friend on the day you arrived at the inn," she said.

Mac nodded. "That was the first time I've ever been accused of trying to deliberately run someone down. I don't mind telling you, I was pretty confused for a minute or two there."

"They were frightened, Mac, and that fright definitely contributed to their decision to take this class." Before he could protest, Louise added, "What happened was not something that you did deliberately. Ethel and Florence are both older women who like their independence but also need to feel a sense of security. Very little out of the ordinary happens here in the country, so when something new or startling occurs, it has a greater effect on us."

"Like my breezing into town riding a motorcycle." He sounded more subdued now.

"Something like that, yes. Before you arrived, I think the only motorcyclists—bikers—my aunt and her friend had ever seen were in the movies." She smiled a little. "I could say the same. And in the movies, the people who ride bikes are usually the bad guys."

Mac laughed. "Now it all makes sense. If only you ladies knew . . ." he shook his head and laughed again.

"I'd love to know the joke," Louise prompted as she pulled the Caddy into a space next to the General Store.

"I have no idea how to be a 'wild one,'" Mac told her. He took out a handkerchief and wiped his eyes. "The Ducati is the first motorcycle I've ever owned. I only bought it three months ago, just after I retired, and I had to take lessons to learn how to ride it. Before that, I always drove a nice, safe sedan."

Louise was completely mystified by his admission. "What prompted you to buy the motorcycle?"

"The classic midlife crisis, I suppose. Stay right there." He got out of the car and came around to open her door for her. Then he escorted her into the General Store and got a shopping cart. "What's the first item on your list? Mine is shaving cream."

As Louise did the shopping, Mac pushed the cart for her and picked up a few of the items that he needed. He also talked about his plan to tour all fifty states with his motorcycle.

"When my friends retired, they couldn't wait to go to Europe, but that wasn't for me." He helped her lift a large bag of the environmentally safe cat litter Jane preferred to use for Wendell, and placed it on the bottom rack of the cart. "There are too many places in our own country I've never seen, like Niagara Falls or the Grand Canyon."

"Jane tells me the sequoia forests in northern California really are as magnificent as they are claimed to be," Louise mentioned as she took a bag of litter box liners and added it to the cart.

"I'll have to add northern California to my list." He stopped the cart and politely waited for an older man who was blocking the aisle with his own. "I've always liked the idea of touring America. Not zipping around from city to city in a jet, but really traveling. Driving up and down the highways and back roads, taking in the sights, meeting new people, being able to move on whenever I please."

"It sounds very adventurous." And lonely. Louise couldn't imagine a life without friends and family around her.

The man whose cart had been blocking the aisle at last noticed Mac and Louise. Rather than apologizing, he glowered at Mac, muttered something that sounded unfriendly, and jerked his own cart around to push it in the opposite direction.

Louise couldn't imagine why the older man had reacted so rudely. Mac was dressed casually, but neatly, and looked like any other man in town. "Do you know that man?" she asked him.

Mac glanced over. "Yes, I do. I had to ask him to move his car a few days ago when he double-parked and blocked in my bike. He wasn't too happy about it."

"I see." Louise tried to think of something else to say. "I imagine that you have a lot of places to see when you leave Acorn Hill. How long do you think your trip will take?"

Mac shrugged his shoulders. "Probably the rest of my life."

Louise nearly dropped the box of cat treats she had taken from the shelf. "That long?"

"This is a big country." He gave her a broad smile. "I bet I know what you're thinking."

"Everyone seems to these days," Louise said. "I never knew before that I am this transparent."

"It's more like an educated guess than reading your mind. My friends all said I was crazy too." Amusement colored his voice. "A couple of them got together, took me out for dinner after my retirement party and tried to talk me into seeing a therapist. They thought my selling the house and everything I owned, as well as buying a motorcycle, was, and I'll quote here, 'a cry for help.'"

Louise wondered how she would react if Alice or Jane did such a thing. It had been difficult enough for her to cope with Jane's youthful wanderlust, and then not to worry when Jane had left home to fulfill some of her dreams.

"I'm sure they were only worried about you." She

paused. "Did you *really* sell your house and everything you owned?"

"Lock, stock and barrel. What I couldn't sell, I donated to charity." Mac gave her a serious look. "All the things were what people told me that I needed to have, not what I actually wanted. I also didn't want to leave anything behind that someone else would have to look after for me. All I own now is the Ducati, enough clothes to get by, a decent bankroll and my time."

"How does your family feel about these plans of yours?" Louise had to ask.

"I only have one brother, and he and his wife didn't take it too well at first." Mac's smile dimmed. "They still don't, truth be told."

"I'm sorry." And she was. Louise knew that family could be the greatest of supporters, as well as the harshest of critics.

"My brother is a stockbroker, a very good one. He has his wife and kids and exactly the life he's always wanted. I've never had that. Here, let me grab that for you." Mac took a package of light bulbs from one of the top shelves that Louise was stretching to reach.

"What did you want, Mac?" Louise asked.

"While I enjoyed my work, I wasn't born wanting to be an investment banker—it wasn't my dream. I think you should try to live your dream at least some part of your life. Mine was this bike and riding cross-country with it." He sighed. "Somewhere in his heart my brother understands that, even if he will never approve of my choices."

A wife and children might have made a difference in Mac's life, Louise thought. Family always made a person more willing to put down roots. "I know you're a bachelor, but did you ever once think about getting married?"

Mac shrugged. "The right lady never came along. There was a time when I regretted that, but over the years I became convinced that I was never meant to be a husband either."

As they walked into the produce section, Louise saw that the older man who had blocked the aisle earlier was walking through the area, muttering to other customers and nodding his head at Mac. In a short time everyone within the immediate vicinity stopped what they were doing to look at Louise and Mac. The stares were not friendly.

"I thought you grew the fruits and vegetables you use at the inn in those beautiful gardens of yours," Mac said, dragging her attention back to him. "I've seen your vegetable garden. It looks better than most produce sections."

"We do. Well, almost everything. Jane has a taste for the exotic now and then." Louise focused on her shopping list. "Such as this week. She needs star fruit, mango and fresh coconut."

Mac went over to the specialty fruit bins and picked up a green foam tray with two halves of a coconut under plastic wrap. "These are as fresh as you'll find this far north of Florida."

The older man had already spoken to the two women standing on the other side of the bin, who looked at Mac while they exchanged whispers. Over by the refrigerated juice case the older man now stood talking in a low, disgruntled voice to the produce clerk.

Pauline Sherman came around the corner, talking on her cellular phone. She appeared a little distracted as she stopped directly in front of Louise without seeing her.

"Swiss steak?" Pauline sorted through her cart, which was heavily laden with groceries. "No. Because I thought you said Swiss cheese, Stanley. No, I won't. Yes, dear. I will. See you tonight." She switched off the phone and threw it into her purse, giving the purse a look of dislike before she noticed Louise. "Hi, Louise."

"Pauline, how are you?"

The younger woman dragged a hand through her hair. "I forgot my list. Again." Before Louise could reply, Pauline dropped her hand. "I'd better get going or I'll be late. Take care, Louise." She hurried away.

Louise stared after her. She felt something was troubling Pauline, and whatever it was seemed to be growing worse.

"How many mangoes does Jane need?" Mac called out to her.

"I'll look for those," Louise said to him. "Why don't you take the cart and get in line at the check-out?"

"Wait, I've found the star fruit." Mac said.

"Hello, Louise." Florence Simpson came to her side. She was carrying a small hand basket in which she had a carton of skim milk and a box of toast rounds. "Did the manager get in a new shipment of bananas? The ones they had for sale last week were dreadfully green. I couldn't eat them for three days after I bought them."

"I can't say, Florence." Louise looked up as Mac brought the coconut and a produce bag with several orange-yellow star fruit to the basket. "You remember Mr. Wilde, our guest at the inn."

Florence nodded to Mac. "Good afternoon." The sound of a loud whisper caught her attention. The produce clerk looked very unhappy as the older man said something low but vehement. What he was saying clearly wasn't pleasant. The clerk looked torn between politeness and distress.

Louise felt a tension headache beginning to creep up the back of her neck.

"The bananas look good this week, Mrs. Simpson, but there are no mangoes, Louise," Mac said as he placed the fruit in the cart. He seemed indifferent to the hostile looks being sent in his direction. "Do you need anything else?"

"No." Louise forced a smile. "That should do it."

"What are you looking at, Gladys?" Florence abruptly called to one of the women by the fruit bins. "Haven't you ever seen a man shop for produce before now? Oh, I forgot, your husband doesn't shop."

"Neither does yours, Florence," Gladys said, sounding rather miffed.

Louise turned the cart around. "It's all right, Florence. We'll be going now."

"Just a minute, Louise." Florence turned her attention to the clerk and the older man. "Acorn Hill is supposed to be a friendly town that welcomes visitors. Some of us, a great many of us, depend on the goodwill of our visitors to make our living, isn't that right, Harvey?"

Harvey Racklin, of course. Louise recognized the name but had never met the man. Alice had mentioned him because she knew his son Clyde, who ran a taxi service in Potterston and regularly sent cabs to pick up fares in Acorn Hill.

"Whatever are you fussing about, Florence?" The woman named Gladys uttered a nervous titter. "No one has said anything to that man."

"That is my point, Gladys. You're all standing around gawking and whispering about him, but I've yet to see one of you welcome him to our town. This is how you do it." Florence turned to Mac. "Welcome to Acorn Hill, Mr. Wilde." She glared at Gladys. "Now, is that so hard?"

Harvey made a snorting sound. "Fool woman."

Florence's eyes narrowed. "Let me tell you something about a fool, Harvey Racklin. 'A fool finds no pleasure in understanding, but delights in airing his own opinions'" (Proverbs 18:2).

"Well, I suppose you'd know," Harvey muttered.

Gladys tittered.

"Yes, I would, as I've been very free with my opinions over the years," Florence snapped. "I've just finished taking special counseling, as it happens. I wrote a personal essay on that verse from Proverbs. Any time you want to talk about the difference between understanding and opinions, you just come on over to my church. Rev. Thompson will be happy to talk to you."

Louise closed her eyes for a moment. *Lord, please stop her. Please.*

"What in tarnation were you doing in counseling?" Harvey demanded to know.

"I'm trying to become a better Christian. I'm trying to find some genuine tranquility in my life." Florence sniffed before she added, "You'd benefit from something like that yourself, Harvey." She looked over at the women by the fruit bins. "That goes for you, too, Gladys. When was the last time you had anything good to say about your sister?"

Gladys looked aghast. "Florence!"

"Mrs. Simpson." Mac put a hand on her shoulder. "It's all right. No harm done here." He smiled at Harvey and Gladys. "Sorry to interrupt your shopping. Have a good day."

Florence insisted on walking with them to the checkout line, where she hovered like a bodyguard behind Mac. Anyone who gave Mac even the slightest look received a scowl from Florence.

"This really isn't necessary," Louise said quietly to her aunt's friend.

"I disagree," was all Florence said. She appeared ready to do battle with anyone who might snub Mac.

Pauline Sherman happened to be the customer in line ahead of Louise, Mac and Florence. She paid for her groceries with a credit card, but her card was rejected. Pauline made a frantic search in her purse for her checkbook and then checked her wallet.

Guessing that the younger woman did not have enough cash to pay for her order, Louise stepped forward. "Pauline, may I help?"

"No," Pauline said sharply. She looked at the cashier. "I'll be right back." She hurried out of the store without her order.

The manager had to be summoned to void the order and Pauline's bagged groceries placed to one side. The cashier smiled at Mac as he began unloading the items out of the cart for her to scan. "Did you find everything you were looking for, sir?"

He grinned at Louise. "Everything, plus a little more I wasn't expecting."

Chapter Eleven

Mac seemed more amused than upset by the incident with Florence and the customers at the General Store, and said nothing more about it during their other stops or when he and Louise returned to the inn. Louise decided not to mention it to her sisters, though she felt sure that her aunt would hear all about it from Florence, if not from one of her other innumerable sources for gossip in town. Yet the incident stayed on her mind, so much so that the next day she found herself calling Rev. Thompson to discuss what had happened with Mac.

"I can't say I'm exactly surprised, since Florence is very proud of her success in trying to be a better Christian," Rev. Thompson said after she had given him the details. The head pastor of Grace Chapel was one of Louise's good friends as well as her primary confidante outside her own family. "I'm sorry that one of your guests had to be involved, though. Is Mr. Wilde upset?"

"Not at all," Louise said. "In fact, he seems to have shrugged off the entire incident." It was too bad she couldn't do the same.

"I know Florence may not always be the most diplomatic of souls, but what she did for your guest was an unselfish act," Rev. Thompson said. "I also find her public revelation that she has been in counseling encouraging."

Louise couldn't see why. Florence constantly fretted over her standing in the community. Her public announcement about being in counseling might invite some unpleasant comment. Louise mentioned this fear to the minister.

"Obviously I can't discuss details, since matters of counseling are private, but you shouldn't worry about how this will affect Florence," Rev. Thompson assured her. "I believe that she has learned that what you are is far more important than what people think you are."

"I don't mean to pry," Louise said. "It's just that I don't want Florence to suffer because she stood up for Mac Wilde."

"That's not prying, Louise," Rev. Thompson advised her. "That's loving concern for another."

After she ended the call, Louise straightened the area around the reception desk. Alice had gone to work, Mac had left for the day and Jane was upstairs involved in some project. No phone calls came in. The inn remained quiet.

Wendell wandered out of the study where he had been snoozing and perched on the front windowsill to look out at the birds. The tabby loved to nap in the sunlight, so it wasn't long before he stretched out again, tucked his nose between his front paws and fell asleep.

"If this keeps up," Louise said to herself, "*I* may go take a nap."

As if on cue, the front door of the inn opened, and a man dressed in a dark suit walked in. He was short and rather stout and had sharp eyes and a trim, heavily silvered beard. His head was bald and shone as if it had been polished. He looked around for a second before spotting Louise and walking up to the desk.

"Good afternoon," the man said. He had a mellow, deep

voice and the ready smile of a man who has met many people and has enjoyed doing so. "My name is Davis Utley, and I'm here looking for a friend of mine. Do you have someone staying here by the name of MacElroy Wilde?"

"Mr. Wilde is presently a guest at the inn," Louise acknowledged, "but I'm afraid he's not here at the moment. Would you care to leave a message or a business card so that he knows you called on him?"

The man looked uncertain. "I'm not sure," he said. "I talked to him before he left on this trip, and we had planned to meet in this area. I got in early, and when I called Mac's answering service, they told me he was already in Acorn Hill, staying here at the inn."

Louise felt curious, but it wasn't her place to ask questions. "Did you need accommodations, sir? We do have some rooms available."

"Thank you, but no. I'm staying at a hotel in Potterston. I have some business there." He took out a card holder, and then gave her a speculative look. "I know this sounds a bit odd for me to ask, but how is Mac?"

"Mr. Wilde is in fine health and, as far as I know, he has been enjoying his stay here with us." Louise took a pen from the drawer and offered it to him. "Perhaps you might write the name of your hotel and a phone number on the back of your card? That will give Mr. Wilde a chance to contact you directly when he returns."

Davis did so and handed the card back to her. On the face of the card was printed the name of a bank that Louise knew had branches all over the country. She also noted the man's beautiful Rolex watch and its heavy gold cuff links. Davis Utley appeared to be a man of considerable wealth.

"Mac and I were in the banking business together for years," Davis said in a conversational tone. "I also considered him my best friend."

Considered. Now there, Louise thought, was a telling word. "It is pleasant to see and catch up with old friends."

"It would be, if I weren't so concerned about him." He gave Louise a measured glance before continuing. "It's his state of mind I'm worried about. That's why I asked how he was."

Louise looked over Davis's shoulder as the inn door opened a second time, and Mac Wilde came in, so quietly that Davis did not hear him. "Mr. Utley, perhaps you should discuss this with Mr. Wilde."

"Too much information, huh? I apologize, ma'am. Frankly, I don't know what to think about Mac." He made a frustrated gesture. "The thing is, he just threw away everything he's worked for during the last thirty years. Sold his house, his furniture, practically everything he owned, and then he goes out, buys this motorcycle and decides to ride it cross-country. Just like that." Davis snapped his fingers. "He's going to ruin his life, if he hasn't already."

Louise didn't know what to do or say. She saw Mac reach back, open the front door and close it, this time with more noise, so that it would seem as if he had just come in at that moment.

Davis turned around. "Mac!"

"In the flesh." Mac came over, ignored Davis's outstretched hand and embraced the shorter man. "You're a sight for sore eyes, Dave. You lose a few pounds?"

"I've been hitting the driving range a few nights a week," Davis said. He looked over his friend. "You've thinned out some too. I see you finally got a tan."

"Ride through the country instead of sitting at a desk all day, add a little sunscreen, and you got yourself a tan," Mac said easily. "When did you get into town? I didn't expect to see you until next week."

"I finished up in Cleveland earlier than I'd expected."

Davis drew back and saw the flame-decorated helmet Mac carried. He gave a nervous laugh and tugged on the lapel of Mac's jacket. "So this the new style for you. What do you call it? Biker wear?"

"It's just a windbreaker and a safety helmet. Leather isn't my thing." Mac clapped a hand on his friend's shoulder. "How much time do you have before your next meeting? I've got to tell you about this trip I took last week through Amish country. Incredible ride."

"I thought you'd, uh, just keep going," Davis said.

"I'm going to spend a few weeks here while I get used to riding the bike for long periods of time," Mac told him. "Some of the stretches of highway out West can be pretty long, and I want to make sure I'm up to them. There are plenty of open roads around here in the country where I can ride around, see what it's like to spend all day on the Ducati."

Louise suggested the men sit in the parlor, where they could talk in comfort and privacy. They refused her offer to make tea or coffee for them, and she closed the door and returned to the front desk. It wasn't long before the two men came out of the parlor, and Mac saw Davis to the door.

Davis hesitated at the door, seeming reluctant to open it. He gave Mac a long, hard look. "Think about what I said, okay?"

"I'll call you tomorrow," was all that Mac promised. When his friend left, he glanced over at Louise. "Would that offer for a cup of coffee still be open?"

"Of course." Louise took off her reading glasses and set aside the ledger she had been checking. "Come into the kitchen."

It only took a few minutes for Louise to make the coffee, during which Mac told her about his friend Davis.

"Smartest financial analyst I've ever known," Mac said as he sat at the kitchen table. "That man can look at an account spread sheet and figure ten different ways to cut costs and make more profits for everyone involved. Taught me how to keep from slicing my shots on the golf course, but then he's one of the best amateur golfers in D.C."

"He seemed like a very nice man," Louise said as she brought their coffee to the table. "Are you an avid golfer too?"

"I played every week, but I've never liked the game," Mac confessed. "It was something I learned how to play, and play well, because my clients loved it. Most middle-aged bankers and financial managers golf. Also, Davis is my friend. Sometimes you just do what your friends like to do, to be a pal."

"My father occasionally played golf with some of his parishioners," Louise recalled. "He said it was a sport that required a man to have the patience of Job."

Mac chuckled. "When I started playing, Davis had to spend weeks to get the hook out of my stroke. I thought he'd brain me with his nine iron a few times."

"How long will your friend be in town?" Louise asked.

"Couple of weeks." Mac refused cream and sugar and sipped his coffee as it was.

Wendell strolled into the kitchen to investigate what was going on and walked up to Mac. After a few sniffs, he rubbed his dark-striped head against Mac's trousers.

"Oh, Wendell, no," Louise said as the family pet jumped up onto Mac's lap and curled up.

"It's okay, I like cats." Mac scratched the back of the delighted tabby's neck. "Davis didn't come here just to do business or look in on me. He wants to talk me into going back to Washington with him."

"I gathered as much. What will you do?"

"Not what Davis wants. He has this idea in his head of what my retirement should be. Namely, a carbon copy of his own." Mac cradled his cup in one hand and petted Wendell with the other. "He's already talking about what we'll do when he takes his retirement next year. I don't know what he was thinking, but I can't ride off into the sunset on a golf cart, even if he's driving it."

"You might still spend time together," Louise suggested. "Off the golf course, that is."

"I'm not like Davis anymore. I was, once," Mac said. "Like him, I worked hard, made money, did everything I was expected to do. The pitiful thing is, hardly any of it was what I really wanted. That shouldn't be the story of my life, Louise."

"You said it would take time for your brother to accept your choices," Louise reminded him. "Davis may need that as well."

"Davis can do as he likes." Mac finished his coffee. "That's the real difference between us. I don't particularly care for his life, but I would never try to tell him what to do with it. Funny how hard it is for most people to accept a lifestyle different from their own."

"We want the best for those we care about," Louise said. "My daughter Cynthia, for example, has a wonderful career in publishing. She's healthy, happy and ambitious. She lives in a lovely little apartment and has many interesting friends. She's active at her church and in her community."

Mac nodded his approval. "Sounds like the perfect daughter."

"I think she is, until I get on the phone with her. Then I listen to myself asking all sorts of intrusive questions. Is she getting enough rest, is she working too many hours, is she drinking too much coffee or losing too much weight?" Louise shook her head.

Mac ran his hand over his neck. "Then she starts in on you, I'll bet."

"You would not believe it to look at her, but that child is *twice* the nag that I am." Louise smiled. "My point is that wanting the best for someone sometimes blinds us to everything but the worst, or what we imagine is the worst."

"In Davis's eyes, that's where I am." Mac stood and took his cup to the sink and rinsed it out. "The worst possible place I can be." He shut off the faucet and turned to her. "He's my best friend, but this is my life we're talking about. The rest of my life. How can I make him see that?"

"Show him what it means to you," Louise advised, "and perhaps that will open his eyes."

Sleep proved to be elusive for Louise that night, and after an hour of lying wide awake in her bed, she gave up the battle and went downstairs for a cup of warm milk. In the kitchen she found Jane, sitting at the table and skimming through a magazine.

"Insomnia?" Jane asked.

"Yes. I've just been tossing and turning." Louise took some milk from the refrigerator, poured it into a cup and put the cup into the microwave to heat. She found a small note on the counter. "Rose called?"

"She invited you, me and Alice to come out to Bellwood Farm tomorrow," Jane said. "The Majeskas have found some replacement panels for their big top and are having a tent-raising party."

"Mr. Majeska told me about how they do that. We should try to attend, if we have the chance." Louise glanced at her. "Have they scheduled their performance?"

Jane shook her head. "No, according to Rose, their elephant is still not ready to perform, so they're holding off." She rolled her eyes. "Must be *some* elephant act."

"It likely is," Louise said. "So what are you still doing up? Are you excited about going to the tent-raising?"

"Actually, I'm trying to find some new recipes to keep Alice on her diet." Jane indicated the magazine. "She's craving chocolate, so I thought I'd try something with carob. If you use the right recipe, carob tastes very much like chocolate."

"Poor Alice." Louise glanced at the clock on the wall and saw that it was just after midnight. "Will she *ever* lose those last two pounds?"

"Give me another week to work on her," Jane said grimly. "Please watch what you eat in front of her, too, if you would. She's in the diet danger zone, and one good binge could put her right back where she was when we started this."

"Heavens, no." Louise immediately resolved to eat nothing more fattening than a cracker in front of Alice. "The girl has suffered enough."

Jane flipped a page and studied it. "Hey, here's a recipe for carob brownies that sounds pretty tasty."

Louise opened the cabinet to get some nutmeg to grate on her milk and saw the little round tin of loose white tea she had purchased from Wilhelm Wood. She held it up for Jane to see. "Did you know that white tea isn't white?" she asked. "It's sort of a silvery green."

"I know that white tea is supposed to do wonders for your skin, if you make a mask of it," Jane said absently as she folded over the page with the carob recipe and flipped to another. "So what's causing your insomnia, sweetheart?"

Louise thought of her conversation with Mac. "Do you ever regret leaving home when you were younger, Jane?"

"Not often." Jane seemed puzzled by the question. "I sometimes wish I had come back to visit Father and Alice more often, but I needed to get away from Acorn Hill. Leaving then made it possible for me to appreciate now what I didn't when I was young."

Mac did not have the advantage of youth now, as Jane had once had. "If you had stayed, do you think you would have regretted it more?"

"Yes, I do." Jane peered at her. "What's this all about? You're not thinking of ditching me and Alice and the inn and taking a cruise around the world, are you?"

"No, I'm very happy with our life here." Louise put her cup on the table and sat down. "One of Mac's friends, a man named Davis Utley, came by the inn today."

"And?"

"He's deeply concerned about Mac's plans." Louise told her about what Davis had said and how Mac had overheard. "What amazes me is how calm and accepting Mac was. He already knows that his family doesn't approve, and then to stand there and listen to his best friend say that he's wasting everything that he has worked for and ruining his life . . ."

"It's Mac's life," Jane said promptly. "One man's ruin is another man's freedom."

"It's not quite that simple. I remember how I felt when you made the decision to leave home." Louise nodded at Jane's surprised glance. "I felt so helpless and so angry with you. I wanted to lock you up in your bedroom. Permanently. I think I might have tried, if Father hadn't intervened."

"I always wondered why you were so upset that last week I was home," Jane said. "You hardly spoke a word to me."

"Before Cynthia was born, you were more like my daughter than my sister." She reached over and covered Jane's hand with her own. "I felt that my little girl was going out into the world and that I wouldn't be there if she needed me. I was utterly terrified."

Jane's expression softened. "You're going to make me cry, aren't you?"

"I need to say this to you." She patted Jane's hand. "I should have realized then how important it was for you to go. You were a young woman, not a little girl. I should have respected your decision and trusted you to look after yourself. I didn't, and sometimes I still don't. For that I apologize, my dear."

Tears sparkled in Jane's eyes. "That did it." She reached over to hug Louise.

Someone made a grumpy sound, and Louise and Jane looked over to see a drowsy-looking Alice standing in the kitchen doorway.

"I was having this strange dream about something pulling me through a top hat, but my stomach started rumbling so loudly that it woke me up," she said, and yawned. "Am I allowed to have some cocoa on my diet?"

"No," Jane said. "Too much sugar."

"A glass of milk and two cookies?"

"A glass of skim milk, yes, cookies—" Jane shook her head. "You really shouldn't eat this late at night, but if you must, you can have carrot or celery sticks, plain. No dressing and no salt."

"That explains the top hat dream," Alice said as she went to the fridge.

"How so, dear?" Louise asked.

Alice brought the carton of skim milk and a bag of carrot sticks to the table, where she regarded them with a woebegone expression. "I'm turning into a rabbit."

Chapter Twelve

The next day Louise called Bellwood Farm to accept Rose's invitation. The Bellwoods were delighted and arranged to meet the sisters at the circus area at 2:00 P.M. that afternoon.

"Mayor Tynan is satisfied with how Aldo and Ilsa are handling the safety issues, and Hannah has clearly recuperated from the birth," Rose told them, "so the Majeskas decided to hold a special performance while they're here in Acorn Hill."

It was five minutes to two when Louise drove into the parking area outside the entrance to the midway.

"Wow, it's so much bigger than I imagined," Jane commented.

"Oh, look! A tiger!" Alice said, as she looked out the passenger window.

Louise looked at the vehicle being driven around the entrance and saw an enormous black, white and orange striped cat pacing inside the cage built onto the trailer. "It certainly is a large one."

Rose and Samuel were waiting for them in front of the old fire truck, which was now set up at the front gate to serve as a ticket booth. Both of the Bellwoods greeted the Howards warmly and walked with them down the midway.

"It's a privilege to watch something like this," Samuel said. "Usually townies aren't permitted on the grounds until the circus is ready to put on a show."

"Townies?" Alice echoed.

"That's what the circus folk call us people from town," Rose explained.

Alice looked eagerly at the concessionaires, who had already started stocking their booths with treats. "I haven't had cotton candy in years."

Rose chuckled. "The circus people call that floss."

Jane put a hand on her shoulder. "Cotton candy—floss—is made of sugar. Pure, one hundred percent, thigh-widening, diet-destroying sugar." She steered her to the other side of the midway. "You can have some fruit when we get home."

"Caramel apples!" Alice said, looking at the temptations of another stand. "Some of them are double-dipped in caramel and chocolate." She gave Jane a defensive look. "What? They're made of fruit. Mostly."

"You'll step on the scale tomorrow morning," Jane warned, "and shriek in horror at what it reads. I know I will."

Alice gave the candy-coated apples one last, lingering look. "We could buy matching earplugs."

Louise watched as performers and helpers went about their business. "It was very kind of the Majeskas to invite us on such a busy day."

"All of our kids and their families are here too," Rose told Louise. "My daughter even came home from college for the weekend so she could see this."

Most of the circus people began gravitating toward the now empty space where the temporary practice tent had stood. Some carried huge rolls of canvas, others coils of rope. Two men drove a vehicle Samuel called a "spool truck" that was also heavily laden with tent canvas. Still others were rolling up their sleeves, prepared to help. Louise saw the tops of the tent stakes, which had already been driven into the ground, and watched the gigantic form of Hannah as she was brought out of her pen by her trainer.

Alice's eyes widened. "Look at how beautiful she is."

The Asian elephant was an awe-inspiring sight. She was so large that her trainer, a slim, fair-haired man of average height, seemed like a doll next to her. The elephant's gray, wrinkly skin appeared old and sagging, but Louise could see that it was kept scrupulously clean. Hannah's ears were not as large as those of an African elephant, but they had a pleasing shape and moved often as if to catch nearby sounds. Incredible as Hannah was, the circus people seemed to pay little attention to her, treating her as if she were simply another member of their troupe.

Louise could not do the same. Hannah's movements were almost unearthly, so slow and deliberate, and her sheer size made it impossible to compare her to anything else. Yet Hannah seemed completely placid and responded to every hand signal made by her trainer.

"I wonder how much she weighs," Jane said to no one in particular.

"Mr. Majeska told me that she weighs over ten thousand pounds and is nine and a half feet tall and nineteen feet long," Louise told her. "Even you'd have your hands full trying to feed her, Jane."

"Oh?" Jane looked intrigued. "Is she a picky eater?"

"Hannah is a vegetarian," Louise said. "As her cook, you'd have to provide one hundred and fifty pounds of hay, fruit and vegetables for her every day."

Jane whistled. "She *does* pack it away." She glanced at Alice. "That was an observation, not a suggestion."

"All I wanted was one little caramel apple," Alice murmured.

"Poor Alice," Jane said, and then turned her attention

back to the giant creature. "Why doesn't she have tusks like elephants do in the movies?"

"Not all female Asian elephants do," Alice told her. "Her baby probably doesn't have them, either."

"Where is the baby, Louise?" Jane asked.

"They're keeping the little one in a pen until it can be trained," Louise told her.

"That's better than a caramel apple," Alice said. When her sisters looked at her, she added, "Not the baby, the birth itself. I read a sad article in a nature magazine about the decrease in the elephant population. There are only about thirty thousand Asian elephants left in the wild. Even though they live about fifty years, females usually only give birth once every four to six years."

"Why is that?" Louise asked.

"I'm not sure, but the gestation period for an elephant baby is nineteen to twenty-two months. That probably has something to do with it. In addition to their low birth rate, elephants are still killed by poachers for their meat or tusks."

"Okay, another question, if Hannah is the only elephant in the show, how did she get pregnant?" Jane asked.

"I can answer that one," Louise said. "Hannah's trainer, who is also her owner, decided to breed her. Aldo arranged for her and her trainer to spend a few weeks with a male Asian elephant from another circus."

"Can't the zoos do something like that?" Jane asked.

"Zoos have been having a much more difficult time breeding Asian elephants, according to Mark Graves," Alice said, mentioning her friend, the chief veterinarian for the Philadelphia zoo. "Mark and I have talked a lot about elephants. They've always been one of his favorite animals. There is some controversy over whether they are better off being in zoos or performing, but maybe Hannah proves that circus life really is better than captivity for them."

Aldo and Ilsa were busy directing the assembly of the big top's panels, so the Bellwoods and the sisters went to the folding chairs that had been set up for spectators. There Louise, Jane and Alice greeted Rose and Samuel's children and grandchildren and sat down to await the tent-raising and to discuss the upcoming performance for the townspeople.

"If all goes according to plan, they'll be putting on a regular show," Samuel told them. "Aldo sets up grandstand seating all around the walls of the tent. Their capacity limit for one show is three thousand, so there will be plenty of room."

"Everyone is so curious about the circus that I'm sure they'll sell out," Alice said. Her gaze moved past Samuel. "Look at what Hannah's doing." She caught her breath. "Goodness."

The elephant had bent her front legs so that she was kneeling forward on the ground. At the same time, she had her long trunk wrapped around her trainer, and was helping him climb up onto her back. When he was sitting astride her neck, the trainer uttered a strange word and gently tapped Hannah's flank with the stick he carried. Slowly the elephant stood up.

"Why does that man talk to the elephant in another language?" Jane wanted to know.

"Hannah's trainer is called a mahout," Samuel said, "and he speaks to her in Hindi. Hannah came from India, where she was also trained, and none of her original mahouts spoke English."

"Excuse me." It was Dilly. Today he was dressed in worn jeans and a denim work shirt, but still sported the red foam ball on the end of his nose. "Could I borrow the fair lady pianist for a few moments?" He bowed and held out his hand to Louise.

Jane and Alice laughed as Louise rolled her eyes. She

accepted Dilly's hand and allowed him to lead her over to where the calliope stood gleaming in the sunlight.

"How did you find out I was a pianist?" Louise asked him.

"Ah, circus people can find out anything." He laid a finger beside his red clown nose. "Especially when we catch little kids who, when they aren't trying to sneak in a circus to have a look at the animals, are piano students. Some of whom really hate playing 'Twinkle Twinkle Little Star,' shall we say."

"That's my Charlie, always singing my praises." Louise shook her head and laughed.

Dilly helped her climb up onto the new platform on which the calliope stood. He had placed a short bench seat in front of the keyboard and invited her to sit down with him.

"Is this a test of my musical ability?" Louise asked.

"Samuel mentioned how much you admired this old blowhard," Dilly said, "so I thought you might like to try it out yourself."

The keyboard, which was only half the size of standard piano's, looked alien to her. "I don't know quite where to start."

"Middle C is the same on a calliope as it is on a piano," Dilly said, showing her that and the other range of notes she could play. "The compressor allows enough air distribution for you to play six notes simultaneously. If you can play any more than that, I'll definitely sign up to take piano lessons from you."

Once Louise had tried out the keyboard and become familiar with the ranges, she played an old ragtime tune. Dilly grinned, and when she had finished, followed it up with one of his own.

As they played rounds on the calliope for each other, some of the performers paused by the platform to listen. Louise was impressed by Dilly's dexterity and the number of old pieces he had memorized. He was able to play music written by composers as diverse as Brahms and Billy Joel, and he used no sheet music.

"How long have you been playing?" Louise asked as they took a break.

"Since I was a kid," Dilly said. "I spent most of my childhood running away from foster homes, but a few I stayed in had pianos. When I was seventeen, the Majeskas came to town. I wasn't in a great place at that time, and I always dreamed of running away with the circus, so I did."

"Indeed." Thinking what might have happened to a boy on his own, Louise found this more disturbing than adventurous.

"At least, I *tried* to." Dilly looked over to where Aldo was supervising the big top tent's assembly. "I wrote my age as twenty-one on the job application they made me fill out. I was such a First of May—a circus rookie," he added at Louise's blank look. "Aldo interviewed me and told me that he would hire me, except that there was no room in his troupe for liars and runaways."

"So he saw through your deception." Louise felt a pang of sympathy for the young man. "What did you do?"

"I almost ran off again before the Majeskas talked me into doing things the right way. Aldo took me to see my foster care case worker, who helped emancipate me so that I was no longer in state custody," Dilly said. "Aldo put me on the payroll, but I had to go to the circus school just like any other kid here. Aldo and Ilsa have treated me like their own son. Ilsa found out I was musical and taught me to play the calliope. She used to be a windjammer—a calliope player—before her arthritis got bad."

A sad story, but one that seemed to have a happy ending, Louise thought. "Do you like the circus life?"

"I love it. I've never had a family. Now I belong to a huge one. I've learned so much from these people too." Dilly removed his clown nose. "I was mostly living on the streets and getting into trouble before I came here. I don't know why the Majeskas took me in, but they changed my life. Saved it, too, I think."

"I'm glad, Dilly."

"Me too." He smiled at Louise. "So how about you? Want to run away with the circus?" He popped his clown nose back on his face, and then played scales up and down the calliope's keyboard. "You could be my relief calliope player. All the popcorn, candy floss and hot dogs you can eat."

"Now *that* is an excellent bribe," Louise said, running her fingers along the edge of the wind chest's polished wood. "I'm almost tempted."

Dilly played another classic piece of circus music from memory, but something caught his attention and he stopped abruptly in the middle of the tune.

"Not him again," Louise heard him say under his breath. She followed the direction of his gaze with her own.

A man was standing outside Hannah's pen. He was dressed in shabby-looking clothes and had a stained, soiled baseball cap pulled down low on his forehead. In his hand was a pine tree branch, and he was jabbing it at Hannah's baby, jerking it out of reach every time the little elephant tried to take hold of it with her trunk.

Louise's gaze shifted. The tent-raisers were taking a break and passing out soft drinks from a large, ice-filled barrel while Hannah and her trainer were walking as if to return to the pen. No one but Louise and Dilly had yet seen the man tormenting Hannah's baby.

"I've got to stop him." With an acrobatic vault, Dilly jumped off the platform and ran toward the pen.

Louise saw the elephant stop several yards away from the pen. The man, who was laughing and still teasing Hannah's baby, remained completely oblivious to the presence of the adult elephant. When Hannah lifted her trunk as if to grab the branch, her trainer tapped her side with his stick, and she lowered it.

By that time Dilly had reached the man and wrestled the pine branch away from him.

"Hey," the man protested. "I was only playing around with it. Gimme that back."

"This is not a petting zoo," Dilly said, his tone as flat as his expression was stern. "Please leave."

"I said I was only fooling with it." The man tried to grab the branch, and when Dilly threw it away, he shoved the clown into the pen's fence, which made a buckling sound.

Goliath appeared, seemingly out of nowhere, and planted his massive form between Dilly and his attacker.

"We do not permit fighting here," the roustabout informed the man politely. He swept his hand toward the midway. "You will go away now. You will not be welcome back."

"So?" the man sneered. "I'm not afraid of you. You can't make me do nothing."

"This is true, I cannot." Goliath pointed past the man's right shoulder. "She can."

The man turned around to see Hannah and her trainer standing a few feet behind him. The trainer uttered a short, sharp word, and Hannah lifted one of her tree-trunk sized legs, as if to step on something.

"Hannah weighs five tons," Goliath told the man, still sounding very polite. "How much do you weigh?"

The man turned pale and scrambled backward, nearly falling. "Get that thing away from me!" he shouted.

"A drifter," Samuel muttered as he came to stand beside Louise. "That's unusual, but I'm sure Goliath and Dilly will take care of him."

"There won't be a fight, will there?" Louise asked, appalled by what had already happened.

"No, circus people only do that in the movies," Samuel

said. He nodded toward Goliath, who along with Dilly had taken hold of the drifter and was marching him toward the midway. "Any troublemakers around here will be shown the door, so to speak. If they refuse to leave or try to pick fights with the performers, Aldo has trained security people on hand who can subdue them and haul them off to the nearest police station."

"I never would have imagined that people would come to a circus to cause trouble," Louise said. "This is a place for children and families."

"There are people who cause trouble wherever they go," Samuel said with a certain amount of resignation. "It's best to be prepared for it."

Louise walked with Samuel back to where her sisters and Rose were talking with Aldo and Ilsa.

"The tradition of performing in a ring came from the days of ancient Rome," Aldo was telling Jane and Alice. "The word *circus* means circle or ring."

"I didn't know the Romans had circuses," Alice said. "I thought they just had all those awful gladiator fights in the coliseum."

"The modern circus can trace its origins back to combat spectacles, like those that were held in the coliseum," Aldo said. "In addition to the gladiator bouts, the Roman emperors imported many exotic animals, like tigers, lions and even elephants to entertain their bloodthirsty audiences. Of course, this entertainment usually pitted one animal against another."

"Or the animals against the Christians," Jane said.

Aldo nodded. "It was not, perhaps, the best of beginnings, but eventually the circus evolved into a less violent spectacle. When civilization descended into the Dark Ages, and people once again lived in isolation from each other, circus performers left their permanent arenas and became the first traveling people."

Louise was fascinated by Aldo's knowledge of circus history and listened attentively as he described how the jongleurs, gypsies and minstrels from the Dark Ages were responsible for shaping the acts that would become standard for modern circuses.

"At first, most of those vagabond entertainers traveled alone, but over time they banded together in troupes. There was little law in those days, but much safety in numbers." Aldo smiled. "The troupes began taking regular routes through the countryside, always stopping at fairs and tournaments where they would be welcomed rather than chased away by suspicious locals."

"The gypsies had the hardest time, for everyone considered them thieves," Ilsa put in. "But they gave the circus fortune-tellers and dressage, or riding acts. They, too, understood the life of a traveler."

"Circus people were the first traveling people," Aldo said again.

"Aldo thinks this, because his family comes from circus people," Ilsa said to Louise. "Gypsies were—are—my people, and I know they were the first traveling people."

Her husband gave her an exasperated look. "They were not."

"Do not have us talk about who is descended from the lost tribe of Israel," Ilsa advised Louise. "That one makes us yell."

The first of what would become the modern circuses, Aldo told them, came into being in the eighteenth century, when Philip Astley, the son of an English cabinetmaker, fell in love with horses.

"Instead of becoming a carpenter like his father, Astley joined the military and served in the Dragoons," Aldo said. "He was a big, brave man who loved adventure, and during his career performed many acts of courage that made him a famous war hero. When he returned to England and civilian life, he wished to open a riding school, but a soldier made little money in those days, and he could not afford to. To raise money for his school, he began performing in trick riding exhibitions, the first dressage acts. He did so well that he was not only able to open his school, but he also bought land near Westminster Bridge, and there established the very first circus with performances held in a ring."

"I know some circus trivia," Jane said. "What was the name of the first circus held in America, and where did it put on its first show?"

Louise and Alice looked at her and answered simultaneously. "The Ricketts Circus, in Philadelphia." The answer was information every native Pennsylvanian knew.

Jane scowled. "Okay, smarties, but which American president was the first to attend the circus and sell one of his horses to the owner?"

"Thomas Jefferson?" Alice guessed.

Jane glanced at Louise, who only shrugged. "George Washington," Jane said triumphantly. She turned to Aldo. "If Mr. Astley started with one ring, who added the other two?"

"That happened right here in America. It was the development of the railroads that enabled the circus to easily travel the great distances between cities and towns. Wherever there were train stations, there were many people, and that meant much larger audiences than before. The big top came into being at this time, and circus owners hired more performers and added new acts to draw even more people to the show. All of this could not be fit into a single ring, so a second was added, and then a third."

Aldo explained how the arrival of a circus became an event, and the ways owners played up anticipation. "The setup or twenty-four-hour man would always ride ahead of the show. He would find the right spot for the circus to raise the tents. He'd mark it, and then go all around town pasting up playbills announcing the performances. As you have seen in our trailer, Louise, the early ones were all hand-painted and lettered. When the circus train arrived, the performers would unload everything onto beautifully painted wagons, leave the station and ride through town like a parade. It was the caged wagons with the animals, as well as the calliope, that brought people running to see the spectacle. In some ways the parade was the opening act."

Aldo told them how James Bailey and P. T. Barnum created the largest circus in the world, appropriately billed as "The Greatest Show on Earth," while five brothers named Ringling bought and consolidated many small circuses until they were prosperous enough to buy Barnum and Bailey's show.

"When was the flying trapeze invented, Aldo?" Jane asked.

"The first trapeze artist was a Frenchman named Jules Leotard, who performed his act for the first time in 1859, at the *Cirque Napoleon* in Paris. He had a solo act in which he swung from one bar to another and even performed a somersault in mid-air. It was called 'flying' by those who watched, since Jules seemed to fly through the air. It was he who inspired the song 'The Daring Young Man on the Flying Trapeze.' In time other performers were added and we had the first trapeze 'flyers' and 'catchers.'"

"Leotard." Jane tilted her head. "Was the leotard named after him?"

"He invented it," Ilsa said. "Because of the demands of his act, he made a one-piece garment that allowed him unrestricted movement."

"Leotard made it skin-tight to show off his physique," Aldo said. "He called it a *maillot*, but in time it became known as the leotard."

Alice chuckled. "I always suspected that those things were *not* invented by a woman."

"We are lucky, my Ilsa and I. We were born into the circus life, and we never wished to do anything else with our lives. With shows closing and consolidating as they are today, we are lucky to still be able to live our dream." Aldo saw the performers gathering around the assembled canvas panels, and Hannah's trainer leading her back to the center pole, and stood. "Come, Ilsa, it is time to put the roof on our new house."

Ilsa nodded, but Louise noticed the older woman seemed not as happy as her husband. She also moved slowly as she rose from her chair, as if in pain.

Louise recalled the circus retirement community brochure she had seen arrive for the Majeskas during her first visit to the circus, and she felt sorry for the couple. They deserved a chance to enjoy their golden years in some comfort, and that was something the circus they loved could not provide in large measure. Yet with so many people depending on the circus for their livelihood, retirement seemed out of the question.

Everyone must make sacrifices, Louise thought. *Even people who live their dreams.*

Watching the big top being raised was thrilling. The panels of canvas, now stitched together, stretched out like enormous sails. How quickly the task was performed astonished Louise.

"That tent looks bigger than our whole *town*," Alice said as the roustabouts went inside the big top to secure the "guys," which Samuel identified as the broad, heavy cables that supported the center and quarter poles, and provided anchor lines for high-wire rigging.

Hannah, who was no longer needed for the heavy work, was led back to her pen by her trainer. Rose and Samuel agreed to take their grandchildren to see the new baby, and Jane asked to tag along. Louise decided to go with Alice to check on Ilsa, who along with Aldo had gone to their RV.

"She's having a problem with arthritis, isn't she?" Alice asked as they walked over to the Majeskas's RV.

"Dilly mentioned something about it," Louise said. "I don't think Aldo is in the best of health, either. His limp seems to be a little worse than the last time I visited." She saw the Majeskas sitting outside the RV at a small patio table, but judging by their expressions, it appeared as if they were having an argument.

"I can't believe they travel all over the country the way they do, as old as they are," Alice commented. "Not that I think age should keep someone from doing something he loves. It's just, with age comes health problems. Health problems that a traveling lifestyle won't help improve."

As they drew nearer, Louise saw Ilsa lying on a chaise longue-style lawn chair and Aldo gently massaging her hands and scolding her.

"No more fighting about this now," Aldo told his wife. "Your hands are very swollen, darling. You should take the medicine."

"I don't like pills," Ilsa replied, but she sounded as if she were in considerable pain. "I am not changing my mind, Aldo. We cannot do this to our friends. A gypsy would never do such a thing."

"We are not gypsies, my heart," Aldo said.

"I am, and you are married to me, so I make you one. Now, I will go inside and rest for an hour." She rose with stiff movements and hobbled up the steps of the RV.

Aldo's sad expression vanished as soon as he saw Louise and Alice. "Ladies, forgive me for abandoning you. My wife was not feeling well."

"I'm a nurse, Mr. Majeska," Alice said. "Is there anything I can do?"

"No, she will take her medicine, rest and feel better. Please, sit down." He gestured to the lawn chairs. "Miss Howard, you were asking something about the photos of Hannah we have on display?"

"Yes, I noticed that Hannah always has her trunk up in every photo," Alice said.

"That is an old circus superstition," Aldo told her. "It is bad luck to photograph an elephant unless she has her trunk up, so the good luck does not run out."

"Are there other special things circus people do for luck?" Alice asked.

"It is more what we will *not* do, for fear of bad luck. We never touch peacock feathers, or whistle while getting dressed for the show." Aldo smiled. "In the old days, you could never look back during the circus parade into town. My grandfather thought it was such a terrible thing that he would make anyone who did so clean the animal cages for a week."

Louise saw the brochure for the circus retirement community on the table next to Ilsa's chair, and wondered if that was what Aldo and Ilsa had argued about. "I haven't had the chance to thank you for inviting us to the tent-raising," she told Aldo. "It has been a truly enjoyable experience."

"It was our pleasure to have you here," he assured her.

Alice picked up the brochure. "Oh, a community for retired circus performers. Have you ever visited it, Mr. Majeska?"

Aldo nodded. "Many of our old friends live there now, so we stop by whenever we are near." He gave Louise a wry look. "You must have heard what my wife said. She is right, of course. We cannot be so selfish to think of ourselves. All of our money is tied up in the show. We could not retire unless we close it and sell off everything we have."

"I understand that you love the circus, but you have to be realistic," Alice said softly. "How much longer can you and your wife continue to travel?"

"I don't know," he admitted. "But we cannot close the show. We have over a hundred people depending on us for their livelihood. If we shut down and sell out, they will be left with nothing."

Louise thought that since most of the performers were younger people, they could relocate and find jobs . . . except for the Bratwicks and Goliath. Because of their physical differences it would probably be hard for them to obtain employment anywhere except in another circus.

Aldo was watching her. "You understand, yes?"

"Yes, I'm afraid I do." On impulse, Louise took hold of his hand and Alice's. "Would you mind if I say a prayer now, Aldo?"

The old man smiled. "That kind of help I always accept," he said.

Louise closed her eyes and prayed, "Dear Lord in Heaven, You always provide for us. It was Your Son, Jesus Christ, who said to us, 'Come to me, all you who are weary and burdened, and I will give you rest' (Matthew 11:28). Bring comfort and healing to our new friends, Aldo and Ilsa, whom we lift up to You now. Bless them and help them in their struggles and keep them close to Your heart, through Christ our Lord, Amen."

Chapter Thirteen

S ince this lovely weather seems to be here to stay for a while, Florence and I would like to have a tea in the inn's garden," Ethel said to Louise the next day. She had come to the inn after Sunday service at the Chapel to see if her nieces would be willing to host the gathering.

"A tea for whom?" Louise asked.

"The members of the Seniors Social Circle." Ethel mentioned a date. "Can we have it here on that date, or do you have something planned?"

"I'll have to check with Jane, of course, but the inn is free on that day," Louise told her after checking the inn calendar. "But I thought your group met only once a month."

"This is a special occasion," was all Ethel would tell her about the meeting. "Now, where's Jane? I want to discuss the menu with her. Everyone loves her cherry vanilla scones. They definitely must be included."

The inn had hosted the meeting for special occasions several times in the past, and Jane had no problem with doing the extra work, so it was planned for the following Thursday. As it happened to be one of Alice's days off, she volunteered to help serve, and Louise was left to wonder what her aunt was up to now.

The next afternoon, as Louise walked out to collect the mail, she saw Florence Simpson coming out of the carriage house. This was not unusual, as Florence often visited Ethel, but there was something in the way she hurried to her car that piqued Louise's curiosity.

"Do you know what is going on with Aunt Ethel and Florence?" she asked Jane as she brought their mail to the front desk.

"No idea." Jane held her hands out for the bundle and began sorting through it. "They've decided to change the menu for their tea again. They seem really nervous about this meeting. Oh—here's a letter from Cynthia. It was stuck in the middle of these ads." She handed Louise an envelope. "What's your theory?"

"I'm afraid to speculate." Louise opened the envelope and drew out the photos her daughter had enclosed. "Oh, look at this." She handed Jane the top photo, which showed a living room furnished with an eclectic mix of furniture and styles, all in dramatic combinations of scarlet, black and white. "This came out just as she told me it would."

Jane peered at it. "That's really an interesting effect."

"It's just flea market makeovers," Louise said with a chuckle. "It's the thing now to buy old, broken-down pieces from flea markets or rummage sales, fix them up, paint them fresh colors and otherwise make them look new."

Jane raised her eyebrows. "Sounds like what we've done with the inn here. So how come this trend isn't named after us?"

Louise patted her cheek. "Because we're not hip young editors living in a one-bedroom city apartment and trying to furnish it on a minuscule budget."

"Ah." Jane nodded.

Eager to look through the rest of the photos and read Cynthia's letter, Louise pushed aside her curiosity about her aunt, Florence and the upcoming meeting. But the next evening Alice also mentioned seeing Florence pay Ethel a visit.

"She and Aunt Ethel must have been locked up in the carriage house all morning," Alice told her sisters over dinner. "When I went out to get something from my car about three hours after I saw Florence go into Aunt's house, Florence was leaving. She rushed away so fast that she didn't even see me wave to her."

Louise frowned. "I wonder what they were doing."

"I have no idea." Alice gestured in the direction of the carriage house. "I asked Aunt Ethel this afternoon, but she said they were just visiting."

Florence visited the carriage house the following day, too, and again spent several hours with Ethel before hurrying off.

"I'm sorry, but I have so much to do, girls," Ethel told her nieces that afternoon as her reason for refusing their invitation to join them for tea. "I can't believe the meeting is tomorrow."

When their aunt left, Jane eyed Louise. "Okay, something is definitely going on."

Louise sighed. "Yes, and I suppose that we'll find out about it with everyone else, tomorrow."

The day of the meeting dawned bright and warm, without a cloud in the sky. Mac left the inn early to visit his friend Davis in Potterston, so once Louise had finished her usual morning chores, she went to help Jane with preparations for the meeting.

"Auntie wanted a formal tea," Jane said as she took a pan of miniature muffins out of the oven and set them on a rack to cool. "Do you think that means everyone will show up in Easter dresses and big floppy hats?"

"I hope not," Louise said, thinking of Florence's love of themed events. She reached for the cookie jar, which Jane kept stocked with fresh-baked treats, and frowned. "Where are the cookies?"

"There are only a few left in the jar. I put the new batches over . . ." Jane paused and frowned. "Where is the cookie jar?"

"That was what I meant."

"It was right here." A sudden, gloomy look came over her face. "Oh, Alice."

"Alice?"

"She must have eaten what I had left in the jar." She stripped off her oven mitts and pressed one hand to her forehead. "I can't keep her on this diet, Louise. I give up."

"I'm sure Alice didn't eat the cookies," Louise said. She checked the dishwasher, but the jar wasn't in it. "Maybe she accidentally knocked it over and broke it." It wouldn't be the first time one of them had broken something in the kitchen.

Jane removed the lid from the kitchen trash bin and inspected the contents. "No sign of it here. Just forget about it. I don't want to make her feel guiltier than she already must feel." She went to the garden door and walked outside.

Louise followed her sister out to where Alice was setting up the tables for the meeting. "Jane, ask her what happened to it."

"I don't need to know," Jane said.

Alice looked from Louise to Jane. "Know what?"

"Nothing." Jane gave her a sad smile and went over to adjust one of the chairs.

"Alice, we have a problem," Louise said. "We need to ask you about something."

"I told you, it doesn't matter, Louise," Jane said. "I understand. Really I do. The caramel apples at the circus were too much. It pushed her over the edge." She turned to Alice. "I know it wasn't your fault."

The phone inside the inn began to ring.

"Jane, I don't have the faintest idea of what either of you is talking about," Alice said, giving Louise a skeptical look before she walked inside.

Jane blocked Louise's path as she went to follow their sister. "You're just going to make her feel worse for breaking her promise to me, and then she'll go on another binge."

"Alice would not break her promise," Louise said, hoping that was true.

"Look, there were only three or four cookies in that jar. And yes, they were the kind I make with the extra big chocolate chips, but it's not so bad. She could walk off the extra calories in, I don't know, a couple of days." Jane sighed. "Unless she's been binging at work too."

Louise frankly was so weary of Alice's diet and Jane's obsessing over it that she thought *she* might have to go on a binge. "Let's talk to Alice about this."

Louise went around Jane, walked back into the inn and found Alice on the phone at the front reception desk.

"That's all right, Pauline. I know you're busy. I'll give them the sheets next week. Wednesday, not Tuesday. Yes, I'm sure. You too. Bye now." Alice hung up the phone and glanced at her sisters. "That was Pauline Sherman. Briana and Tiffany didn't make the ANGELs meeting last night because Pauline thought it was held on Thursdays."

"The ANGELs meetings have always been held on Wednesdays," Louise said, puzzled by this.

"Pauline knows that. She's been bringing her daughters to ANGELs meetings for well over a year now." Alice looked troubled. "She sounded really upset about it. I could hear Tiffany in the background complaining about missing the meeting too." She turned to face Jane. "Now, why do you look like you've just lost your best friend?"

Jane gave Louise a frustrated look before she said, "We know about the cookies, Alice."

"Oh right, I meant to say something to you about that last night. The temptation was really starting to get to me." Alice smiled. "Is it okay with you?"

"Okay?" Jane's eyes widened. "Sweetheart, I know this has been tough on you, but I am not okay with this. Think about all our hard work. All those weeks of watching every portion and counting every calorie. All those bike rides you've been taking."

"What about them?" Alice asked, looking bewildered.

"Jane thinks that you ate the cookies that were left in the cookie jar," Louise explained.

"Oh, really?" Incredibly, Alice grinned.

Louise decided to go and visit Cynthia the next time someone went on a diet. "Alice, please, don't provoke your sister. She is ready to burst into tears as it is."

"I would never do such a thing, Louise. Come in here with me, both of you, and I'll show you what I did." Alice led Jane and Louise back into the kitchen, where she opened a cabinet, revealing the cookie jar stored in the back. "Here it is," she said to Jane.

"Oh, no," Jane moaned. "She's showing me where she hid the evidence. Make her stop, Louise."

Alice made a decidedly unladylike sound, took down the jar and opened it. "Look inside. Count them, if you like. All five are still in there, and not a single chip is missing."

Jane's expression turned comical. "But—but—"

"I put the cookie jar in the cabinet last night so I wouldn't see it every time I walked into the kitchen." Alice cradled the jar in her arms. "As I said, the temptation was killing me."

"Well done, Alice." Louise folded her arms and looked at Jane.

"Thank you, Louise." Alice handed the jar to Jane. "Now, say, 'I'm sorry that I doubted you, Alice.'"

Jane looked truly contrite. "I'm sorry that I doubted you, Alice," she repeated.

Alice patted her arm. "'I will trust you to keep the promises you make, Alice.'"

"I will trust you to keep the promises you make, Alice," Jane said, rolling her eyes at Louise.

Louise saw Alice's eyes twinkle just before she said, "'You may have all the cookies in the cookie jar, Alice.'"

"You may have—wait a minute!"

Alice laughed. "It was worth a try."

Fifteen members of the Seniors Social Circle arrived to take part in Ethel and Florence's tea in the garden. The group, which met monthly to share fellowship and discuss Christian issues, seemed just as puzzled as Louise by the change in their usual meeting schedule.

"Good thing I check the answering machine every day," octogenarian Edna Grassnickle said as she took a seat next to Ginny Clovis, one of her friends. "Otherwise I'd have missed this." The elderly woman spoke a little louder than was necessary.

"Edna's got a new hearing aid," Ginny said to Louise, as explanation. "She is having it adjusted, but the doctor hasn't quite hit the right setting for it yet."

"I heard you just fine, Ginny." Edna inspected the table, and the three-tier cake plate loaded with a variety of Jane's baked goods. "Very prettily done. Nice to see that young sister of yours didn't waste all her time on making silly things out of suet at that fancy cooking school."

"Yes, thank you, Edna." Louise was careful to keep a straight face.

"Hello, ladies." Mayor Lloyd Tynan stopped by their table. Instead of one of his smart suits, he was wearing a sweatshirt, matching pants and sneakers. It was the sort of thing someone wore to an exercise class, Louise thought, not a church group meeting.

"Mayor Tynan." Edna gave him a measured look. "Don't you have something nicer to wear to a meeting than that getup? You look ready to take out the garbage."

"Edna," Ginny admonished.

"I do have better clothes, Edna." Lloyd knew better than to be offended by the older woman's outspokenness. "I'm helping out Ethel with some sort of demonstration, and she asked me to wear this." He turned to Louise. "Have you seen your aunt? She's not over at the carriage house."

"Not yet, Lloyd." Louise scanned the garden and saw a familiar red head coming around from the side of the house. "I think this is Aunt Ethel now."

Ethel and Florence were dressed in the same informal exercise wear as Lloyd, and as they greeted their friends they began passing out pamphlets. Once everyone had one, the two women went to the front of the tables and Ethel read a verse from the Bible to open the meeting.

"What's going on?" Alice whispered to Louise when the prayer was over. "Why are they dressed like that?"

"I don't know," Louise said. "I'm almost afraid to ask."

"This special meeting of the Seniors Social Circle will now come to order," Florence called out. "Did everyone get a pamphlet?"

"I don't eat omelets at two in the afternoon, Florence Simpson," Edna said in a querulous tone. "I don't care what that girl learned in San Francisco, that's breakfast food." She frowned as Ginny leaned over to murmur something to her. "A *what*? Oh, never mind." She flapped one hand. "Go ahead, have your eggs. I'm going to try some of these pretty little cakes."

Ethel gestured for Lloyd to come and stand beside her. "The reason we called you all together today was to talk about the rights and safety of senior folks in the community.

For years we've depended on law enforcement and our children and grandchildren to protect us, but that hasn't always worked. Now there are other options available to us."

Jane came out of the kitchen and walked over to join Alice and Louise. "Everyone having a good time?" She saw Ethel, Florence and Lloyd and frowned. "Why are they dressed like that? Lloyd looks like he's ready to move furniture."

Louise just shook her head, suspecting now that her aunt intended to share some of her new expertise with the other seniors.

"Self-defense," Ethel said, confirming Louise's fears, "is not just for young people anymore. Florence and I joined a class over in Riverton, and we're going once a week now. Our instructor has taught us that we don't have to feel afraid for our safety anymore. The techniques take practice but, Lord knows, we can all use the exercise, and after a time it can even be fun."

"Gun? What's this about a gun?" Edna asked Ginny, loud enough for everyone to hear. "If Ethel Buckley has a gun, then I want one too. Not the killing kind, but I'll take a good BB rifle. I was a crack shot when I was a girl, you know."

Ginny patted Edna's hand. "Dear, Ethel said that self-defense can be *fun*."

Jane choked back a laugh, and Alice produced a cough to cover hers. Louise simply smiled on the outside and cringed on the inside.

"The pamphlet we've handed out is for the class in Riverton, but if there are enough people interested, our instructor, Officer Dana Starkey of the Riverton Police Department, may hold a class right here in Acorn Hill," Florence said. She sounded excited by the prospect.

"Today we're going to demonstrate some of the techniques we've learned," Ethel said. "The first one is what is called a 'one-two-three grip breaker,' which helps you escape someone who has taken hold of you." She turned to Lloyd. "Lloyd, grab my wrist."

The mayor, who was smiling and seemed unconcerned, reached out and took hold of Ethel's wrist. "Like this?"

"Yes, that's very nice, Lloyd. Watch closely now, this will be fast." Ethel bent her knees as well as the wrist Lloyd was holding. "One." She quickly pulled her arm up in a motion that appeared as if she meant to throw Lloyd's arm around her neck. "Two and three."

The move broke Lloyd's hold on Ethel's wrist quite effectively, but also knocked the mayor off balance, and he stumbled to right himself. In doing so, he bumped into one of the front tables, upon which Jane had set out the punch bowl and extra cups.

"I'd better go put a stop to this," Jane said, and walked toward their aunt.

Florence stepped over to Lloyd's other side. "Another technique is to use whatever happens to be in your hand or around you." She showed the group the bunch of keys she held in her hand. One of the keys was positioned between her thumb and middle finger. "If you've been out at night and you're walking to your house, or to your car, you should always carry your keys like so. Then you can use them to disable an attacker." She took hold of Lloyd's shoulder and moved the keys quickly in front of his face. "Like so."

Still recovering from the first technique, Lloyd instinctively jerked backward away from the keys and threw his arm out. "Florence! What are you—"

Three things happened at that moment. Ethel ducked under Lloyd's flung-out arm and bumped into the punch bowl table. Jane came rushing up, startling Florence, who crashed into the table from the other side. A wave of punch went through the air and landed on Jane and Lloyd.

Ginny let out a cry of horror. "Oh no!"

Louise and Alice stared, as did everyone else, as trickles of the punch that had soaked Jane and Lloyd from head to toe dripped onto the garden path where they stood.

Edna turned to Ginny. "Forget about that BB rifle," she said to her friend, almost shouting now. "I want to go to one of those classes with Ethel Buckley."

"I talked to Aunt Ethel last night, and she promised me, no more demonstrations," Louise said to Alice as they drove into town. "She also called to apologize to Jane."

"I hope she called the mayor too," Alice said. "Poor Lloyd. She and Florence should have warned him or practiced with him ahead of time or something. He had to pour that punch out of his sneakers before he could get into his car and drive home."

Ethel and Florence's demonstration had definitely made an impact on the members of the Seniors Social Circle, who had not kept the comical situation to themselves. Next to the circus's upcoming performance, self-defense using party punch was the most talked-about topic in town, as Alice and Louise discovered when they stopped in the Coffee Shop for a late lunch.

"Hi, Louise, Alice." Hope Collins came over to their table. "May I take your order?"

Louise ordered a small salad and soup. Alice said, "I'll just have a salad and please put low-calorie dressing on the side."

"Will do," Hope said as she wrote on her order pad. She looked around and lowered her voice. "You should know that there's a wild rumor going around town about your aunt and the mayor."

"I expected as much." Louise gave her a weary look. "What is it?"

"My sources say your aunt dumped a bowl of punch over

Mayor Tynan's head during a church meeting," Hope said, trying not to grin. "He was reported to have been flirting with Florence Simpson."

"Some punch was accidentally spilled on Mayor Tynan and our sister Jane during a church meeting," Louise corrected. "He did not flirt with Florence or anyone else." Knowing Hope was one of the hubs of information in town, she added, "Anything you can do to stamp out inaccurate rumors would be greatly appreciated."

"Gotcha." With a cheery smile, Hope went to put in their order.

"I can't believe people think Aunt Ethel or Mayor Tynan would act that way," Alice said, sounding huffy. "Why do people insist on blowing things all out of proportion when they gossip?"

"This is a small town, Alice," Louise reminded her. "Gossip, as Sissy Matthews says, rules."

Louise and Alice enjoyed their lunch and were able to set straight a few other customers who came over to talk to them about the doings at the church meeting. They paid their check, and Louise left a generous tip for Hope, telling herself that it was for excellent service and in no way constituted a bribe. After completing several errands, they walked down to Sylvia's Buttons to pick up some lace that Alice needed for a craft project that she had planned for her ANGELs.

The diminutive bicycle built for two parked outside Sylvia's should have been a tip-off, but Louise didn't connect it to the Bratwicks until Billy and Bobbi came out of the fabric shop.

"Hi, Mrs. Smith," the brother and sister chorused.

"How are you, Billy, Bobbi?" Louise took a moment to introduce Alice. "Still working on your costumes?"

"We've compromised," Bobbi told her. "Instead of brats or fairies, we're going to be medieval jesters." She produced a fold of harlequin-checkered fabric from the shopping bag she carried.

"Anything is better than being brats," Billy assured Louise. He looked over at their bicycle and groaned. "Bobbi, we have a flat tire?"

"We didn't have one when we got here," Bobbi said, going to look at the deflated tire.

Pauline Sherman, who with her husband and daughters was walking out of the Good Apple Bakery, spied Alice and Louise and called to them. Her daughters walked across the street to another shop, and Pauline left her husband standing in front of the bakery and trotted over.

"Alice, I'm so glad I ran into you." Pauline, who had dark circles under her eyes, appeared more harried than the last time Louise had seen her. A few strands of hair had escaped her uneven topknot and hung on either side of her face. "Briana and Tiffany told me that they needed something for next week's meeting, but they couldn't remember what it was."

"The girls volunteered to bring some chenille stems for the craft project," Alice told her, "but that was for the last meeting, which they missed."

"Oh." Pauline's face fell. "I'm sorry. I don't know how this month is getting away from me. Next thing you know it will be Thanksgiving—it isn't this week, is it?" She released a nervous laugh and tried to tuck the unruly strands of hair behind her ears.

"The tube's torn," Billy said in a disgusted voice, drawing the women's attention. "We'll have to get a new one, Bobbi."

"Hello." Obviously charmed by the Bratwicks, Pauline gave them a warm smile.

"Pauline, this is Billy and Bobbi Bratwick. They're performers with the Majeska circus." To the Bratwicks, Louise said, "This is our friend, Pauline Sherman."

"You wouldn't happen to have a spare tire tube on you, would you, Mrs. Sherman?" Bobbi joked. "It would come in handy right about now."

Pauline looked at the bike and frowned. "I have a spare tire in my car, but I don't think it would fit," she responded in kind. "We don't have a bike repair shop here in town, either. I'm sorry."

"Looks like we're hoofing it back to the show, Sis," Billy told Bobbi.

Before Louise could offer the Bratwicks a ride, Pauline said, "We can run you back to Bellwood Farm, if you like. It's on our way home, and my car has a big trunk, so you won't have to leave your bike here."

Louise saw that Stanley had joined them in time to overhear his wife's offer.

"Pauline, what are you saying?" Stanley asked. "It's four-fifteen. Briana and Tiffany are going to be late for gymnastics, and we have that appointment—"

Pauline didn't look at her husband, and her smile became stiff and forced. "Yes, I know, dear, but these people need some help getting back to Bellwood Farm. I offered to give them a ride."

"That's very sweet and thoughtful, honey." Stanley looked over at Billy and Bobbi without much enthusiasm. "But you can't do that."

Pauline gave him a strange look. "Stanley, I just did."

"What I mean is that it's nice of you to offer, honey, but you have other commitments." Stanley looked impatient now. "Remember what we talked about last night, and how you promised me that you would make a real effort to keep your commitments to me and the girls?"

"I remember," Pauline said through very tight lips. "Darling, it will only take a few minutes to drive over to Bellwood Farm. These people are stranded."

"Sweetheart, the girls' gymnastics class is on the other side of town, and you promised to drop me at the club afterward," Stanley complained. "You're going to have to run by the house, too, to let the dog out. We wouldn't want any more accidents on the carpet, now, would we?"

"No." Pauline's gaze shifted as Briana and Tiffany walked up to stand beside their father. Both girls were happily munching on cookies. "I guess we wouldn't."

"Mom," Briana said, "don't forget to get some garlic bread for dinner tonight."

"Garlic bread." There was a fearsome glitter in Pauline's eyes now, and she was gnawing at her bottom lip. "Dinner."

"The bakery was fresh out of the bread we like, and you did promise me and the girls you'd make spaghetti and meatballs for dinner tonight," Stanley said. "You can get started on it when you go home to let the dog out." He looked at the Bratwicks. "Sorry we can't—"

"Oh, no you don't, Stanley Sherman." Pauline whirled around and confronted her husband. "That does it. I am done. Finished. *No more*."

"No more what?" Stanley seemed perplexed.

"No more running home to make spaghetti and meatballs. No more letting the dog out. No more buying garlic bread. No more taking you to your club so you can work on your abs. You don't *have* any abs."

"Mom!" Horrified, Tiffany almost dropped her cookie.

"Why are you yelling at Daddy?" Briana asked.

Pauline stared at her daughters. "And you two. No more getting up at four in the morning to make three dozen cupcakes—and decorate them—because you forgot to tell me until the night before that you needed them for school."

Alice stepped forward quickly. "Pauline, maybe we should—"

"Excuse me, Alice, but this is a family matter." Pauline faced her husband again. "No more, Stanley. Do you understand me? No more being your unappreciated servant. No more getting the groceries and the laundry and the errands done and then finding out you've thought up more for me to do. No more killing myself trying to accomplish everything you expect me to do every single day." The last sentence was almost shouted.

"Pauline!" Stanley was totally shocked. "What are you saying?"

"I am saying that I am fed up. I'm going to leave you. See? This is me leaving you." Pauline took the car keys out of Stanley's unresisting hand and turned to the Bratwicks, who were staring at her open-mouthed. "I'd still like to give you a ride to the Bellwood Farm. Are you ready to go?"

Bobbi didn't bat an eyelash. Billy, recognizing Pauline was on the edge, simply nodded.

"Good-bye, Stanley." To her daughters, Pauline said, "Briana, Tiffany, be good for Daddy."

"Honey." Stanley had the distressed look now. "I didn't know that you weren't feeling well. Come on and I'll take you home and you can have a nice rest. The girls and I don't have to have spaghetti and meatballs tonight. You can make it tomorrow night."

Alice and Louise cringed.

"Stanley? You can go jump in a lake." To Bobbi and Billy, Pauline said, "If you'll bring your bike over to my car here, we'll put it in the trunk."

Louise left Alice with the stunned members of the Sherman family and walked with Pauline and the Bratwicks to Pauline's car. "My dear, please. I know you're very angry with your husband, but don't walk away like this. Think about what you're doing."

"Louise, I just did. For the first time in fifteen years, God help me." Pauline opened the car trunk and helped Billy put the bicycle inside.

Louise had never seen a person pushed past the limits of

all patience, but obviously that was where Pauline was now. "Pauline, stop. You can't leave Stanley and the children here without a car."

"Can't I?" Pauline made a mirthless sound. "Stanley has money. He can call a taxi from Potterston to take him and the girls home."

Louise opened her mouth to speak, but Pauline shook her head. "Make sure he knows that I meant exactly what I said. I am leaving and I am *never* coming back."

A few moments later, Louise stood watching helplessly as Pauline Sherman drove away with the Bratwicks.

Chapter Fourteen

"Pauline did not come home last night," Ethel said to her niece over coffee late the next morning. "Briana and Tiffany haven't stopped crying since she abandoned them in the middle of town. Stanley is just beside himself trying to cope."

Louise felt a certain amount of sympathy for Stanley Sherman, but she couldn't excuse him from his part in causing the tragic situation. "Does anyone know where she has gone?"

"No. I've called everyone I can think of, but no one has seen her." Ethel gave her a worried look. "Louise, maybe we should call the police and report this. Maybe they can issue one of those PCBs for her."

"APBs, Aunt, and Pauline isn't missing. She hasn't committed a crime. She left her husband." Louise only wished she had been able to persuade the younger woman to calm down yesterday.

"Her daughters too." Ethel sniffed. "What sort of woman walks out on her family like that?"

Louise recalled what she had glimpsed in Pauline's eyes as she stalked away from Stanley and her daughters. "A very unhappy one." She sighed. "Sorry, Aunt, I must get ready for Pastor Thompson. He will be here for me any minute now."

Louise usually accompanied Rev. Thompson each week on Friday to Potterston Hospital to visit patients and provide spiritual support for them and their family members, but this week he had asked her if they could delay their visit one day, since he had a number of other appointments to keep on Friday. Louise had agreed, and so she and Rev. Thompson were making their hospital rounds on Saturday.

It had been difficult at first for Louise even to walk into a medical facility, as hospitals always reminded her of her husband Eliot's last weeks of life. With the pastor's help, however, she had come to look forward to the weekly visits. Nothing, she discovered, helped to heal the wounds of the past as much as helping others who were presently suffering.

Louise also enjoyed Rev. Thompson's company. Kenneth was a quiet, rather austere-looking man who had not impressed the Howards when he first came to Acorn Hill. Happily, it had not taken long for Louise and her sisters to discover that Rev. Thompson's gentleness and wisdom was equal to that of their beloved father, Daniel. It was now impossible to think of anyone but Kenneth taking over as head pastor of Grace Chapel.

"I believe we did some good today," Kenneth said as they started the drive from the hospital back to the inn. They had met with a young couple whose child had been born with a heart defect and had talked with them about the strain of facing surgery for their newborn. "Mr. and Mrs. Acheson are feeling much more optimistic. Thank you for thinking to ask the surgeon to come in and explain the procedure in less complicated terms."

Louise nodded. "Sometimes those huge medical words sound more frightening than they are."

The pastor glanced at her. "I hope I didn't take you away from more pressing matters. You seemed a little preoccupied with your thoughts on the drive to the hospital."

"Actually, you have kept me from dwelling on some

unhappy people with difficult problems," Louise said. "The sort that are not so easily solved."

Rev. Thompson nodded. "Can you tell me about them?"

Louise briefly described how Pauline had left her family, and why the Majeskas could not take the retirement they badly needed. She mentioned her aunt and Florence Simpson, too, for she still felt troubled about their continuing with the self-defense classes.

"Perhaps I take my own happiness for granted," Louise admitted, "but it disturbs me to know so many who are unhappy with their lives."

"Satisfaction with life is hard-sought and rarely found," Rev. Thompson said. "We are bombarded with unrealistic standards from the media and have expectations that exceed those of any society in the past. I often think life would be far less muddled and confusing if we could turn the clock back fifty or sixty years and enjoy simpler times."

"Those simpler times, Pastor, could be complicated too." Louise knew that only too well, having lost her mother at a time that should have been idyllic for the Howard family.

"If I may borrow one of my grandfather's favorite expressions, you seem to sail on an even keel, Louise." He smiled, which relaxed and softened the stern lines of his features. "I've always admired your equilibrium."

She felt quite flattered, for she had fought long and hard to establish the balance in her life. "I can't take sole credit for it. I was fortunate to have a father who instilled in me and my sisters the necessity of purpose in life but also allowed us the freedom to discover for ourselves what our purpose would be. His love and, more importantly, his guidance gave us the confidence we would need as adults." Louise sighed. "I wish everyone had a father like ours. Or a minister like you."

"Thank you," Rev. Thompson said. "I stopped by Viola's bookstore the other day, and saw she's added a new shelf for how-to and self-help inspirational books. Many of them are quite good. So even for those who don't have such parental guidance or don't enjoy the fellowship of a church, there are sources of comfort and wisdom."

"Yet Pauline Sherman still left her husband, and the Majeskas cannot bring themselves to retire, and my aunt is dousing people with party punch." Louise shook her head.

"When Catherine passed away," Rev. Thompson said, referring to his late wife, who had inspired him to become a minister, "there were friends of mine who thought I should abandon my calling and do something less spiritually demanding. Their logic was reasonable. I had lost my beloved wife, why should I burden myself with the cares of others at such a time? For a time, Louise, I was truly tempted. There were days when it took all my resolve simply to get out of bed."

Louise tried and failed to imagine Kenneth as anything else besides a minister. "No one would have blamed you."

"That is the worst temptation of all to succumb to, you know—the one for which no one will ever blame you." Rev. Thompson made the turn onto Chapel Road. "Finding the balance between duty and self-fulfillment is something we face nearly every day and that will likely never change until we join our Father in Heaven. The Bible is where I always find the guidance I need, as well as the counter-weights. It contains the building blocks of purpose, as in 2 Peter: 'His divine power has given us everything we need for life and godliness through our knowledge of him who called us by his own glory and goodness. Through these he has given us his very great and precious promises, so that through them you may participate in the divine nature and escape the corruption in the world caused by evil desires'" (2 Peter 1:3-4).

Louise knew the verses, for they preceded three from the same chapter in the Bible that Daniel Howard had cherished and had quoted often to his daughters.

"'For this very reason, make every effort to add to your faith goodness,'" she continued, "'and to goodness, knowledge; and to knowledge, self-control; and to self-control, perseverance; and to perseverance, godliness; and to godliness, brotherly kindness; and to brotherly kindness, love'" (2 Peter 1:5–7).

Rev. Thompson chuckled as he drove up in front of the inn. "Amen to that, my friend."

There was an unfamiliar black Mercedes Benz convertible parked just in front of where the pastor had stopped. Louise discovered its owner when she walked inside and into the front hall.

"Yes, all right," Davis Utley was saying to Mac. "I wouldn't mind a driving vacation myself."

Louise nodded to both men and slipped into the kitchen to give them some privacy. The men's voices carried, however, and she still heard every word they said.

"So what's the problem?" Mac asked him.

"All good vacations have to come to an end, Mac," Davis said. "You seem to view this harebrained idea of yours as an alternative lifestyle."

Mac chuckled, then asked, "Why couldn't it be?"

"For a Hell's Angel, I suppose it is, but you? Come on, man, you're talking about riding the back roads of all fifty states. Who knows how long that will take?" Davis asked. "Speaking of time, I've got a meeting in thirty. I've got to go."

"While I've got all the time in the world, buddy," Mac told him. He didn't seem fazed by his friend's disapproval. "You should think about trying that mindset sometime. Might change your life."

"I've already had my crisis, thanks." Davis uttered a terse laugh. "Buying a convertible at my age was daring enough. My ex-wife was livid, but only because she hadn't thought to do it first." The humor faded from his voice. "Don't do this, Mac. There's still time to turn it around. If you don't, you're going to regret it."

"If I do, I'll call you and tell you that you were right. Let me walk you out to the car."

In the kitchen, Louise put on the kettle. A few minutes later Mac appeared at the door. "Would you care to join me?" she asked him.

"I'd love to. I've been a coffee drinker all my life, but this inn is making a tea addict out of me." He spied the round tin and read the label, or tried to. "Panda tea?"

"White tea." Louise gave him a brief description of the tea and its properties. "Is everything all right with you and Mr. Utley?"

"No, as you probably overheard. Davis has now gone from questioning my sanity to deciding I no longer possess any." Mac rubbed a hand over the back of his neck. "He is more stubborn than I thought. He's called me every day since he got into town, trying to persuade me to sell the Ducati and run back to the golf course before someone notices I'm not teeing off."

Louise set two mugs on the table. "But you're still planning to take your tour."

"I'm more determined than ever."

Over cups of white tea Mac told her about the new route he had planned for himself. "Since it's close to winter, I thought I'd head south. The only time I've ever been to Georgia was for half a dozen business meetings in Atlanta, but I never left the city. Sometimes I hardly left my hotel. Do you know that Stone Mountain is only fifteen, twenty miles due east of Atlanta? I thought about that every time I saw it as I flew into the city, and yet I never went there."

"It's a lovely place," Louise said. She and Eliot had taken Cynthia there when her daughter was younger. She recalled that Jane had taken a more recent trip to the natural wonder.

"My sister told me that they have a laser show at night there now."

"Lasers on Stone Mountain." Mac chuckled. "See what I've been missing?"

Louise couldn't treat the matter with levity, not when it involved such a radical change. "What if you do discover, as Mr. Utley predicted, that you regret making this decision?"

"I don't think that's possible, Louise." Mac took his wallet from his jacket pocket and removed a photograph from it. "This is from my retirement party. Davis and all my friends threw it for me. Best hotel restaurant in D.C."

Louise took the photo and studied it. There were some thirty men standing in a group around Mac. All were dressed in handsome suits. All looked prosperous. "They look like good people."

"They are, but they're not happy. Davis is divorced and has an ongoing problem with his weight. Bob, the one standing next to me, has gone into rehab three times for his alcoholism. Jonathan, the fellow there in the tan jacket, has had surgery for heart problems and bleeding ulcers."

Louise glanced at him. "Is investment banking that stressful?"

"You have no idea." Mac grimaced. "Half of them will die of heart attacks or strokes, probably while they're still wearing a suit and working overtime. The others will end up in some retirement community where their main focus in life will be improving their golf handicaps."

"I see your point." She handed the photo back to him. "But it doesn't have to be that way for everyone."

"I've been a good citizen, paid my taxes and done my part for society. I donated the proceeds from the sale of my house and furniture to a scholarship fund at my alma mater. I was never blessed with a wife or children, but I've made sure my immediate family is financially set. Why shouldn't I be allowed to do as I wish now? Why can't I look for the adventure that I've always wanted, before I'm too old to make the trip?"

Louise couldn't think of a single argument to make.

"Would you mind if I showed you my bike?" Mac asked.

"I've seen it—"

"No, I mean *really* show it to you. Tell you about it." He gestured toward the front of the inn. "Davis won't go near it, and I'd like someone from my age group to see what a beautiful machine it is."

"I'm flattered, but . . ." What was she afraid of? It was a motorcycle, something that gave Mac a great deal of pleasure and happiness. What would it hurt to walk up to it and have him tell her why? "I'd be delighted."

Louise went with Mac to the drive, where the motorcycle was parked.

"This is a Ducati Sports Touring ST3, imported from Italy, where the bikes are made," Mac told her as he rested a fond hand on one of the handlebars. "Three valve, one hundred and seven horse power L-twin engine, six-speed, tubular steel trellis frame with custom paint on the tank, fairing and fenders. Duke here is fully outfitted for cross-country touring, too, from tires to instrument panel."

Louise was bemused by Mac's recital. "Duke?"

"Most bikers name their ride, uh, give their bike a name. Mine is Duke, after John Wayne. That's who I feel like, every time I ride off on it. I have to restrain myself from yelling out 'Yee-ha.'" Mac lowered his voice. "Don't tell your aunt, but I've never actually watched that Marlon Brando movie. Plus I can't wear black leather. Most bikers do, since it gives some protection in a fall, but it makes me sweat."

Louise chuckled. "I see."

Mac told her a little about the history of the Ducati, widely considered the "Ferrari of motorcycles." "It all started during World War II in German-occupied Italy, when an

Italian lawyer built a little pull-rod engine to be attached to a standard bicycle.

"Farinelli knew that pedal bikes would likely be the only means of transportation most Italians could afford after the war. The little pull rod engine he built made a high-pitched, yapping sound, for which he christened the engine *Cucciolo*, which means 'little puppy.'"

Louise learned that the first Ducati motorcycles were made primarily for the racetrack, as motorcycle races were very popular during the post-war years.

"By adapting Formula 1 engine designs, Ducati began turning out bikes that were not only the fastest in the world, but the most innovative in design," Mac told her. "Today the company still adheres to the motto, 'Try it on the racetrack first.'"

"You aren't going to try to race, are you?" Louise asked, her eyes filled with concern.

"If I were thirty years younger, I might be foolish enough to try," Mac said, shaking his head, "but I'm content simply to ride off to find adventure." He glanced at her. "I know all this motorcycle talk is probably deadly boring, but I love this machine. I feel as if I've earned it and the right to do as I please. What do you think?"

Louise didn't agree with Mac's concept of adventure. Life, as she well knew from her marriage to Eliot, could be just as adventurous under quieter, more sedate circumstances. But she was in no position to judge him. "I would say you have the right to live your own life as you see fit, Mac."

"Thank you." He seemed gratified to hear this. "If a woman like you can say that, then I think there's hope for Davis."

"What sort of woman am I?" Louise asked, wondering if he meant to flatter or insult her.

"You're a traditionalist," Mac said. "Not the type to run out and buy a motorcycle or do anything on impulse. I'd say you're very careful with your decisions, and you look for a long time before you leap."

Louise couldn't deny any of it. In fact, she was proud of it, and Rev. Thompson had even praised her for it. "Does that seem like a failing to you?"

"Not in the slightest. I admire women like you, Louise. You have strong feelings for your family and have formed extensive ties to your community. You are the foundation on which this country was built. The things we want, however, are complete opposites." Something flickered over his features. "Maybe that's the problem. Davis sees me as a reflection of himself."

"Yet he isn't planning to tour America by motorcycle," Louise pointed out.

"Davis couldn't do something like that because he's grown to love the same trap that I was caught in. He doesn't see his life as dominated by the accepted standards. He thrives on it." Mac looked at his reflection in the front fender chrome. "For my pal Davis to understand where I'm at, he might need to—forgive me—walk on the 'Wilde' side."

"Perhaps." Louise thought of what she and Rev. Thompson had discussed earlier. "I don't think that we should abandon everything because our dreams are unfulfilled and growing old scares us. There are always troubles, and chasing your dreams may add to them. Age, unfortunately, is inescapable."

Mac cocked his head. "You speak like a lady who has been down that road a time or two."

"My love of music once consumed me. I had a real talent and seriously contemplated devoting my life to it." She thought of Eliot's gentle face. "Then I fell in love, and what I had always considered my dream suddenly seemed empty and pointless. I chose love over a dream. Or maybe, Mac, they are just two sides of the same coin."

"I wish I had the experience to agree or disagree." Regret tinged his expression. "I waited, and I looked, but love never came my way."

"I lost mine, at least, temporarily," Louise told him. "My husband went home to the Lord ahead of me, but I will never regret spending my life with him instead of chasing that dream of music. Not for a moment."

"Louise!"

Louise and Mac turned to see Ethel Buckley hurrying up the drive.

"Louise, thank heavens. I've just gotten word on Pauline Sherman, and she's fine. Well, all things considered. You're never going to believe where she is."

"Excuse me, Mac." Louise pushed aside her slight annoyance with her aunt's interruption and gave her attention to Ethel. "Where is Pauline?"

"She's at Bellwood Farm. Not with Rose and Samuel, but with those people." When Ethel saw that Louise didn't understand, she added, "Pauline has run away to join the circus."

Chapter Fifteen

On the following Thursday, when Pauline Sherman had been gone for almost a week, Louise and her sisters discussed the matter and agreed that someone should speak to Pauline about her decision to leave her family. Alice and Jane agreed that that someone should be Louise.

"I would go, but I'm sure that I'll just remind her of Briana and Tiffany," Alice said. "Most of the time we only see each other at ANGELs meetings or when we're working on some project for them."

"Under the circumstances," Louise countered, "I think Pauline *needs* to be reminded of her children." Of all the victims in this tragedy, the Shermans' daughters deserved to suffer least and were likely suffering most.

"It'll just make her feel more guilty, which will make her angrier," Jane said. An odd emotion darkened her eyes. "I'd run over there and talk to her, Louise, but I don't know her that well. I'm also not the most diplomatic person in the world."

"When was *I* elected to be the family diplomat?" Louise challenged.

"You can be," Jane said, ". . . when you try . . . very hard."

"Jane, that is not helpful," Alice said. "Louise, you took

Bible study classes with her. You know her fairly well, and you don't represent any unhappy associations for her."

Although Louise saw her sister's point, she was still not overjoyed at the prospect of serving as mediator. She felt sorry for the Shermans, but thought Rev. Thompson was a more appropriate candidate for the task and said so to her sisters.

"Not the pastor," Alice instantly disagreed. "Pauline has always been a little intimidated by Kenneth, and she would be mortified if he went out there. No, it's better if you go, Louise. Pauline respects you, and you won't frighten her. You might be able to reason with her better than anyone."

It would help if I knew what to say.

As Louise drove out to the circus show grounds at Bellwood Farm, she felt torn about Pauline Sherman. On the one hand, the conversation she had shared with Mac had given her a little insight into the mind of someone rebelling against life choices. On the other hand, Mac Wilde was not turning his back on anything but a lifestyle. Pauline had, technically, deserted a husband and two children. That, Louise felt, was far more serious.

The consequences, too, might be unpleasant for everyone involved. Given the intricacies of modern divorce law, which recognized the rights of fathers as well as mothers, anything might happen. It would not be entirely unexpected if Stanley divorced Pauline and sued for full custody of their daughters. Since Pauline had left him, he might be granted it.

I have no experience with this sort of thing, Louise thought. *None of my friends ever left her husband or would even think of leaving their children. Jane should have come instead of me.*

Jane, whose unsuccessful marriage had ended in divorce, was closer to Pauline's age. Jane also had more empathy for people who did things that were regarded as socially unacceptable. Yet Jane's divorce had been very painful for her, Louise knew. *That might explain that look she had in her eyes when she said she couldn't go. Maybe Jane doesn't want to relive one of her own worst experiences.*

When Louise parked at the circus show grounds, one of the roustabouts told her that she could find Pauline working in the costume tent, where she was helping the show's seamstress.

"Hello?" Louise stepped through the entry to the tent. Inside were racks upon racks of garments in a dazzling range of colors. Most of the costumes were heavily decorated with sequins, beads, feathers and other elaborate trims.

"Something I can help you with, ma'am?" a middle-aged woman said as she emerged from behind one of the racks carrying a stack of skin-colored leggings. She had a pincushion strapped to her wrist and a yellow measuring tape draped around her neck. Several loose, red and blue sequins sparkled in the short curls of her silver-black hair.

"Hello, I am Louise Smith. I was told that I could find Pauline Sherman here," Louise said.

"I'm Hester, the seamstress. Pauline is in the back, doing some mending for me." The seamstress nodded toward the far end of the tent. "Are you a friend, or a relative?"

Louise smiled. "A friend of the family."

"Right." Hester gave her a shrewd look. "Come to talk some sense into her?"

"I would like to talk to her, yes," Louise said carefully. She didn't want Pauline to overhear them discussing her as if she weren't there.

"Good luck, honey. I told her everything negative I could think of about circus life, and I couldn't get her to budge an inch. Tell her I'll be back in a half hour." The woman slipped out of the tent.

Grateful for the privacy the seamstress had given them, Louise walked back to where a small section of the tent had been partitioned off with costume racks and stacked plastic garment bags.

Here a sewing machine stood with a waterfall of shiny blue spandex thrown across its short table. Something else was soaking in a bucket of soapy water. Like confetti, sequins and beads in every color of the rainbow littered the hard-packed dirt and grass of the tent's floor.

Louise thought of the Shermans' home. It was a large modern house set back from a quiet country road among beautiful oak trees. Although she had never been a guest, Alice had described the décor as tasteful and lovely. *She would give up that home for this?*

On a folding chair sat Pauline Sherman, dressed in clothes that clearly had been borrowed, a faded T-shirt and overly large work denims. Her pretty brown hair was gathered into an untidy ponytail on the very top of her head, which made her look painfully young.

"Hello, Louise," Pauline said, looking up from her work. She was using a needle and stout thread to tack a loop of flashy gold braid back onto the shoulder pad of a vivid red silk jacket. "What a surprise to see you."

Louise had expected tears, perhaps even some anger, not an easy smile and a cheerful hello. "I thought I'd stop by and see how you're doing."

"I'm doing fine. Your Aunt Ethel told you I was working here now, didn't she?" Pauline used a pair of scissors to snip off a thread. "The way that woman collects information, she should work for the CIA."

"Yes." Louise knew Pauline was joking, but still felt slightly embarrassed. *What am I doing here?* "I met Hester out front. She said that she would be gone for half an hour."

"That should give you plenty of time to lecture me," Pauline said, nodding. "What will it be first? Pauline, how could you leave your husband, or Pauline, how could you abandon your children?"

Beneath the light, casual tone in her voice, Louise detected pain. "My dear, I am not here to lecture you."

"Good. I'm a little busy, you see. I've got a real job now." The younger woman set aside the jacket she was repairing and stood. "Besides sewing, I'm going to perform. Hester and I worked on my costume last night. Would you like to see it?"

Without waiting for Louise to answer, Pauline went to one of the garment racks and removed a pretty dress with a vivid pink bodice, green skirt and white accents. The entire dress was covered with sequins sewn in diagonal lines across the fabric, which gave the effect of slashings of silvery rain.

"I've never owned a dress with sequins all over it. I don't own this one—the performers all share—but isn't it just the loveliest thing you've ever seen?" Pauline turned the dress this way and that so Louise could see all sides of it. "So much prettier than those silly costumes I used to make for myself out of Mother's old cocktail dresses."

"It is stunning." *And*, Louise thought, *Pauline will look stunning wearing it.*

"Hester is fitting me with my leotard tonight," Pauline continued as she ran her hand over the spangled material lightly, almost lovingly. "They make most of their own costumes and undergarments. The leotard is made of very thin, flesh-colored fabric for my arms and legs. You'd think when you see a presenter from the audience that she has nothing under a little bitty dress like this, and her arms and legs are bare. Fact is, almost all of them wear leotards. Like ice skaters at the Olympics do."

"I didn't know that," Louise said. "At least you won't get cold if you're wearing something underneath." *Lord*, that *has to be the least intelligent thing I've said all year.* "What does a presenter do, exactly?"

"It's a bit like what showcase models do on television game shows. You dress up, walk out and elegantly present each act in the ring while the ringmaster announces it. Like this." Pauline demonstrated by producing a dazzling smile and slowly waving one arm to the side.

Louise frowned. That sounded more like a made-up job than a real one. Had Aldo offered it to Pauline because he needed a presenter or because she desperately wanted to join the show?

"Do I need to practice more?" Pauline asked, suddenly anxious.

"No, it looked quite . . . professional." Louise smiled. "Is there a big demand for circus act presenters?"

"Mr. Majeska seemed really happy to hire me to be his. Wasn't that nice of him to do that, since I showed up here out of the blue?" Pauline said. "I've never had a real job before this."

"You took care of your family, Pauline," Louise corrected. "You worked very hard at it too. No one would ever deny that."

"I mean a real job, with a paycheck. Stanley gave me an allowance, as if I were a child, but that was for the household expenses. I had to ask him for money if I wanted something for myself. Then I had to explain why I wanted it." A stubborn expression came over her face. "Now I'll just be making my own money, and I can buy anything I want with it."

Louise seized the opportunity to talk about her family. "Stanley, Briana and Tiffany must be so worried about you. Have you called to tell them where you are and that you're safe?"

"Why should I? They don't care about me. They only care about what I do for them." Pauline shoved the hanger with her new costume back onto the rack. "I suppose they sent you. Are they sorry now that their slave is gone?"

"Stanley did not send me, and I'm sure that he and the girls have never thought of you as their slave." Pauline's flippancy worried Louise. "You should consider how they're feeling right now. They must be just as upset as you are."

The younger woman didn't seem to hear. "You're not supposed to treat other people like that. Especially not people who love you more than anything in the world." Unshed tears made her voice sound thick and indistinct.

"My dear." Compassion flooded Louise's heart. "It doesn't have to be this way."

"I apologize, Louise. I don't mean to weep all over everyone." Pauline found a tissue in her pocket and blew her nose in it. "I'm still a little emotional about what took place."

"It's never too late to admit that you've made a mistake or to make amends for what's happened." Louise came and put her arm around the younger woman's hunched shoulders. "The first step is to turn your troubles over to the Lord through prayer. He's always there for you. Let Him shoulder some of your burden."

"I never had time to pray," Pauline said sadly. "Isn't that funny? I wanted to, but there wasn't room on the schedule for it. Even when I was in church, when everyone else was praying? In my head, I was going over my list of things to do for the day. I wonder if God listened to that. I bet He got tired of hearing it. He knows I did."

"Pauline, if you would trust in the love of your family to work things out, and see this through—"

"Is that what you think? That it was a mistake for me to leave Stanley and the girls?" Pauline drew back and uttered a semi-hysterical laugh. "Oh, no. My biggest mistake, Louise, was not doing it *sooner*." She flung out her arms. "I am free here. Free as a bird."

Louise was trying to think of what to say to this when Billy and Bobbi Bratwick rushed in.

"Pauline, we need the first aid kit," Bobbi said, pointing to a large white medical chest set under the sewing machine table. "Dilly took a fall in the big top, and he's been hurt."

"Mr. ... Piccadilly," Dr. Andrew Meecham said, reading from the ER chart in his hand, "does not have a fractured skull. He does have a mild concussion, some abrasions and two fractures in his left wrist."

Louise, who was waiting in the ER lobby with the Majeskas, felt an instant sense of relief.

An hour earlier she had rushed with the Bratwicks inside the big top tent and seen Dilly sitting next to the center pole holding his arm. While the show's medic fashioned a sling for Dilly's arm, Bobbi told Louise how the young musician had fallen while climbing the pole to secure some rigging for the trapeze act.

"I'm fine," Dilly insisted, until Louise came over and saw the condition of his wrist, which was swelling up and turning purple at an alarming rate. "I just banged my head on something as I came down." He felt the bleeding bump on his forehead. "Give me a minute."

The Majeskas insisted Dilly go to the emergency room at once, and Louise had offered to drive him and the circus owners to Potterston Hospital.

Now, here in the ER, Aldo and Ilsa were teary-eyed with joy and relief.

"Thank you, Doctor," Aldo said. "Dilly is like our son."

"May we see him?" Ilsa asked anxiously.

"Sure. Nurse?" Dr. Meecham had one of the assessment desk nurses escort the Majeskas back to the treatment room where Dilly had been taken. Louise noticed the frown creasing the doctor's brow.

"I'm Alice Howard's sister, by the way," Louise told him. "Thank you for the apples you sent to us. They were delicious. My sister has been cooking up a storm with them."

He produced a tired smile. "Anytime you want more, let me know. My family keeps sending me crates of them."

"Dr. Meecham," Louise glanced toward the treatment room, "is there something else wrong with Dilly?"

"There are some other issues, but I can't go into details."

He gave her a sympathetic look. "You'll have to discuss it with him."

Louise thanked Dr. Meecham, promised to say hello to Alice for him and went back to the treatment room, where Aldo and Ilsa were trying to convince Dilly to get back on the treatment table.

"There's nothing they can do," Dilly was saying to Ilsa. His wrist was heavily bandaged, and there was a large, ugly-looking bruise surrounding the scraped but fading bump on his forehead. He was so pale that every one of his freckles stood out and his hair seemed to blaze. "I'll have them slap a cast on it and in six weeks I'll be good as new."

Aldo looked quite upset. "You must have this surgery."

"Our medical insurance coverage is limited, Aldo," Dilly said. "I can't cover the deductible, and they won't do the surgery without it."

Louise thought of Dilly's hands dancing across the calliope's keyboard. "How much is the deductible, Dilly?"

The young man grimaced. "Two thousand dollars."

"We will find the money," Ilsa assured him. "You will stay and get well."

Dilly sighed. "Ilsa, that kind of money is very hard to find."

"He is right, my dear," Aldo said slowly.

"It doesn't matter," Dilly insisted. "Forget about it, Aldo. I'll wait and save up, and maybe next year I can have it done."

"I'm no doctor, but I would guess this is the type of surgery that can't wait." Louise glanced at Ilsa. "Could you secure a loan for him?"

"Banks do not lend money to traveling people," Ilsa said. When Aldo gave her a surprised look, she added, "Awhile ago I tried to arrange a loan for Dilly to buy the circus and let Aldo and me retire. No one would lend us a dollar."

"Ilsa, you never said anything like this to me," Aldo protested. "I thought retiring was an idea you hate."

"I hate leaving our show," Ilsa corrected. "Retirement I would love, but we can never have it and keep the show running."

"It's no use arguing about this." Dilly reached for his shirt.

"Excuse us." Aldo led his wife out of the treatment room and into the hall.

"Dilly, would you be able to raise the money you need for this surgery by having extra performances?" Louise asked. "Or taking up a collection among the performers, perhaps?"

"No one in the show has much extra money," Dilly explained. "They need what they have to pay for their personal stuff. What we make from our performances has to be used for the animals, vehicles and equipment. Aldo and Ilsa have never really made much of a profit, and what they have made, they have given to performers who had one emergency or another." He looked over as the Majeskas came back into the treatment room. "If you'll help me with my shirt, we can go home, Ilsa."

"No, Dilly. You stay and have this surgery." Ilsa looked terribly sad. "You will not be able to perform. Aldo and I have not said before, but there are two others who have decided to leave the show."

"This late in the season, there are no replacements to find," Aldo explained to Louise. "After we have the performance for the people of Acorn Hill, it will be time."

"Time to do what?" Dilly said, although from his stricken expression he already knew the answer.

"We are closing the show and putting it up for sale," Ilsa said, very gently.

"How awful," Jane said when Louise told her about the Majeskas' decision the next day. "Isn't there something we can do to help?"

"I offered to contribute, but this is about more than

Dilly's surgery," Louise said. "Aldo and Ilsa simply cannot keep up with the demands of circus life. I think that's why Dilly didn't make much of a fuss. He knows how tired they are. It's a pity it has to end this way."

"What has to end?" Mac asked as he came downstairs from his room. At the same time, the inn's phone rang. Louise answered it while Jane related the details of the circus's closing to Mac.

It was Ethel on the phone. "Louise, Florence and I are meeting in town to do some shopping for her niece's birthday. Would you like to have lunch with us at the Coffee Shop?"

Knowing the circus was closing down had left Louise feeling restless. She also felt guilty over the way she had been avoiding Ethel and Florence lately. "That would be nice, Aunt. What time?"

"We'll meet you at the Coffee Shop at noon," Ethel said.

Mac, Jane and Louise discussed the closing of the circus before Louise went upstairs to get ready for lunch. Two trips to the hospital in one week had her feeling slightly frazzled, so she took her time and dressed carefully. Wearing her favorite light gray skirt and powder blue blouse lifted her spirits a notch, as did putting on her pearl earrings.

Sometimes it helps to dress up a little, Louise thought as she examined her reflection in the mirror.

"You look very nice," Jane said when Louise came downstairs. "Pearls? For lunch at the Coffee Shop?"

Feeling a little self-conscious, Louise touched one ear. "Do I look ridiculous?"

"You do not. A breath of fresh air would envy you." Jane made a shooing gesture. "Go. Have a good time. Do a little window shopping while you're in town. Oh, wait." She pulled a slip from her pocket. "Would you pick this up for me from Wild Things? It's potted plant nutrient for the ferns."

"Of course." Louise put the slip in her purse. "Jane, do

you think it's fair that the Majeskas have to sell off the circus to help Dilly?"

"I think that's their decision," Jane said, "and you need to stop worrying about it."

Louise couldn't do that. She thought about her new friends' unhappy situation all the way into town. Even seeing all the lovely late-summer plants and flowers that Craig Tracy had grouped in the window of Wild Things failed to raise her spirits.

"Jane must mix one teaspoon of the powder nutrient in one cup of water," Craig Tracy told Louise after he rang up the order. "As long as the warm weather holds, she can use it to water her ferns three times a week."

"I'll tell her, Craig." Louise took the sack.

"Good. Now, Louise, what's bothering you?" He swung his hand toward the front of the store. "You didn't smile once at the display, and I spent hours arranging it."

His comment startled a laugh out of her. "Didn't I? It is lovely, as always." She smiled and patted his hand.

"That's more like it," Craig said. "Smile like that every time you walk by my front window, and I'll be a much happier man."

"I'll do my best to remember that," she promised.

Louise walked over to the Coffee Shop and waited outside until ten minutes past noon, but Ethel and Florence did not arrive. Florence's car was parked in a space in front of the antique shop. The store was one of the more interesting places in town to shop. They had probably arrived early and decided to go inside to browse. Neither Ethel nor Florence came out of the shop, however. No one did.

Another five minutes passed, and Louise wondered if the lunch date had been forgotten. *Or maybe they're demonstrating some new self-defense technique for Rachel Holzmann.*

Imagining the damage Ethel and Florence could do in a shop filled with expensive antiques decided the matter for

Louise. She put the bag from Wild Things in the trunk of her car and walked down to the antique shop.

That's odd. Usually the shop's owners, Rachel and Joseph Holzmann, kept their shade up to tempt window shoppers, but this afternoon the shade was pulled down. *Maybe Rachel closed the store for lunch.*

Then Louise saw the "open" sign hanging on the glass panel of the door, so she reached out to try the knob. It was unlocked, and she stepped inside.

Chapter Sixteen

The interior of the antique shop was oddly dark, but Louise could see Ethel and Florence standing together by a table loaded with button-filled mason jars. They were staring toward a man who had his back to them and was bent over one of Rachel's glass-topped jewelry cases.

"You're not going to get away with this," Ethel called out. She sounded terrified.

"One more word out of either of you," the man growled, "and I'll lock you two up with the shopkeeper. Just shut up and stay out of my way."

Louise wasn't sure what was happening . . . until the man took a heavy bronze lamp base from a nearby shelf and smashed the top of the jewelry case.

The sound of glass shattering made Louise flinch, and the doorknob slipped from her fingers, causing the door to slam shut.

"What the heck?" The man turned to see Louise and swiftly marched over to lock the shop door. "Go stand over there with them and don't make a peep."

He was still holding the lamp base like a club, so Louise did exactly as he said. After giving her a threatening look, the man went back to the smashed display case.

"Pearls, diamonds," the man said as he began snatching pieces of antique jewelry out of the case. "Looking good." He held up the first few he removed, inspecting them.

Louise saw that there were four watches on his left wrist. He nodded to himself and began grabbing handfuls of brooches, earrings and necklaces to stuff in his pockets.

A curious paralysis came over Louise. *Does he have another weapon?* The thief certainly had not hesitated to use the lamp base to smash the glass. *What will I do? I can't even move. Lord in Heaven, help me.*

From her memory came the voice of Daniel Howard as he read the passage from the Bible that he quoted whenever one of his daughters was anxious about something. *Be strong and courageous. Do not be terrified; do not be discouraged, for the Lord your God will be with you wherever you go* (Joshua 1:9).

Louise's gaze moved to Ethel and Florence, who stared at the thief as if mesmerized. *I have to get them out of here. And where is Rachel? He said he locked her up.* If she concentrated on the other women, she wouldn't feel so frightened. She would be able to do something.

But how could she do anything without attracting the thief's attention?

"Help," a faint female voice called from the back of the shop. "I'm locked in the storeroom." The sound of a fist beating on the inside of a door made soft, muffled thuds. "Please, come and unlock the door. Is anyone out there? Help!"

That was Rachel Holzmann's voice. Louise recognized it immediately. There was no sound from Joseph, but often only one of the Holzmanns worked in the store during the week. It appeared that Ethel, Florence and Louise were the only other occupants of the shop.

Florence eased her arm from Ethel and took a step forward. "Young man, you put those things back right this minute, and leave here."

The thief ignored her as he rifled through the last of the

jewelry and then straightened up. Louise had the presence of mind to go to her aunt, who was staring at the man with unblinking eyes and holding her purse like a shield against her chest.

"Aunt," Louise whispered. When Ethel gasped, she placed a finger against her aunt's mouth to indicate silence, and pointed to the door. "We have to get out."

Ethel only shook her head and shrank away when Louise tried to guide her toward the door. She was too frightened to move or to try to leave.

Louise understood that only too well. *Don't scare her. Don't push. Be calm. Think.*

"Did you hear me?" Florence said, her voice a little louder now. "Those things don't belong to you. Stop that this instant."

Louise couldn't call out to Florence. The man had told them to keep quiet, and God only knew what he would do if they didn't obey his order. And she couldn't run out to find help and leave the two women alone with the thief, not when her departure might provoke him into doing something even more dangerous. She spotted the extra phone extension Rachel had on one of the back walls of the shop.

I'll call for help. As silently as she could, she moved toward it.

"Young man." Florence took another step forward and her voice became strident. "You have no right to steal from these people and vandalize their store. If you stop and put everything back we won't call the police."

Louise smothered a groan. *Lord, Florence, don't try to bargain with a criminal.*

"Didn't I tell you to keep quiet?" The thief pounded a fist against Rachel's old-fashioned register, making the cash drawer slide open.

"I happen to know a police officer from Riverton," Florence said, her voice shaking a little. She had the same look on her face as she had had when she defended Mac at the General Store, Louise thought, wondering where on earth Florence was finding the nerve to speak so. "Officer Dana Starkey. She will arrest you."

"Yeah, sure, if I was in Riverton." Once the thief had removed all the bills from the drawer, he turned around to face Florence and Ethel. "You old biddies get in the back now," he snarled as he thumbed through the bills as if to count them. "I'll lock you up with her, and nobody will get hurt."

Louise flinched as she suddenly recognized the thief. It was the drifter who had teased Hannah's baby and tried to hurt Dilly.

Florence stayed exactly where she was, Louise saw, which blocked the thief's only exit from the store. She grabbed the phone and quickly dialed 911.

"Hello," she said as loudly as she dared, Florence's words to the thief covering the sound of her own. The operator asked her to state her emergency. "There is a robbery in progress at the Acorn Hill Antique Shop. Please hurry, the man is still in the store."

"Hey," the thief shouted. "Where's that other one?"

"I'm not going in the back unless it's to let Rachel out," Florence said. "Why don't you stop this before you end up in jail?"

Louise left the phone off the hook and moved back toward her aunt. She didn't know what else to do but she would not leave Ethel standing alone to face the thief's wrath.

"Where were you?" the thief yelled as soon as he saw Louise.

"Just over there," she said, gesturing vaguely. "You have what you want. Take it and go."

Florence turned her head and gave Louise an incredulous look. "He can't take Rachel's jewelry and money. It doesn't belong to him." Hysteria was in her voice, making it squeaky.

"Get in the back so I can put you in with her," the thief ordered.

"My aunt is too frightened to move," Louise said. "Just go."

"Yeah, right. Come on, you old biddy, you first," the thief said as he walked up to Florence. When she didn't move, he grabbed her arm and shoved her to one side.

That proved to be the thief's undoing.

Whack!

The sound came from Florence hitting the man in the head with her purse. "How dare you!" she shouted and hit him a second time. "Don't you dare put your hands on me like that again." *Whack!* "I'll make you regret the day you were born." *Whack! Whack!* "And *who* are you calling an *old biddy*?" *Whack! Whack! Whack!*

"Lady!" The thief put up his hands to deflect the impact of Florence's heavy designer purse. "Cut it out!" He swiped one of his hands at her, only to jerk it back and howl after her purse landed on his wrist.

Ethel made an angry sound and before Louise could stop her, rushed up to join Florence.

"You horrible man!" Ethel shrieked as she slammed her purse into the thief's shoulder. "Don't you touch my friend!"

Whack! Whack! Whack! Whack!

The thief was soon cringing under the flurry of purses slamming into his head, face and shoulders. He roared out a protest and then dodged as if to run, but his foot caught on one of Rachel's Persian rugs and he fell into the side of a display case. A large antique globe fell, hitting him squarely on top of the head, and he slumped down to the floor, dazed.

Louise went to the door of the shop, unlocked it, wrenched it open and shouted for help. Within seconds a large man ran across the street to her.

It was Jack O'Hara, the Animal Control Officer from Potterston. "What is it, Mrs. Smith?"

"A thief, inside." She held the door open wider and was relieved that it was Jack who answered her cry for help. The Animal Control Officer, Louise knew, had once been in the U.S. Marine Corps and was very fit and strong. "I've already called 911."

Jack O'Hara hurried inside, assessed the situation and went to Ethel and Florence. "Whoa, ladies, looks like you have everything under control."

Jack's voice seemed to stun the two women, who lowered their purses and stared at one another with wide eyes.

"Aunt?" Louise rushed over to her to see if Ethel was hurt, and then checked Florence. Neither woman was speaking. "Aunt Ethel," she said, a little more sharply.

"I'm fine, Louise." Ethel sounded like a ghost of herself.

Florence nodded slowly. "So am I."

"I forgot every single thing I learned in self-defense class." Ethel swallowed hard. "Just like that." She stared down at her purse, some of the contents of which were protruding from three different tears in the vinyl sides. "I couldn't move until that man shoved you, and then I couldn't even think about what I was doing." She regarded Florence. "Do you think Officer Starkey will be angry with us?"

"I don't know." Florence regarded her own purse, which was battered and hanging by one strap from her hand. "I just had this strap repaired, and it broke again. Fancy that."

In the meantime, Jack had hauled the thief to his feet. After tying his wrists behind his back with a Victorian drape cord, Jack turned to Louise. "Let the 911 operator know that I'm here and that I've secured the perpetrator."

Louise went to the phone and discovered that the 911 operator was still on the line. After explaining the change in the situation and learning that police were only moments away, she hung up and went to the back storeroom to let out Rachel Holzmann.

"Louise, thank God." Rachel sounded hoarse, probably

from calling out. "A man came in and said he had a delivery. When I walked back to open the delivery door, he grabbed me and shoved me in here."

Louise put an arm around Rachel and helped her to the front of the store, where two police officers were handcuffing the thief. There was some confusion at first as the jewelry and money were removed from the thief's pockets, and Rachel, Florence and Ethel all tried to speak at once.

Jack came to stand beside Louise. "Am I wrong, or did these two little old ladies just foil a robbery by using their purses?"

"Yes," Louise said, feeling just as amazed. "But if I were you I wouldn't call them 'little old ladies.'"

"He locked poor Rachel in her storeroom," Florence was saying to one of the officers. "He threatened me and Ethel, and then he grabbed me and pushed me."

Ethel lifted her purse and shook it. "I guess he'll think twice about doing that again."

The sight of the purse made the thief cringe. "They're crazy, both of them. I didn't do nothing to them, and they attacked me. Get them away from me," the thief begged the police officers.

After the thief was led from the shop, Rachel glanced at the smashed display case and the open, empty drawer of her register, and then turned to face the women. "Ethel, Florence, I'm so sorry this happened. I don't know what to say except, well, thank you."

Ethel was the first to start smiling. "Did you see his face when you smacked him in the head with your purse, Florence?"

Florence nodded and gave a girlish giggle. "I thought his eyes were going to pop out of his head."

"I felt like my feet were stuck in concrete, until he tried to grab you." Ethel chuckled. "Then all I remember was seeing red and rushing up to him."

Florence nodded. "You whacked him pretty good."

"You were more accurate," Ethel said. "Just like you are in class. Oh, we have to go back to class at least one more time now, Florence, to show off our technique."

"Our purse technique," Florence repeated, and began laughing.

"Class?" Still pale and shaken, Rachel looked from Ethel to Florence, trying to understand what was being said. "Technique?"

Louise put an arm around the shop owner's shoulders. "Don't ask."

No one in town had to ask about the foiled robbery. After Louise, Ethel and Florence had given their statements to police, the women decided to go over to the Coffee Shop to have a very late lunch.

Lunch became an opportunity for Ethel and Florence, the new heroes of the day, to hold court.

"I should call Jane and Alice," Louise said. There had been no time back at the antique shop, after giving a statement to the police and helping Rachel to clean up the broken glass from the case the thief had smashed. "Someone might call the inn and say something, and they'll assume the worst."

June Carter, the owner of the Coffee Shop, brought over three cups of her strongest brew. "Lunch is on the house today, ladies."

"June, that's not necessary," Louise said. She was already uncomfortably aware of how much attention they were getting from the other patrons.

"On the contrary, Louise. In my book, it is." She gave them a broad smile and held her pencil over her order pad. "How about three of my lunch specials and some fresh-baked pie?"

Once June had taken their orders, Louise excused herself to use the pay phone. June intercepted her and escorted her back to her little office, where she was told to use the restaurant's phone.

Resigned to being treated like visiting royalty, Louise called the inn and quickly related the details of what had happened to Alice.

"Oh, Louise." Alice sounded ready to cry. "I'm so glad no one was hurt. When are you coming home?"

"I'm going to have lunch with Ethel and Florence, to give them time to settle down, and then we'll follow Florence home before we drive back to the inn," Louise said. "Give me an hour or so."

When Louise walked out of the office, she saw that nearly every patron in the diner had changed his seating. Customers were now gathered around the table where Ethel and Florence sat, their meals and drinks left behind on their tables.

"I thought we were done for," Ethel was telling her new audience. "If looks could kill, Florence and I would be knocking on the Pearly Gates right now."

"Did he have a gun, Ethel?" June asked as she stood holding a full coffee pot. She seemed just as fascinated as everyone else.

"No, the police didn't find a weapon on him, but Florence and I didn't know that. We, of course, assumed the worst and could only pray he wouldn't . . ." Ethel pointed her forefinger at her temple and brought her thumb down like the hammer of a gun being fired.

Louise wondered idly if she should ignore Ethel or give in to her impulse to run out of the coffee shop and head for home.

"We were completely helpless too," Florence put in, "at his mercy, if he had any, which I'm sure he didn't." She rubbed the spot on her arm where the thief had grabbed her.

Ignore her. The throbbing in her head made Louise go to the counter, where Hope was wiping up a water ring left by a glass.

The waitress gave her a sympathetic look. "Headache?"

"Is it that obvious?" Louise pressed her fingers to her temple.

"You look a little wrung out," Hope said, "and not everyone thinks a robbery is as good as starring in an action-adventure movie." She reached under the counter and produced a small tin of aspirin. "These should help. Two do the trick whenever my head starts pounding."

"I'll just have one," Louise said, as aspirin sometimes upset her stomach, which was already in the shape of a pretzel. "Thank you, Hope."

Louise took the pill with a glass of water that Hope brought her. She glanced back at her aunt, who was describing the thief in detail while drawing some sort of diagram on one of the paper napkins now. "I'm surprised how well she recalls all that. All I can remember was the distance between me and the phone, which was roughly equivalent to the length of South America."

Hope smiled. "Everyone reacts differently in a crisis. The last place I worked at was held up by a couple of armed robbers while I was working the dinner shift. They had on ski masks and carried these huge guns. We were so busy that I didn't see them until people at the tables started ducking and covering their heads."

"Dear Lord." Louise stared at the waitress. "Was anyone hurt?"

"No, we gave them every penny we had, even the coin tips we carried in our apron pockets." Hope tugged on hers as emphasis. "The great thing was, we had a silent alarm button on the floor, and the manager had the presence of mind not only to press it, but to stand on it so they didn't see it. When the robbers left the restaurant, the police were waiting outside." Hope grimaced. "I couldn't stop shaking for a full day after that. I pray I never have to go through that sort of thing again."

"May I second that?" Louise asked.

"Absolutely. Although, you know, it was a good experience in a way," Hope said. "It made me more aware of my surroundings and my safety. I'm much more cautious now when I walk out to my car or answer the door at home."

"This is the purse," Florence was saying as she held up her bedraggled handbag for all to see. "I just had the strap repaired, thank goodness, and that was the only thing that gave. You can see Ethel's purse didn't hold together as well."

Ethel solemnly displayed the tears in the side of her own purse.

"That's why you should always buy a good quality handbag, ladies," Florence said to the women listening. "You never know when you're going to need that kind of durability."

June stopped by the table to look at the purses. "My, my. With all the junk we girls carry around in them, I bet they left some hefty bruises on him too."

"He'll think twice before trying to push around another woman," Florence predicted.

"Are you going to buy another purse like this one," June wanted to know, "or are you going for something bigger and heavier?"

"I don't want another purse." The suggestion made Florence look indignant as she clutched her battered purse in her arms as if it were her single most prized possession. "This purse saved my life. I am never carrying anything else."

Ethel looked less convinced that she wanted to keep hers.

Louise turned to Hope. "On second thought, may I have that second aspirin, my dear?"

Chapter Seventeen

Recovering from the robbery attempt, which had turned Ethel and Florence into much-lauded crime-stopping heroines, was not so easy for Louise. Her tension headaches, which normally were only occasional, came every day of the week following the crime. Of course, it didn't help that she kept reliving the horrid event in her mind, unable to think of anything but how dangerous the situation had been and how recklessly her aunt and Florence had behaved.

Everyone else seemed to think that the purse defense was brave or hilarious. This reaction only made Louise more upset. Comical as Ethel and Florence's actions appeared, they also might have caused the situation to become much worse. To her, there was nothing humorous about being involved in a serious crime.

The worst effect for Louise was realizing that she had allowed herself to grow blissfully unaware of the outside world. She always had been cautious when she lived in Philadelphia, particularly after Eliot's death. No woman who lived alone in the city could afford not to be. Yet, since moving back home, she had allowed her guard to relax. That their small, peaceful community could be visited by crime was something that she had not believed. Or, perhaps, she had refused to believe it. Acorn Hill was her childhood home, and the happy memories of the years she had spent here had colored her vision of it.

That vision was distorted now. Louise wasn't even sure she could ever bring herself to go back inside the antique shop again.

Alice and Jane initially praised Ethel for her bravery, but when their aunt went home, they expressed some of the same concerns Louise had. That made Louise feel a little better. Alice also noticed how upset Louise was and quietly did what she could to provide loving sisterly support. Jane, who also seemed a little shaken by the reminder that Acorn Hill had no special immunity to crime and violence, threw herself into a flurry of baking, the results of which were all Louise's favorites.

Yet no matter how the sisters tried to compensate for what had happened, the robbery attempt seemed to hang over them like a dark cloud, silent, threatening and unmoving.

"I'm going to have to diet soon," Louise warned one morning as Jane passed to her a platter of tiny, beautifully decorated pastries.

"If you do, I'm moving back to California, where people hire professionals to help them diet, instead of making their sisters do it," Jane told her. She looked across the table at Alice. "You are not to touch those pastries. In fact, you should not even inhale the aroma."

Alice wrinkled her nose. "With one pound to go, do you think I would?" She picked up her spoon and applied it to the citrus half in front of her. "I like grapefruit. Grapefruit is my friend. Sugar is my enemy. I love my enemy."

"*Alice.*"

"Just kidding. Although if you leave those pastries out where I can see them, I will thump you." She gave Louise a sudden, apologetic look. "Sorry."

"It's all right." Louise looked at the pastries and felt her stomach clench. "I'm not very hungry this morning, Jane. I think I'll take my coffee and sit in the garden for a little while."

Louise went to sit on one of the benches that Jane had put along the garden path. The sun was shining as brightly as if it were mid-July, but Louise could only stare blindly at the flowers and wonder if she would ever feel safe again.

"Hey." Someone nudged her. "Move over."

She looked up at Jane, who was carrying a book in her hands. She moved over to let her sister sit down beside her, but wished Jane had stayed inside. Her sisters meant well, of course, but some things could not be mended with pastries and diet jokes. "I'm fine, dear."

"No, you're not. You've been having one headache after another since last week. You walk around like a lost ghost, and you hardly say a word to me or Alice. You didn't even try my pastries. I'm beginning to feel quite put out."

"I'm sorry." And she was. "I have a lot on my mind."

"No kidding. Well, I've had enough of this, Louise. I've tried baked goods, and they haven't made a dent in this depression of yours. You leave me no choice but to take drastic measures." Jane opened the book, which was a Bible. "Isaiah."

Louise suppressed a smile. "Isaiah is drastic?"

"It is when I have to quote from it at seven o'clock in the morning in the garden." Jane flipped through some pages, and then began to read. "'When you pass through the waters, I will be with you; and when you pass through the rivers, they will not sweep over you. When you walk through the fire, you will not be burned; the flames will not set you ablaze. For I am the Lord, your God, the Holy One of Israel, your Savior'" (Isaiah 43:2–3).

Louise sighed. "Amen."

Jane closed the Bible. "There's more. I can tell you how God gave Egypt for our ancestors' ransom and brought their children from the East. Isaiah has plenty of that kind of thing. I'm not afraid to use it if I have to."

"You shouldn't make jokes about the Scriptures," Louise warned.

"I'll make you a deal," Jane said. "I'll stop being irreverent and subjecting you to random bits of Biblical wisdom, and you will stop acting as if the end of the world is scheduled to arrive next Tuesday on the red-eye."

Had she been acting that way? Louise felt stricken. *It is not the end of the world. It is a different view of it.* And she hated what she had seen in those terrifying moments in the antique shop.

"Maybe I need to walk softly and carry a bigger purse." Louise rested a hand against her forehead.

Jane's expression mellowed and she put an arm around Louise. "Sweetheart, it happened. It was ugly and dangerous and very frightening, and I wish it had happened to anyone else, but it didn't. It's over now. It's done with. You have to let it go."

"I know that." She put her head on Jane's shoulder. "I'll try."

"You know what upsets me? You're the real hero and no one realizes it," Jane said in an ominous tone. "I've half a mind to call the *Nutshell*."

Shame welled up inside Louise. "Yes, I felt so very heroic, standing there like a statue."

"No, you didn't. I talked to Ethel after it happened. When she was done bragging about how she pummeled that thief with her purse—which, by the way, was about the *stupidest* thing anyone could have done in the midst of a real crime—she just happened to mention that you got to a phone and called 911." Jane rubbed her hand in a soothing circle over Louise's shoulder. "You risked your safety to call the police, Louise. In the middle of a robbery, no less. Your spine must be made out of pure steel."

"I couldn't think straight, and I certainly couldn't twitch a muscle," Louise admitted. "Then I remembered that verse from Joshua that Father always read to us when we were frightened by something. I heard him so clearly, Jane. It was almost as if he was standing there right beside me, encouraging me."

Jane kissed her cheek. "Maybe Father was." At Louise's blank look, she added, "If anyone is our guardian angel and watching out for us, it's Father." She lifted the Bible again. "Now, come inside and have some of those wonderful pastries I made for you, or I'll start reading again. You know how much I love Galatians. And Philippians."

Louise gave Jane a little smile, but she had already determined what she had to do. "Please, quote from them any time you like."

Ethel answered the door of the carriage house after Louise's first knock. "Hello, Louise. Do you need something? I'm on the phone."

"I'd like to speak to you for a few minutes."

Her aunt opened the door wider. "Well, come in, and I'll tell Florence I'll call her back later."

Louise followed her into the cozy little house and sat down to wait as Ethel finished her call.

"Louise is here. No, she didn't say. I suppose so. I have a few things I'd like to say to her. Yes. All right, you too. I'll call later. Bye."

Ethel came out of the kitchen and sat across from Louise. "Florence's friend Delia has her facts mixed up. She thinks I hit that thieving scoundrel first, when it was Florence. I think we might have to do an article for the paper to set the record straight." Ethel inspected her. "You don't look as if you've slept a wink since it happened."

"I haven't slept very well this past week." Louise had rehearsed what she wanted to say to her aunt, but those careful, reasoned words abandoned her. "I've been having nightmares. I keep seeing glass shattering and jewelry glittering."

"I've had a few bad nights too," Ethel said, shifting as if she felt restless. "But I don't mind. We got him."

"Is that how you see it? We *got* him?"

"Florence and I got him," her aunt said. "You ran for the phone."

Louise closed her eyes and took a deep breath before looking at her aunt again. "What you and Florence did could have had terrible consequences for all of us. That thief could have been armed with a knife, or a gun, and if he had been, your purse attack could have provoked him into using it."

Ethel gave her an indignant look. "But he wasn't armed!"

"You didn't know that, did you?"

Her aunt's jaw sagged, and then she stood up. "I have to call Florence back. Is that all you have to say to me?"

"No, that's not all." Louise rose to her feet. "I love you, Aunt."

Ethel sniffed. "Excuse me for saying so, Louise, but sometimes it's hard for me to tell. Like now, when you're criticizing me."

"I love you, and I am having nightmares because of you. You did a brave, foolish and terribly dangerous thing." Louise walked forward and put her hands on her aunt's shoulders. "This time, no one was hurt. The man was arrested and will most likely go to prison. This time, we were lucky."

Her aunt wouldn't meet her gaze. "This is a nice town. Maybe there won't be a next time."

"Maybe there won't, or maybe tomorrow you'll walk into the bank or the General Store, and someone will be committing a crime." Louise tried to steady her voice. "Maybe the next criminal that you hit with your purse will turn around and shoot you."

"He tried to hurt Florence." Ethel's eyes shimmered. "What was I supposed to do? Stand there and watch?"

"I don't know. I don't think I will ever know what was the right thing to do." Louise touched her aunt's cheek with a gentle hand. "All I know is that I never want that to happen again."

Tears spilled down Ethel's cheeks. "Neither do I."

Louise hugged her aunt and held her. "We love you and we want you here, with us, Ethel. Please remember that."

Ethel didn't want Louise to leave after that. She insisted on making some iced tea and sharing some of her prize-winning peach tarts. They sat and talked as they had not for a long time.

"Florence and I are not quitting the self-defense class," was one of the things that Ethel told Louise. "We might know how to use our purses well enough, but we'd like to find out more about making the right decisions. As in, when we should fight, and when we should be quiet. We'd like to keep independent as long as we can, and this might help."

"I didn't know you were concerned about that," Louise said, although she remembered wondering why her aunt had lately been making so many disparaging remarks about her age.

"We're not getting any younger." Ethel looked at the age spots on the back of her hands. "Growing older is never easy, Louise, especially not for active women like us. We want to live with dignity and take care of ourselves. I should be able to come and go as I please. Florence shouldn't feel scared to go out shopping for a new outfit on her own."

"Perhaps Florence should get over her obsession with her wardrobe," Louise suggested, "as I must get over my obsession with your peach tarts."

"Her wardrobe is her armor. The peach tarts are

irresistible." Ethel smiled wryly. "I know Florence drives you to distraction, but she likes buying all those fancy handbags and designer clothes because they make her feel safe. The same way I like living here and knowing all the news from town because it makes me feel a part of things. I imagine your playing your music is the same thing as my hearing a good story or Florence wearing a new outfit."

Louise frowned. "I guess I never thought of it that way."

"We all have to find our own way, Louise." Ethel reached over and covered her hand. "It's good to know that my niece cares enough to come and get me whenever I wander off in the wrong direction." She got up and took a book from a shelf and brought it to the table. "This is a book of old hymns that Viola gave me, and there's one in it by John E. Bode that I keep thinking about since the robbery. Do you mind if I read it?"

Louise shook her head.

Ethel opened to a bookmarked passage and began to read:

> O Jesus, I have promised
> To serve thee to the end;
> Be thou forever near me,
> My Master and my friend.
> I shall not fear the battle
> If thou art by our side,
> Nor wander from the pathway,
> If thou wilt be my guide.

Louise felt hope welling up inside her, as if from a hidden source released by the words. "That's beautiful, Aunt, and very wise."

Ethel nodded. "It may not be as impressive as an over-the-shoulder throw, but it does make me feel safer."

She offered Louise another peach tart. "Like you."

∽

Louise slept well that night after speaking from her heart to Ethel, and woke up feeling refreshed. After she finished her early morning chores, she volunteered to take the desk, and so she was the one to answer the phone when Rose Bellwood called.

"Hannah's baby is missing," Rose said without preamble. "The lock on the gate to her pen must have been damaged by that drifter when he shoved Dilly into it," Rose explained. "This morning they found the gate open and the baby gone."

"Where is Hannah?" Louise asked.

"She's still at the circus. Hannah is trained not to leave the pen without her mahout, and she was probably asleep when the baby wandered off last night."

"Has someone contacted Animal Control?"

"Yes, that was our first call. We've also alerted the police and Mayor Tynan. They're mobilizing as we speak. Hang on a minute, Louise." Rose's voice grew indistinct as she answered someone, and then she came back on the line. "We're putting together search parties to look for the baby. Would you or your sisters be available to join us?"

After quickly checking with Alice and Jane, Louise told Rose they all would help with the search, and would drive out to Bellwood Farm as soon as possible. The sisters got ready to leave, putting on the answering machine and calling Ethel to let her know about their plans.

Louise was putting on her sweater when she saw Mac coming downstairs.

"Morning, ladies," Mac said. He saw they were dressed to leave and looked a little confused. "I know I'm a little late coming down. Should I plan on making my own breakfast today?"

Alice and Louise came to a complete halt, while Jane groaned, "We forgot about our guest."

Louise swiftly filled in Mac about the disappearance of

Hannah's baby. "If you wouldn't mind helping yourself in the kitchen," she said after she had explained things, "we'd appreciate it."

"*Eat* when I can go and look for a missing baby elephant?" Mac shook his head. "Breakfast can wait. I'm going with you ladies." He jingled the keys in his pocket. "Why don't you ride with me on my bike, Louise? We could cover more ground faster."

"I think I had better drive my car," Louise said, keeping a straight face. "My sisters won't fit in your saddlebags."

Mac followed them on his motorcycle out to Bellwood Farm, where a large group of townspeople had already gathered. Rose was using a map of Acorn Hill to specify the search areas while Samuel passed out handheld radios to the different teams.

"Mrs. Smith," Goliath called to her. He was carrying the Bratwicks on his shoulders. "Good morning."

Louise left her sisters with Mac and went over to greet her friends from the circus. "We came as soon as we heard," she told the big man. "Has there been any sighting of the baby?"

"No, and when a little one that big disappears, is not good." Goliath sounded depressed. "It is the third we were expecting."

"The third?" Louise didn't understand.

"Bad things," Goliath explained. "For circus people, they always come in threes." He hesitated before adding, "You know how Dilly smash his wrist, and the Majeskas are closing our show. Hannah's baby is the third bad thing."

"I see." Louise looked up at Bobbi, who was teary-eyed and sniffling, and offered her a tissue from her purse.

"It's so awful," Bobbi said. "Billy and I are going to have to go back home and live with our grandparents. They love us, but they won't let us practice our tumbling. My grandmother wants me to take a typing class so I can be a *secretary*." She shuddered visibly.

"Better a secretary than a telephone operator, which is what Grandfather wants me to do," Billy said gloomily. "We've got to find a new show, Bobbi. How many tumblers our size do you think there are out there?"

Louise noticed Goliath's frown. "Will it be very hard for the performers to find new work?" she asked him quietly.

"Some of us, yes. Some, no." Goliath made a see-saw gesture with his hand. "There are shows, but not many. There are arenas, carnivals, Atlantic City, Las Vegas." He shrugged, causing the Bratwicks to clutch at him. "Sorry, my friends." To Louise, he said, "There is always work, if you look for it. But there is only one Majeska, and there will never be a show like this again."

Louise spotted Davis Utley approaching Mac and her sisters, who were speaking to Rose and looking at the town map. "I will keep you in my prayers," she told the circus people.

"Pray a lot, Mrs. Smith," Bobbi asked her softly.

"A waitress in town said everyone would be out here looking for a missing elephant, and I figured I'd find you in the middle of it," Davis was saying to Mac as Louise joined them. "This beats looking for golf balls off the ninth hole, I guess."

"We've got our search area assignment," Jane told Louise, and pointed out the section of woods where they would be starting. "Rose says not to approach the baby or try to restrain it in any way, but to call in to her on the radio."

"Where did all the radios come from?"

"The Majeskas passed them out. All of their employees use them during performances, to coordinate things." Alice checked her watch. "The baby has been missing for over eighteen hours, with no food, so the trainer thinks we might find it in distress."

"I should be able to cover more ground on the Ducati," Mac said. "Davis, why don't you ride with me?"

"Ride with you?" Davis echoed. "What are we, ten-year-old kids?"

"You'll never understand me until you take a ride on my motorcycle, old buddy," Mac challenged. "You're not afraid, are you?"

"Afraid?" The shorter man's chest puffed out. "Give me a break, Mac. That's a teenager's toy."

"Then come on," Mac said. "I brought my spare helmet, we'll see if it fits over that thick skull of yours."

Chapter Eighteen

Louise and her sisters searched the Bellwood property with the other volunteers until noon, when everyone had agreed to rendezvous at the farmhouse. Rose insisted on making lunch for everyone who participated and had enough sandwiches, salad and lemonade set out to satisfy a small army.

"I have to feed people in times of crisis," Rose said to Louise as she helped her pass out paper plates and disposable utensils. "My mother is the same way."

"We've got some of our best local hunters out there," Samuel told Louise later, as she sat at one of the picnic tables that the Bellwoods had set up for the searchers. "They're all good trackers, and we hope they will pick up her trail before sunset."

Louise could see that he was worried. "It will be harder to search for her in the dark," she said.

"It's not only that. The baby is so young that she doesn't know how to forage properly. The trainer thinks she'll eat whatever she comes across." Samuel gazed out at the tree line. "If she gets hold of something . . ."

He didn't have to complete the thought for Louise to understand the danger. She knew only too well how many poisonous plants and berries there were in the woods. "We'll find her," Louise said softly.

The task, however, proved to be much more difficult than anyone had imagined. The woods around Bellwood Farm were extensive, and many places were thick with brush, which made progress slow. Louise had also never realized how exhausting it was simply to walk and look for a lost animal. The warm weather worked against the searchers, making it necessary for everyone to stop frequently to rest and to drink the water Rose had provided in bottles.

It was also puzzling how something as large as a baby elephant could vanish without a trace. None of the farmers on the tracts surrounding the Bellwood property had caught so much as a glimpse of Hannah's baby.

The Howards searched until an hour before sunset, when the authorities took over for the volunteer search parties. Louise was so tired that she gratefully let Jane drive her and Alice in her Cadillac.

"I will never be so happy to go to bed," Alice said, and groaned as she stretched out her legs. "I think I must have walked off at least five more pounds."

"You can have whatever you want for dinner," Jane said generously. She looked at Louise, who had been staring out into the growing darkness of the sky. "This wasn't too much for you, was it?"

"It was more exercise than I've had in some time," Louise said. "I was thinking about Dilly and the calliope."

"He'll be released from the hospital before the circus's final performance," Alice said. "Because he has surgical pins in his wrist, he'll be in a hard splint for a couple of weeks."

That meant Dilly wouldn't be playing the calliope for the circus's last performance. Because of her arthritis, Ilsa couldn't fill in for him, either.

I could stand in for him, Louise thought, feeling her heart lighten a small degree.

"I heard a couple of the roustabouts talking, and the other two clowns have quit the show to take jobs with another circus," Jane said. "With Dilly unable to perform, that means no clowns at the last show, unless someone can fill in."

"That's a shame," Alice said. "Speaking of missing persons, did you see Mac before we left the farm?"

"I heard his motorcycle in the distance a few times, but I never caught sight of him or his friend," Jane said. She peered ahead. "I spoke too soon. Looks like they beat us here."

Mac and Davis were standing in the driveway, both holding helmets and talking. Mac waved as Jane parked the Cadillac a short distance from them.

"Any luck?" he called out.

"No, she's still out there somewhere," Louise said. She noted the grubby condition of Davis's suit and the coating of dust on his face. "Mr. Utley, would you care to come inside and freshen up?"

"I'd appreciate it, ma'am." Davis looked at Mac. "It will also get me away from my crazy friend here, who is trying to talk me into buying one of these monster machines."

"You loved riding around with me today, Davis," Mac said with a laugh.

"It was different, but I think I'll stick to my nice, comfortable convertible, thanks." Despite his comment and his condition, Davis seemed much more relaxed. "I'll be a good loser and buy dinner tonight, though."

"I bet him a good meal that he'd like my bike," Mac said to Louise.

"No need to pay up just yet, Mr. Utley," Jane said. "I've got a deep-dish chicken pie in the fridge, and Rose made us take some salads and things home. Have dinner here with us."

While Louise and her sisters put together the meal, the men went upstairs to clean up. Jane's chicken pie, which usually lasted three meals for the sisters, was judged large enough to serve as an entrée. The Caesar salad and ambrosia Rose had given them rounded out the meal nicely.

"I have some citrus cooler in the fridge, or iced tea if the men would prefer that," Jane said. She handed a stack of plates to Alice and handfuls of utensils to Louise. "I'll warm up things, you two set the table."

Louise was thinking of what she might play on the calliope while she and Alice set places for everyone at the dining room table. When they returned to the kitchen, Alice stopped and held up her hand for silence.

"What is it, dear?" Louise inquired.

"Can you hear that noise?" Alice asked.

"No, I don't hear anything unusual," Louise said.

Alice pointed toward the window that faced the vegetable garden. "There! Did you hear that rustling noise?"

Louise went to the window, but night had fallen and it was too dark outside to see much of anything. "Likely it is a little breeze going through the leaves."

"I don't think so. Leaves don't sound that way." Alice went to the back door and opened it.

Louise heard the curious sounds clearly now, and joined her sister at the door.

"That's not leaves rustling." She listened again. "That sounds like . . . chewing."

Alice turned her head from one side to the other, trying to catch the sound's direction. "I think it's coming from the vegetable garden."

Jane, who had gone upstairs to change, arrived just in time to hear the news.

"There's something in the vegetable garden," Louise told her. "Something that is chewing or eating."

"Not another mole," Jane wailed. The one mole that had invaded her garden in the past had proved to be nearly impossible to catch.

"It's too loud to be a mole." Louise held a finger up to

her lips, and eased out the door to the garden. She did not turn on the exterior lights, but gestured for her sisters to follow her.

Quietly they walked toward the vegetable garden, which was illuminated by the light from the moon overhead. The rustling, tearing sounds were very loud, and Alice stayed close to Louise.

"Over here." Jane moved ahead.

Louise lost sight of her and nearly stumbled. "Jane." She clutched the support of Alice's arm and peered into the shadows. "Where is she?"

"Louise." Alice pointed with a trembling finger at a shape rising near the decorative cabbage border that led from the garden.

The moonlight showed the outline of the figure, which was hunchbacked and thick-bodied. Louise felt her heart pound as she thought she saw a snake fall on top of one of Jane's decorative cabbages and then, inexplicably, wrench it from the ground and lift it.

Suddenly the dimensions and shape of the creature made sense, and Louise had to stifle a laugh. Standing by the path next to what was left of Jane's winter decorative plantings was the most sought-after creature in the county.

"Is that . . ." Jane barely breathed.

Louise nodded.

Hannah's baby paid no attention to the sisters, but went on happily munching on the cabbage she had pulled from the ground with her trunk.

While Alice kept watch in the garden, Louise and Jane tiptoed back into the house and called Rose Bellwood, who promised to have the circus people come over to retrieve the baby elephant immediately.

"Thank heavens you found her," Rose added after she

had told her husband to contact the authorities to call off the search. "Aldo and Ilsa will be so relieved. As will poor Hannah."

Soon Goliath and several other men from the circus arrived with a transport truck.

"Dear Madam." Goliath insisted on shaking Louise's hand. "Thank you. Hannah is so heartsick without her little one. Thank you a thousand times."

Louise was surprised when instead of nets and ropes, Goliath used the cabbage leaves to lure the baby elephant into the truck. Hannah's baby did her mother proud by going along quite docilely.

"So much for my decorative border," Jane said as they waved good-bye to the circus people.

"There's still plenty of time to plant more," Louise said. "How often do you have the chance to feed and rescue a runaway baby elephant?"

Jane yawned. "Not very often, I hope. They eat a lot more than moles do." She closed the door behind them. "After dinner I'm going to collapse on the nearest flat surface."

"Me too," Alice said with a sigh, resting a hand against the small of her back.

Unlike her sisters, Louise felt oddly energized. After dinner she sent Jane and Alice off to bed, but stayed to help Mac and Davis with the clean-up, which they insisted on doing in return for the meal. The two men chatted about the search and Mac's motorcycle and speculated on how the baby elephant could have wandered so far away from the circus show grounds. They also asked Louise about the reasons behind the show's closing, which she related in brief detail.

"I wonder what they'll do with the animals when they sell off their assets," Davis said as he dried a dinner plate. "Can't be easy to find a home for a five-ton elephant and her baby."

Mac nodded. "If they were raised in captivity, they can't be returned to the wild. We have no elephant preserves here in North America either. A zoo would be the only place they could go."

"That might work," Davis said. Like Mac, he didn't seem tired, and was showing no inclination to leave.

Louise was happy for them. She never liked seeing good friends at odds with each other, and it was evident that Mac and Davis had come to some sort of understanding. Even if they had not reconciled their differences, they were showing respect and affection for each other, which was the foundation of friendship. *Now if only that could happen for Pauline Sherman.*

"Thank you for helping, gentlemen. We have decaf coffee and some pastries, if you'd like to sit and talk in the parlor," Louise suggested after the last clean dish was put away.

"That would top off the evening, I think." Mac glanced at Davis. "I have a few things I'd like to discuss with you, if you're not in a hurry to get back to your hotel."

"Hurry back to an empty room in a posh hotel and watch cable TV while I try not to eat all the contents of the mini-bar?" Davis chuckled. "Next time I'm anywhere near Acorn Hill, ma'am, I'm making a reservation at your inn. I like my luxuries, but there isn't a five-star hotel in the country that can boast having a baby elephant in their gardens."

Louise smiled. "That was a one-time-only event, Mr. Utley, but if you do stay with us, I believe you'll find something to keep you entertained." The phone at the reception desk rang, and she went to answer it. "Good evening, Grace Chapel Inn, Louise Smith speaking."

"I'm sorry to call so late, Mrs. Smith," a tired male voice said. "But I would like to talk to you about my wife."

It was Stanley Sherman, Louise realized. "Of course." She smiled at Davis and Mac as they walked past the desk on their way to the parlor. "How may I help you?"

"I heard through the grapevine that you went out to that . . . circus place . . . to talk to Pauline." He cleared his throat. "I was just wondering if she happened to tell you when she was coming home."

"No, I'm sorry," Louise said honestly. She couldn't bring herself to tell Stanley that Pauline had no intention of returning home at all.

"I don't know what to do, Mrs. Smith. Briana and Tiffany refuse to go to school and cry themselves to sleep every night. My office is in five kinds of a jam because I can't get to work. I tried to do the wash today and all my athletic socks are pink now." Anger entered his tone as he added, "Didn't she say anything about when she's coming home?"

"Mr. Sherman, that's a conversation you need to have with your wife," Louise advised.

"Call me Stanley, please. Pauline won't answer her cell phone, and she obviously isn't reading my text messages." Stanley sighed. "Why doesn't Pauline want to return my calls?"

Louise smothered a sigh. "May I make a suggestion?"

"Sure, I guess."

"Go to the Majeska circus, see your wife and talk to her in person," Louise said. "I think you'll find a face-to-face conversation is harder for her to avoid than a phone call or a text message."

"I don't know what to say to her. She said all those crazy things and left." Now he sounded genuinely perplexed. "Why would she say we treated her like a slave? We never made her do anything. She could sit around the house all day if she wanted to."

"Did she know that, Stanley?" Louise asked. "Did you ever give her a day off?"

"We have a very busy life," Stanley protested. "I work full-time, Briana and Tiffany are active in after-school and church activities, and Pauline had all that time on her hands. It's not as if I could do it."

Louise tried to think of how to make Stanley Sherman

see what Pauline had been doing for her family all these years. "Tell me, when was the last time your wife said 'no' to you?"

He uttered a sad chuckle. "Pauline never says no to me. Except that last time, just before she took off with those circus people."

Just as Louise had anticipated. "How many times in the last month have you and the girls asked her to do something for you?"

"I don't know. A hundred. Two hundred. Pauline does a lot of things for us."

"I see." Now for the clincher. "And how many times in the same period has Pauline asked you or your daughters to do something for her?"

There was a long silence on the other end of the line. "I think I see where you're going with this, Mrs. Smith. All she had to do was ask, you know. We love her."

"That, Stanley," Louise said, "is what she doesn't know. In large part, this is her own doing, as she has assumed far too many responsibilities over time without asking for help. Still, you and your daughters have contributed to the problem. Pauline doesn't feel loved or appreciated. She feels invisible."

"That's ridiculous," Stanley snapped. "She has a very comfortable home, she doesn't have to work and we have two beautiful children. Maybe we haven't done much to help my wife, but I assure you, she is the center of this family."

"I have one more question for you, Stanley," Louise said, trying to keep her temper even. "When was the last time you or your daughters have said 'thank you' to Pauline? For anything she has done for you?"

The silence was not as long this time. "I can't remember."

"People who don't feel appreciated also rarely feel loved," Louise said softly. "Imagine trying to do what your wife does. Imagine being expected to do it without being shown any gratitude or affection."

"I don't have to imagine it. I'm already trying to do it," Stanley complained, "and I can't." He heaved a sigh. "I know under the circumstances it doesn't seem like it, but the girls and I never meant to hurt Pauline. We do love her very much. What can we do, Mrs. Smith?"

Louise looked at the circus playbill someone had left on the reception desk and had an idea. "You'll need to buy some tickets."

Chapter Nineteen

I think we're really into autumn now," Jane said to Louise as she came in from taking out the trash. "It's quite chilly." She had on a sweater over a long-sleeved blouse. It had been a week since they had found Hannah's baby in their garden, and the morning temperatures had taken a cooler turn.

"All things must come to an end, including the warm weather," Alice said as she went to the cabinet and took down the cookie jar, placing it back on the counter. "Today is my diet goal day."

Alice's diet goal day, Louise knew, meant the final weigh-in. "I'm almost afraid to ask."

"I'm not. Did you already get on the scale?" Jane asked eagerly. When Alice nodded, she rolled her hand. "Well? How much?"

"I lost eight and a half pounds." Alice grinned.

Jane let out a whoop and threw her arms around Alice. "You did it! I knew you could!"

Alice embraced her affectionately. "I couldn't have done it without you, dear."

"No, you couldn't have." Jane popped off the top of the cookie jar and held it out. "You deserve a reward. Have one."

Alice made a little face. "I'd really rather have some fruit and cereal for breakfast, if you don't mind. Cookies first thing in the morning . . ." She moved her shoulders. "They don't appeal to me that much anymore."

"They don't?" Jane set down the cookie jar, her eyes misty now. "Oh, Alice. I love you."

A little later, when Jane left the kitchen to check on Mac, who was having an early breakfast in the dining room, Louise regarded Alice steadily. "If Father were here, I think he would say something like, 'Your nose is growing longer, Alice.'"

"All right, I would have liked the cookie more," Alice confessed. "But did you see her face when I said that I wanted the fruit and cereal? She almost burst into tears of happiness and pride. That's something I like a lot more than cookies."

Louise had volunteered her services to play the calliope for the Majeskas at the special performance that evening, and they had accepted gratefully, so she left a little earlier than her sisters that afternoon for Bellwood Farm.

Although the performance was not scheduled to begin until dusk, the gates were already open, and there were dozens of people walking down the midway. Electric lights decorated the framework of each booth, and the circus folk, even the roustabouts who were working the show grounds, were wearing jaunty costumes.

Louise decided to walk over to the big top, which was not yet open to the public. There she found Aldo in his shirt sleeves and suspenders, busy directing his men to move the animal cages around to the backyard where they would stand ready until it was time for the performance. Aldo's eyes sparkled with excitement, and the smile he gave her was bright.

"Louise!" He came over to bow over her hand. "I am so happy to see you. You will still play the calliope for us tonight?"

"That's why I'm here." Louise looked over at the calliope wagon, where she spotted Dilly talking to a familiar young man. "Alice told me Dilly had been released from the hospital. How is he feeling?"

"Like new, he tells me," Aldo said. His expression sobered. "The doctor says the surgery went well, and Dilly has a good chance of having complete use of his wrist and hand. This would not have happened if he had not had the operation."

"I'm so glad." Although, in part, Dilly's surgery had meant the closing of the circus so that Aldo and Ilsa could sell off their assets, Louise knew that Dilly was a gifted musician and should have a chance to retain his skills. "I think I'll go over and get warmed up."

"Let me know if you need something," Aldo said before he trotted over to direct another cage into place.

Dilly, who was dressed in regular clothes because of his splint and sling, sported his usual red foam ball on the end of his nose. As Louise walked up to him, she heard him say, "If you don't practice, you'll be playing it forever, Charlie."

Charlie Matthews scowled. "I guess." A flush of guilt spread over his face when he saw Louise. "Uh, hi, Mrs. Smith."

"Hi, Charlie." She exchanged an amused look with Dilly. "I'm filling in for this windjammer here tonight, and I was just going to warm up a little."

"Yeah?" Charlie's face brightened and he gave the instrument a covetous look. "Do you know the calliope is made out of steam whistles? And they used to play them in parades? And there's a guy out in the Midwest who plays one that runs on propane?"

"Propane?" Louise had never heard this.

"He ignites it and makes it shoot fireballs into the sky

while he's playing songs," Charlie said, his eyes dreamy. "Wouldn't it be so cool if a regular piano could do that?"

"Goodness, I can't imagine what that would do to the parlor ceiling." Louise studied her student's face. "You know, Charlie, I think you could still use a bit more practice playing 'Twinkle, Twinkle, Little Star.'"

"But Mrs. Smith, that song is so—" Charlie caught a look from Dilly and his shoulders slumped forward. "Yes, ma'am," he said in a dull monotone. "My mom will make me practice it as soon as I get home."

"I can't wait that long to hear it, Charlie." Louise turned to Dilly. "Could my student use your calliope, just for one or two songs?"

"Sure, he can," Dilly said.

Charlie's mouth formed an O for what seemed like a solid minute. "No way."

Dilly grinned and ruffled his good hand over Charlie's hair. "Way."

Louise had never seen a more delighted piano student than Charlie Matthews that afternoon as he played his practice piece on the calliope. Once he had grown accustomed to the keyboard, he begged to play another piece, and after a nod from Dilly, Louise surrendered the bench seat to him to let him play unaccompanied.

"He's got a knack for the keys," Dilly said as he and Louise listened to Charlie play a warm-up scale. "Although I suspect sports will outrank music on his priority list for the next few years."

"Charlie once told me that he thought it was 'neat' that the piano's keys are black and white." Louise smiled, remembering. "Guess why."

Dilly thought for a moment. "They're the same color as a soccer ball."

"You got it." Louise looked up in surprise as Charlie played the opening notes of "Take Me Out to the Ball Game." "I didn't know he knew that piece."

"Every boy over five does," Dilly said.

Carol and Tim Matthews came over while Charlie was playing, and Louise took great pleasure in applauding with them as Charlie finished the tune.

"Did you hear that, Mom?" he called as he climbed down from the calliope wagon.

"All the way over on the other side of the grounds," Carol assured him. She bent down to hug her son. "Great job, honey."

"Dad." He turned to Tim. "Can you build a calliope for me?"

Tim Matthews studied the instrument, and then clapped a hand on his son's shoulder. "You remember what your Mom said after your Aunt Beth gave you that little drum set three years ago for Christmas?" Charlie nodded. "Well, if I built you a calliope, your mother really *would* tear out all her hair this time."

"Ah, Dad." Charlie kicked some sawdust with his shoe.

Carol gave Tim an ironic look before saying, "They've got a baseball toss game here. The big prize is a brand-new bat. Looks like a Louisville Slugger, but I'm not sure."

"A Louie? For real?" The calliope forgotten, Charlie seized his mother's hand. "I've been practicing my fast ball all summer! Come on, Dad."

Louise waved good-bye to the Matthews family. Men were waiting to move the calliope wagon over to an area next to the big top marquee, so she walked with Dilly down the midway. "Was Aldo able to find someone to replace you in your clown capacity?"

He gave her a rather mysterious smile. "I think so."

On the midway, Dilly bought Louise a cold soft drink and introduced her to several of the concessionaires. For people who were about to lose their jobs, they seemed very happy, Louise thought. There was a contagious sense of excitement all over the show grounds, and it was impossible to feel depressed when one saw all the children rushing here and there to play games and to dart inside the display tents.

"We have to get you gussied up for the performance," Dilly said, leading Louise into the costume tent.

"I don't think I could wear a costume," Louise said, eyeing the racks of glittering garments. "Not one that made me look like a Rockette, anyway."

"The calliope player for Majeska always wears this." From one of the racks Dilly removed a short cape made of red silk edged with gold fringe. "There's a matching hat, too, if you like."

Louise slipped the cape over her shoulders and surveyed herself. The silk was very soft and light. "I think I can wear this without scandalizing my family," she said. She saw the broad-brimmed, feathered red headdress in Dilly's hands. "But no hat."

Hester, the show's seamstress, emerged from a rack. "A windjammer has to have some flash, First of May," she said to Louise. With a deft hand she plucked a spangled red fabric flower from a basket of trims and tucked it behind Louise's right ear. "There, you look like real circus people now."

Dilly grinned. "She sure does."

As twilight slowly descended, more people began to arrive in anticipation of the performance. Strings of electric lights glowed white, red, yellow and blue, casting pools of color onto the sawdust-strewn midway. The scents of cotton candy, roasted peanuts and popcorn grew more intense as they were passed into eager little hands. Voices swelled and ebbed between sudden bursts of laughter that erupted like fireworks around the game booths as people competed for the prizes.

"Come on, Jason!" one boy urged. "Knock that bottle into next week!"

"A carnival glass punch bowl set for the pretty lady in blue," the man working the dime pitch booth said. He handed a large box of the glassware to the thrilled young woman. "Pitch a dime, win something fine."

Louise saw Charlie walking down the midway with his parents, a brand-new wooden bat resting against his shoulder. *Baseball. I'll have to work on a way to use that in his lessons.*

Chapter Twenty

Louise took her place at the calliope and started off with a traditional Sousa marching tune she had learned from Dilly. She was in the middle of the piece when she saw Alice and Jane standing by the wagon. Both were staring up at her red silk cape.

She smiled down at them as she kept playing. "What do you think?"

"You sound wonderful," Alice called back.

"You look like the Phantom of the Opera," Jane said, "only much prettier."

Louise played different traditional circus tunes on the calliope for the thirty minutes up to the start of the show, and then slipped inside the big top to join Jane in the audience.

"Where is Alice?" Louise looked around but did not see her sister.

Jane grimaced. "She got a call and had to go into work."

"Oh, what a shame." Louise knew her sister had had her heart set on seeing the performance.

"I can't believe you're wearing a red silk cape," Jane said, surveying her closely, "and a flower tucked behind your ear. You're not a flower-behind-the-ear and cape person."

"I think it gives me a nice bit of flash," Louise said. At

Jane's startled look, she chuckled. "Think of it as a *temporary* fashion statement."

The interior of the big top was set up in performance style, with three large rings in the very center of the tent. Around the rings was the hippodrome track, which once had been used to showcase the trick riding acts of the early circuses and was now used for the open and closing promenades. All around the filled grandstand seating, men and women dressed in striped shirts and white slacks were selling treats, programs and souvenirs, calling out their wares as they worked the crowd.

"Ladies and gentlemen," a deep voice said over a loudspeaker. "Welcome to the Majeska circus, originally billed in 1859 as *Majeska's Most Magnificent Magical Marvels*, home of Hannah the Performing Elephant, and the entire Majeska family of the most bold, brave and brilliant circus performers in the world."

The audience applauded and buzzed with excitement as the interior lights dimmed, and a spotlight was directed at the center ring.

"Please give a big round of applause for the owner of the Majeska circus and our ringmaster, Aldo Majeska," the announcer called out.

Aldo stepped into the spotlight. He wore a glittering coat entirely covered with gold sequins. On top of his fluffy white hair sat a matching top hat. He spread out his hands and bowed. He then seemed to curl over, but righted himself with a flourish before using his cane to push his hat back up on his head. Everyone laughed at his slightly annoyed expression, and how he went to great pains to dust himself off.

"He should have been a clown," Jane whispered to Louise.

Aldo put a large brass whistle to his lips and blew it three times. Somewhere in the darkness, a drummer performed a roll on his instrument.

"And now, ladies and gentlemen, please welcome our performers, the marvels of the big top, the daring and the delightful, our circus family."

Brassy music played as the performers began entering the big top to promenade around the hippodrome. At first came several beautiful women in glittering costumes, most of whom immediately went to what appeared to be loose ropes hanging down from the rigging overhead.

"Those are the rope dancers," Louise told Jane. "They'll be performing through the first act. Oh, look, there's Pauline Sherman."

Jane gaped. "*That's* Pauline?"

"It certainly is." Louise smiled as the younger woman sauntered by in the dazzling gown she had shown Louise. Tonight her smile nearly outshone her costume. "I hope she does well," she whispered to Jane as she mentally crossed her fingers.

"She looks fabulous," Jane said.

The aerialist performers were followed by Goliath in his strong man costume. The big man carried the Bratwicks on his shoulders. Halfway around the track, Bobbi and Billy pretended to fall, but rolled as they landed and began tumbling all the way around the track. Goliath pretended to chase them, drawing laughter from the crowd when he could not catch the nimble siblings.

The cage wagons came around the rings, and the lions, tigers and monkeys looked out at the audience as if eager to join them. Several of the big cats released very convincing growls. They were followed by a team of six white horses that trotted in perfect unison.

"The star of our show, ladies and gentleman," the announcer called out, "please give a warm welcome to the eighth wonder of the world, our lovely Hannah."

Hannah came lumbering into the tent, drawing a gasp from the crowd. She wore a sparkling headdress and flashing bands around each leg. On her neck was perched her trainer, dressed in an exotic turban and costume. Hannah's baby followed close behind, flanked by two trainers. The little elephant drew cries of delight when the children in the audience saw how she held onto her mother's tail with her trunk.

"So they found a clown after all," Louise said to Jane and pointed to the end of the promenade.

The clown wore huge shoes, a baggy costume and rainbow-colored wig, with a funny face drawn in red and black on a white background. The clown went back and forth trying to shake the hands of the children reaching out from the audience. The only problem was that the clown kept tripping over the oversize shoes, creating comical near-collisions.

"Oh, that's funny," Jane crowed when the clown ended up clinging to one of the quarter poles.

Louise looked down two rows and saw Stanley Sherman and his two daughters seated at the very front. They seemed mesmerized by Pauline, who was now standing by the center ring and smiling brilliantly as she gestured to the rope dancers, who were all hanging upside down and twirling in circles, holding onto their ropes by one leg.

"Good evening," Aldo said when the music and the promenade had finished. "Tonight's show is a historic performance, our very first for the fine people of this town. Many of you, we are told, have children who have never been to the circus. For you, we promise to make this the most glorious, electrifying night you have ever spent."

Drums rolled as multicolored beams of light shot through the tent, catching the sparkling costumes of the performers and making them glitter so brightly that it almost hurt Louise's eyes to look directly at them.

Jane caught her breath, as thrilled as any child in the audience, and grabbed Louise's hand. "What's going to happen next?"

"That is the magic of the circus, Jane," Louise told her. "You never know *what* is going to happen next."

Jane's excitement was infectious, and as the show began Louise found herself just as eager to see what the first act of the night would be. She had forgotten that a three-ring circus, however, meant that three acts would be performed simultaneously.

"Jane, look!" Louise was as astonished as the rest of the audience when the lion tamer, the acrobats and the trick riders took their places in their respective rings.

"Wow!" Jane applauded wildly as the trick riders started off their act with a series of lethal-looking jumps from the ground onto the backs of the white horses as they galloped around the ring.

This is what our lives have been these past few weeks, Louise thought as she watched the acts begin their opening feats. *So many things happening, all at once, and I had to scramble to keep up with all of it.* She took comfort in the fact that although her life might be a three-ring circus on occasion, she wouldn't trade it for the world.

As the lion tamer put his enormous cats through their paces, the acrobats formed a human pyramid three stories high, and the trick riders jumped on and off their galloping white horses.

"Oh!" Like a young girl, Jane covered her eyes, peeked through her fingers, and laughed, all at the same time.

The Bratwicks were featured in the ring after the acrobats. They used props for their gymnastic feats, which had them leaping from what seemed suicidal heights to flip and somersault before landing with perfect accuracy. Louise found her heart in her throat more than once, simply watching them.

There was so much to watch that no one quite knew where to look. As the trick riders left the ring, the rope dancers descended to wind through the air as naturally as if they'd been born with wings. More performers took to the ropes, five men and two women who climbed higher and higher, until it seemed they would climb through the very roof of the big tent.

Louise saw why when the spotlight centered on the platform at the very top, where they began to swing out over the heads of the audience on what appeared to be extremely flimsy bars suspended by two thin cables.

Jane now had her head thrown back, her gaze riveted. "Look, it's the trapeze artists!"

Louise found watching the twirling, flying bodies of the aerialists a bit dizzying, not to mention alarming, and returned her attention to one of the end rings, where the rainbow-haired clown was trying to escape from the Bratwick siblings, whose act the clown had stumbled into. The tumblers grabbed onto the clown's legs, but that didn't stop the clown, who did a complete circuit of the tent with Bobbi and Billy still holding on.

Jane uttered a muffled yelp from behind one hand as two of the trapeze artists performed a double somersault, crossing in mid-air. Shrieks rang out from the audience as one of the flyers nearly didn't connect with his catcher. "My Lord, he almost missed!"

Louise only smiled. She had learned from Aldo that the trapeze artists practiced that feat, making it appear as if the flyer were about to fall. It was then that she noticed the rainbow-haired clown, who had come very close to where she and Jane were sitting. Dilly's replacement was handing out balloons and paper flowers to the children, and smiling at them with a smile that made Louise's eyes narrow. She then saw a short strand of reddish brown hair sticking out from beneath the clown's fluffy wig.

"Jane," she said to her awestruck sister.

Jane was still staring overhead. "*Hmmm?*"

"See that clown there?" She pointed. "Does anything about her strike you as familiar?"

Jane peered. "How do you know the clown is a wom— Alice!"

The clown looked up as if hearing her name and saw Jane and Louise staring at her. She gave them a cheery wave before she produced another paper flower for a goggle-eyed little boy.

"I guess she did have to go to work," Louise murmured.

Halfway through the performance, Aldo called an intermission to allow people to move about, buy treats and souvenirs, and to make visits to the rest area. When all had returned to their seats, the performers exploded into the tent with acts that left even Louise gasping in astonishment.

The show came to its thrilling, three-ring conclusion when Hannah was brought to the center ring. The gigantic creature slowly obeyed the sharply barked orders of her mahout as she balanced on three legs, then two, then one. She lifted her mahout high over her head, where he performed an intricate series of back flips, and brought him safely back down.

The house lights dimmed dramatically, and Aldo's voice, now sounding hushed, came over the loudspeaker. "Ladies and gentlemen, for this next feat, we must ask for complete silence from the audience. If our beautiful Hannah makes a single mistake, it could spell utter disaster for her and her new baby. Quiet now, please."

Voices all around the tent fell silent as Goliath and another trainer led Hannah's baby out to the center ring. Hannah's mahout commanded the elephant to kneel, and had Goliath climb onto her back. As soon as Hannah stood up again, she seized Goliath with her trunk, and lifted him high over her head. Her trainer ordered her to place her back legs on a wide round platform, and to lift her front legs. As her two front feet left the ground, the trainer led her baby directly underneath the big elephant's body, and coaxed the baby to lift one front and back leg for a few moments.

Like everyone watching, Louise held her breath. If Hannah lost her balance, she would drop Goliath and fall on her trainer and her own baby.

"Ladies and gentlemen," Aldo said in a reverent voice as Hannah remained perfectly still, "the star of our show, the strongest elephant in the world, the lovely Hannah."

No one knew whether to applaud or remain silent. In the next second, the trainer led the baby out of harm's way, but Goliath suddenly fell from his precarious perch. Just before the strong man would have hit the ground, Hannah dropped on all fours, snatched him back up with her trunk and placed him gently and safely on his own two feet.

The audience surged in a single wave to their feet, shouting and applauding so loudly that Louise felt the sound as a physical force.

Hannah gave her baby what appeared to be a maternal pat with her trunk before bowing to her audience. The little baby elephant trumpeted, ending the performance the same way it had started—with laughter all around.

Before the audience left the big top tent, Aldo announced that Hannah would select the winning name from the entries for the "Name Hannah's baby" contest, which Louise suspected nearly every child in town had entered.

The entry slips were brought out in a large barrel by Goliath, and Hannah was brought forward to pick the winning slip.

"I hope this poor baby doesn't end up being named 'Spot' or 'Rover,'" Jane said.

"I was hoping Charlie Matthews's entry would get lost," Louise admitted. "He thinks they should call the baby 'Godzillina.' But Ilsa told me not to worry. They sorted out any inappropriate names."

Hannah plucked a slip of paper from the barrel, and there was another eruption of laughter as she held it just out of reach of Aldo's hand. Finally the elephant gave the slip of paper to Ilsa, who had entered the ring.

The elderly woman's hands trembled as she unfolded the paper and squinted at it. "This is a very good name for your baby, Hannah. Thank you." She folded the paper again and made as if to walk out of the ring. When the cries of the disappointed children rang out, she turned as if surprised. "You would like to hear the name Hannah has chosen for her little one?"

Every child in the big top shouted "Yes!"

"Very well," Ilsa said, smiling. "Hannah has chosen to name her baby 'Grace.'"

Sissy Matthews jumped to her feet and shouted, "That's my entry!" in such a loud voice that everyone laughed. Everyone except her brother, who made a horrible face.

"Young lady, would you come down here if you please?" Ilsa gestured to Sissy, who blushed but climbed down from her seat and walked up to the ring. "Now, would you tell everyone here why you picked 'Grace' as a name for Hannah's baby?"

Sissy grinned. "Because she was rescued by Mrs. Smith and her sisters, and the name of their inn is Grace Chapel Inn. Just like our church, Grace Chapel."

The spotlight shifted until it shone directly at Jane and Louise.

"Yes," Ilsa said, smiling at the sisters. "That is the perfect choice."

Louise and Jane sat together, waiting for Alice as the audience began to file slowly out of the big top.

"I can't believe that Sissy Matthews named an elephant after our inn," Jane asked.

"Our inn and our church," Louise reminded her. "I wonder what Father would have said about this."

"He'd say, 'God, please bless this elephant,'" Jane said.

"Yes, that sounds like Father." Louise waved to some friends from church.

"I'm going to make that girl a dozen of her favorite cookies." Jane sat up a little straighter. "Look, there's Pauline Sherman. She looked so beautiful tonight, didn't she?"

Louise watched as Pauline hesitantly walked up to her husband and daughters. The woman's expression changed from diffident to incredulous as she was hugged by her children and soundly kissed by her husband. "I like how she looks even better now, surrounded by the people who love her."

Most of the audience had left, and Alice still had not reappeared, so Jane decided to go look for their missing sister. Pauline and Stanley were sitting on one of the lower bench seats, and Louise smiled when Pauline spotted her. She was further surprised when Stanley gestured for her to join them.

Lord, I'd rather not be a referee tonight, she thought as she walked down the steps to where the Shermans waited. "Hello Pauline, Stanley." She smiled at the two girls before she added, "You looked wonderful tonight, Pauline."

"I nearly threw up," Pauline said blithely. "Twice."

"Oh, dear." Louise wasn't sure what to say to that. "I hope you're feeling better."

"Stanley knew I was scared, didn't you, honey?" Pauline put her arm around her husband. "He looked straight at me and made the silliest face I've ever seen."

"It was really dumb," Briana assured Louise.

"Anyway, it helped me get through my stage fright. But oh, Lord, standing there in front of all those people." Pauline shuddered.

"I'm glad you and the girls were able to make it to the

show," Louise said, exchanging a knowing look with Stanley. "Pauline, I'm only sorry that the show is closing."

"I'm sorry that the show is closing, too, but I'm glad that I'm not performing anymore," the younger woman said fervently. "Now I know I could not do this kind of thing for a living." She gave her husband a tentative look. "Stanley and I are going to get back together."

"We're also going to start family counseling," Stanley said firmly. "If we want it to work this time, we need to talk out our problems and find solutions together."

"Without working Mom to the bone," Tiffany chimed in.

Louise wished the family good luck, and went in search of her sisters. She found them standing just outside the marquee with Aldo and Ilsa Majeska.

"I'm sorry I didn't tell you," Alice was saying to Jane. "I've always wanted to be a clown, and when Rose was talking about getting someone to fill in for Dilly, I jumped at the chance."

"Louise wearing flowers in her hair, you in clown makeup." Jane shook her head. "I feel so left out."

"It's all right, dear," Louise told her. "If you like, when we get home, you can pin all my costume jewelry to your bathing suit."

"But no climbing the Bellwoods' oak trees," Alice said sternly, making everyone laugh.

"We have something to announce to our performers," Aldo said, "and we would like you ladies to be there. Would you come with us?"

After the circus patrons had left, the performers were assembled in the backyard, where they were breaking down their equipment and feeding the tired animals. The Majeskas called everyone together and also asked one of the sound men to hook up a loudspeaker, so the people still working the midway could also hear their announcement.

"My friends, you have never been more dazzling than

you were tonight," Aldo said over the microphone. "As you know, Ilsa and I would like nothing better than to spend the rest of our lives with you. But for us, this must be our final performance."

Louise saw many unhappy faces, but everyone seemed more sympathetic toward the circus owners than upset over their own plight.

"For you, however, the show will go on," Aldo continued. "Instead of closing the show, Ilsa and I have sold it. You all have new bosses now." He shook a finger at the stunned performers. "You do me proud, do you hear me? No slacking off just because they're First of Mayers."

Dilly came out of the crowd. "New owners? Who are they?"

"It is my honor to introduce Mr. MacElroy Wilde and Mr. Davis Utley." Aldo turned and swept his hand out. "The brand-new owners of the Majeska circus."

Louise could not believe her ears, or her eyes, as she watched Mac and Davis walk up to shake Aldo Majeska's hand. Mac was offered the microphone, and he took it with a smile.

"We'll be getting to know all of you over the next couple of weeks, and the Majeskas will be staying on to help us make an easy transition," he told the performers. "I hope you'll all consider staying on with us, because I have never seen a more talented group of people."

Mac told his new employees something about his and Davis's backgrounds. Then he announced that he would be traveling with the show while Davis would look after the financial aspects from his home in Washington, D.C.

"What made you decide to buy the show, Mr. Wilde?" one of the roustabouts asked. "You said that you were an investment banker, but the circus isn't what I'd call a great investment."

Davis laughed. "Give me a chance, and I'll turn that around."

"This will be an adventure for all of us," Mac said. "I can't promise you that we'll all be fabulously wealthy ten years from now, but I'd say circus life is about more than making money. It's about the show, and if we all work together, the show will go on and we'll all do well."

∽

Mac and Davis met up with the sisters back at the inn, where Jane fixed refreshments and Alice finally succumbed to the temptations of Jane's cookie jar.

"I held out for twelve hours," she said proudly to Louise as she took a bite out of one white chocolate chunk cookie. "Through popcorn, peanuts, caramel apples and cotton candy, and playing a clown for several hundred people, I might add."

Louise brushed a crumb from Alice's cheek. "You were marvelous."

Over lemonade in the parlor, Davis was the first to admit that investing in a circus was an unconventional idea at best, and that it had taken Mac some time to persuade him to become his partner, but the change it represented for both of them appealed to him on several levels.

"It's really the best of all worlds. Mac gets to travel, while I can retire but still stay involved in business, which is my love." He looked over at his friend. "We both were looking for a sense of purpose, I think. They may not be carbon copies of each other, but I think it will work out well for both of us." He chuckled. "Heck, wait until the guys at the club find out I'm part-owner of a circus."

Mac toasted him with his cup. "That's the spirit, old buddy. Life is good, even when it's a three-ring circus."

"I can't say that I envy you, Mac," Louise said, "but I

have to agree with your sentiments. Life is always exciting, even when you spend it in a small town."

"Is that right?" Jane pretended to be surprised. "Here, in Acorn Hill? We've probably used up our quota of fun for the next ten years."

"As long as you walk with the Lord and treat every day as an adventure," Louise reminded her sister, "the fun never ends."

Savory Southern Chicken Pie

SERVES SIX

8 ounces pork sausage
4 tablespoons butter
⅓ cup flour
¼ teaspoon salt
⅛ teaspoon pepper
1 teaspoon paprika
Dash garlic salt or powder
1 13¾ ounce can (1¾ cups) chicken broth
⅔ cup evaporated milk
2 cups cubed cooked chicken
1 10-ounce package frozen peas, thawed
1 or 2 cooked potatoes, cubed
1 or 2 carrots, cooked and diced
1 recipe single pie crust

Brown sausage, drain and cut up in small pieces; set aside. Melt butter. Blend in flour and seasonings. Stir in chicken broth and milk. Cook and stir mixture until thickened and bubbly; cook one minute more. Add sausage, chicken and vegetables; heat through. Transfer into casserole. Top with pastry crust and bake at 425 degrees for twenty-five to thirty minutes. Serve piping hot.

About the Author

Faith, family and humor have always been the strong foundation in Rebecca Kelly's life, which is constantly busy but never dull. Encouraged by her mother Joan, a popular local Christian humorist and speaker, Rebecca wrote her first book at age thirteen and hasn't stopped writing since.

When she's not writing or being a mom, Rebecca volunteers in a variety of church projects, including providing aid to the homeless and families in distress. She regularly gives writing workshops to area elementary school students and moderates a weekly writing discussion group on the Internet. An avid quilt maker and conservationist, Rebecca regards her most unusual hobby to be the uncovering of "hidden" quilts, which are nineteenth-century quilts that have been used as batting for newer quilts. She has restored more than fifty to their former glory.s

Rebecca presently resides in Florida with her two youngest children.